THE
GIRLS
I'VE
BEEN

Praise for *The Girls I've Been*

'Slick, stylish and full of suspense'
Sophie McKenzie

'A powerful gut-punch of a book that will leave you reeling long after its final pages. I couldn't put it down!'
Chelsea Pitcher

'Unlike anything I've read before … immediate, gripping, incredibly tense, heart-breaking, heart-warming and FUN! '
Holly Jackson

'I could hardly breathe until I finished. The tension! Absolutely loved it'
Emily Barr

'A captivating, explosive, and satisfyingly queer thriller'
Kirkus

TESS SHARPE

THE GIRLS I'VE BEEN

Hodder
Children's
Books

HODDER CHILDREN'S BOOKS

First published in Great Britain in 2021 by Hodder & Stoughton
First published in the US in 2021 by G. P. Putnam's Sons,
an imprint of Penguin Random House LLC, New York

9 10

A CIP catalogue record for this book is available from the British Library.

ISBN: 978 1 444 96011 2

Text set in Skolar Latin

Printed and bound by Clays Ltd, Elcograf S.p.A.

The paper and board used in this book are made
from wood from responsible sources.

Hodder Children's Books
An imprint of Hachette Children's Group
Part of Hodder & Stoughton
Carmelite House
50 Victoria Embankment
London EC4Y 0DZ

An Hachette UK Company
www.hachette.co.uk

www.hachettechildrens.co.uk

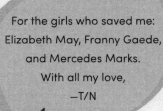

For the girls who saved me:
Elizabeth May, Franny Gaede,
and Mercedes Marks.
With all my love,
—T/N

Part One

———

Truth Is a Weapon

(The First 87 Minutes)

1

It was supposed to be twenty minutes.

That's what I told myself when I woke up that morning. It would be just twenty minutes. We'd meet in the bank parking lot, we'd go in, we'd make the deposit, and it would be awkward, it would be *so* awkward, but it would be twenty minutes, tops.

I could survive twenty minutes with my ex-boyfriend and new girlfriend. I could handle the awkwardness. I was a freaking *champ*.

I even got donuts, thinking maybe that would help smooth things over after last night's make-out interruptus, which I know is downplaying what happened. I get fried dough can't fix everything, but still. Everyone loves donuts. Especially when they have sprinkles . . . or bacon. Or both. So I get the donuts—and coffee, because Iris is basically a grizzly bear unless she downs some caffeine in the morning—and of course, that makes me late. By the time I pull up to the bank, they're both already there.

Wes is out of his truck, tall and blond and leaning against the chipped tailgate, the bank envelope with all the cash from last night next to him. Iris is lounging on the hood of her Volvo in her watercolor dress, her curls swinging as she plays with that lighter

3

she found on the railroad tracks. She's gonna set her brush-out on fire one of these days, I swear to God.

"You're late" is the first thing Wes says when I get out of my car.

"I brought donuts." I hand Iris her coffee, and she hops off the hood.

"Thanks."

"Can we just get this over with?" he asks. He doesn't even look at the donuts. My stomach clenches. Are we really back to this? How can we be back to this, after *everything*?

I press my lips together, trying not to look too annoyed. "Fine." I put the bakery box back in my car. "Let's go." I snatch up the envelope from his tailgate.

The bank's just opened, so there are only two people ahead of us. Iris fills out the deposit slip, and I stand in line with Wes right behind me.

The line moves as Iris walks over with the slip, taking the envelope from me and tucking it into her purse. She looks warily at Wes, then at me.

I bite my lip. Just a few more minutes.

Iris sighs. "Look," she says to Wes, propping her hands on her hips. "I understand that the way you found out wasn't great. But—"

That's when Iris is interrupted.

But not by Wes.

No, Iris gets interrupted by the guy in front of us. Because the guy in front of us? He chooses that moment to pull out a gun and start robbing the freaking bank.

The first thing I think is *Shit!* The second thing I think is *Get down.* And the third thing I think is *We're all gonna die because I waited for the bacon donuts.*

2

The robber—white guy, six feet, maybe, brown jacket, black T-shirt, red ball cap, pale eyes and brows—yells, "GET ON THE FLOOR!"—you know, like bank robbers do. We hit the floor. It's like everyone in that bank is a puppet and he's cut all our strings.

I can't breathe around it for a second, this giant lump of fear in my stomach, chest, and throat. It burns and snags in the soft parts of me, and I want to cough, but I'm scared that'll draw his attention.

You never want to draw their attention. I know this because this isn't the first time I've been here. I mean, I've never been in the middle of a bank robbery, but sometimes it feels like I was born in the line of fire.

When someone points a gun at you, it's not like in the movies. There are no brave moments in those first seconds. It's bone-shaking, pants-peeing *scary*. Iris's arm presses against mine, and I can feel her trembling. I want to reach out and grab her hand, but I stop myself. What if he thinks I'm reaching for a weapon? Everyone and their mother has guns in Clear Creek. I can't risk it.

Wes is tense on my other side, and it takes me a second to realize

5

why. Because he's getting ready to spring at the guy—that's my ex for you. Wes is instinctual and heroic, and has *such* bad judgment when it comes to tricky situations.

This time, I do move. I have to—Wes will get himself shot otherwise. I grab his thigh and dig my nails into his skin, right under the hem of his shorts. His head jerks toward me, and I glare at him, a *Don't you dare do it* look. I shake my head once and glare more. I can practically see the *But, Nora . . .* in his raised eyebrows until he finally slumps down, defeated.

Okay. Okay. Breathe. Focus.

The robber. He's shouting at the teller. The teller—is there only one? why is there only one?—is a middle-aged blond lady with glasses looped on an aqua chain. My mind's in overdrive, noting things like I'll need them later.

He's shouting about the bank manager. It's hard to hear because the teller is full-out *sobbing*. She's all shaking hands and red cheeks, and there is no way the silent alarm got pushed unless she did it by accident. With the gun in her face, she's in full-on panic mode.

Can't blame her. You never know how you're going to react until the gun's out.

None of the three of us have fainted yet, so I figure we're good. For now. It's something.

But when it comes to saving the day, teller's out. Sheriff's not coming unless someone hits the alarm. My eyes track to the left best I can without moving my head too much. Is there another teller hiding somewhere? Where's the security guard? Do they even have one at this branch?

Footsteps behind me. I tense, and Iris lets out a little gasp. I press my arm harder against hers, wishing I could flood reassurance into her through our skin. But when there's a gun, there's not really a lot of that to give.

Wait. Footsteps—rushed. As they pass me, I look up enough to see the sawed-off shotgun in the guy's hand as he circles his way up to the front. It's a slow jolt to my chest, all dread and churning sick. It's not just one guy. It's two.

Two robbers. Both white. Clean jeans, heavy boots. Black T-shirts, no logos.

I swallow with a click, my mouth dry like the desert, my heart doing a tap dance in the rhythm of *We're gonna die! Holy shit, we're gonna die!*

My hands are sweating. I clench them—God, how long has it been? Two minutes? Five? Time goes funny when you're pressed to the floor with a gun swinging in your face—and for the first time, I think about Lee.

Oh no. *Lee.*

I can't get shot. My sister will kill me. But first, she'll make it her life's mission to hunt down whoever shot me. And when she's got a mission, Lee's scary. I speak from experience, because when I was twelve, Lee got me away from our mom with the kind of long con that even the Queen of the Grift didn't see coming. She's in prison now . . . Mom, not Lee.

And I helped put her there.

I can't let fear take over. I have to keep calm and find a way out. This is a problem. Work the problem to fix the problem.

When we came in, who else was in the bank other than the teller? I trace it back in my head. There'd been a woman at the front of the line. Red Cap pushed her aside when he started shouting.

Now she's on the floor to my left, her purse tossed a foot away. Gray Cap had come up behind us. He must have been sitting in the waiting area.

My stomach somersaults when I remember that another person was sitting there—a kid. I can't turn my head enough to see where she ended up, but I glanced at her when I came in.

She's ten, maybe eleven. Does she belong to the woman up front? She must.

But I've got a perfect line of sight on the woman, and she hasn't even glanced toward the chairs where the kid was.

Okay. Five grown-ups or almost-grown-ups. One kid. Two bank robbers. Two guns at least, maybe more.

Those are bad numbers.

"We want in the basement." Red Cap keeps shoving his gun in the teller's face, and it's not helping. It's making her more scared, and if he keeps doing it . . .

"Stop shouting."

It's the first time Gray Cap's spoken. His voice is gruff, not like he's trying to disguise it, but like that's just the way it is. Like years of living have torn the insides out and all that's left is a suggestion of a voice. Instantly, Red Cap steps back.

"Get the cameras," Gray Cap orders. And the one in red scurries through the bank lobby and behind the teller stands, cutting the cords of the security cameras before returning to Gray Cap's side.

Iris nudges me. She's watching them as hard as I am. I press back to let her know I see it, too.

The guy in red may have made the first move, but Gray Cap's the one in charge.

"Where's Frayn?" Gray Cap asks.

"He's not here yet," the teller says.

"She's lying," Red Cap scoffs. But he licks his lips. He's spooked at the thought.

Who's Frayn?

"Go look," Gray Cap orders.

Red Cap's shoes pass by us, and he disappears from the lobby.

I take advantage of the moment, as soon as I'm sure he's out of sight and Gray Cap's distracted by the teller, to turn my head to the right. The kid's under the coffee table in the middle of the waiting area, and even this far away, I can see her shaking.

"The kid," Wes whispers to me. His eyes are on her, too.

I know, I mouth. I wish she'd meet my eyes, so I could at least shoot her some sort of reassuring look, but she's got her face pressed against the ugly brown carpet.

Footsteps. Fear kicks up a notch in my chest as Red Cap comes back. "Manager's office is locked."

The panic in his voice makes it crack.

"Where is Frayn?" Gray Cap demands again.

"He's late!" the teller squeaks out. "He had to go get Judy, our other teller. Her car wouldn't start. He's late."

Something's gone wrong. Whatever they've planned, the first step's been messed up. And when people screw up, in my experience, they do one of two things. They either run or they double down.

For a split second, I think they might run. That we'll get out of this with nightmares and a story that'll give us mileage at every party for the rest of our lives. But then, any hope of that gets shattered.

It's like slow motion. The bank door swings open, and that

security guard I'd been wondering about walks in, his hands full of coffee cups.

He doesn't have a chance. Red Cap—impulsive, shaky, and way too spooked—shoots before the guy can drop the lattes and reach for his stun baton.

The cups fall to the ground. Then so does the guard. Blood blossoms at his shoulder, a small stain that grows bigger by the second.

Things happen in rapid movement, like I'm being sped through a flipbook. Because this is where it gets real. Before the trigger's pulled, there's a slim chance of okay-ness you can hold on to.

After? Not so much.

As the guard falls forward, someone—the teller—screams. Wes throws himself toward Iris and me to shield us, and we curl up tight until we're this muddle of legs and arms and fear and hurt feelings that we really should be putting aside, all things considered . . . and me?

I grab my cell phone. I don't know if I'll have another chance. I slide it out of my jeans pocket as Gray Cap swears, stepping past our tangle on his way to disarm the guard and yell at Red Cap. Wes is leaning on it, so I can barely move my arm, but I manage to tap out a message to Lee.

Olive. Five letters. Definitely not my favorite food. Technically a fruit, just like the tomato.

And maybe the key to our freedom. For as long as I've known my sister, it's been our distress code. We are girls who prepare for storms.

Lee will come. My sister always shows up.

And she'll bring the cavalry.

Phone Call Transcript between
Lee Ann O'Malley and Deputy Jessica Reynolds

August 8, 9:18 a.m.

Deputy Reynolds: This is Reynolds.

O'Malley: Jess, it's Lee. Can you check to see if any silent alarms have been triggered at the bank? The branch on Miller Street, next to the old donut shop that moved last year?

Deputy Reynolds: You on a job? What's up?

O'Malley: Not a job. Nora sent me a distress signal.

Deputy Reynolds: You guys have a distress signal?

O'Malley: She's a teenage girl. Of course we have a distress signal. She told me she'd deposit the money the kids raised last night before coming into the office. I tracked her phone—she's still at the bank.

Deputy Reynolds: Someone mentioned the bank on the scanner earlier, but no alarms have gone off. Let me check . . . Here it is. The bank manager was in a car accident on the way to work. They took him to the hospital. You think Nora's pranking you?

O'Malley: She wouldn't. I'm heading over.

Deputy Reynolds: I'll meet you. Don't go in until I show up, okay?

[Silence]

Deputy Reynolds: Okay?

[End of call]

9:19 a.m. (7 minutes captive)

They're arguing. Red and Gray Cap. Red's freaking as the guard lies there on his back, bleeding into the carpet. Thank God he only got shot in the arm. He'll probably be okay. For now. But someone needs to put pressure on his wound, and they're just ignoring him.

"I told you this was a bad idea. You said no one would get hurt. That we'd just get Frayn into the basement to open the—"

"Quiet," Gray Cap growls, casting a glance toward us.

I keep my head down, but I'm listening to every word.

They've got to be talking about safe-deposit boxes. That's what's in the basement. Those things are gold mines of secrets. People love stashing stuff in there that they don't want anyone else to know about. But if the bank manager is the only person who can access the basement where the boxes are kept . . .

That's why they need him. And if he isn't here?

Boom goes their plan.

No wonder they're panicking hard enough to shoot. Someone might've heard the gunshot, but the bank is the only thing left in this once-full strip mall. And even if no one heard it . . . my text to Lee went through. Any minute, she's going to bring the wrath of O'Malley Private Investigations down on these guys. She'll probably rope in the sheriff's department. They're not great, but they'll bring guns.

More guns aren't always good, though. In most situations, more guns make everything worse. And cops always make things worse. But it's a risk I had to take to let Lee know something was wrong.

"Lock the doors and go watch the parking lot," Gray Cap orders. Red Cap scurries to obey, like he's grateful for something to do.

He's gonna be the weak link here. The mark, if I need one. My mind's skipping like flat rocks on a still pond, trying to make a plan.

"You," Gray Cap barks. Wes stiffens. His chest's still practically in my face, and I can feel his muscles flex as I realize Gray Cap's talking to him. "You're husky. Drag him away from the windows."

Wes glances down at me, just a one-second glance before he stands up, and the look on his face tells me not to worry.

Which, of course, sends me into a freaking tailspin. What's he going to do? He better just follow the guy's directions.

Gray Cap's gun and attention are on Wes as he moves toward the security guard, and it makes my skin crawl. My hand twists in Iris's, and she squeezes, trying to reassure me, but there's none of that here.

Wes bends, hesitating as he tries to figure out the best way to move the guard without hurting him more. He hefts him up in one movement. Wes is tall and strong, and sometimes that helps him, but here, right now, it makes him the biggest threat in this entire bank to those men, and my teeth dig into my lower lip as he turns to look at Gray Cap.

"Where do you want him?"

"Over there." The man gestures with the gun toward the little lobby area, where the kid's still hiding under the table.

My stomach drops, because Wes hesitates. That gun in Gray Cap's hand snaps back to him so fast, Iris sucks in a soft breath next to me.

"Was I not clear?" Gray Cap asks, and there it is. The anger in his voice. I've been waiting for it. Poised on a knife's edge until I heard it.

There's nothing like an angry man with a gun. I learned that early.

"Sorry, man, this is gonna hurt." Wes shifts the guard up, his face twisting as the man lets out a punch of a sound, all pain and fear. Wes handles him as gently as he can—I can see how careful he's being; Wes is always careful—but more blood spills down the man's arm as Wes places him down in the lobby area, away from the glass doors.

Gray Cap grabs one of the heavy posts that holds a sign advertising mortgage loans, tears the sign part off, and threads the metal pole through the handles of the bank's door, making it hard to flee and harder to breach.

This is getting worse by the minute. We don't have police in Clear Creek; we're too small and rural. We just have the sheriff and his six-deputy team, two of whom are part-time, and the closest SWAT team is . . . God, I don't even know. Sacramento, maybe? Hundreds of miles away through the mountains.

"All of you, get over there in the waiting area." Gray Cap gestures to where the guard and the kid are. We obey, and the teller joins us, her face still wet with tears as she stares down at the guard. Iris whips off her cardigan and presses it against the guard's shoulder, and then the teller seems to snap out of it, taking over for her with a shaky nod.

"It's gonna be okay, Hank," she tells the guard. His mouth twists in pain as she tries to stop the blood.

"Are you okay?" I ask the kid. Her eyes are wide and glassy. She jerks her head quickly.

"It's going to be fine," Wes tells her.

"Quiet, all of you. I want your phones, purses, keys, and wallets, everything in a pile, right there." Gray Cap points with the gun to the lobby table.

I place my phone and wallet on the table, Wes following my lead.

Iris sets her wicker-basket purse carefully next to our stuff, the red Bakelite cherries attached to the handle shaking at the movement. She glances at me as she sits back down, a gleam in her eye, and my stomach jolts as I realize what's missing on the table: She still has her silver lighter. I saw her pocket it in the parking lot. And it's still there, tucked in the folds of her vintage dress. The skirt is full, falling over Iris's second-poofiest crinoline, and the dress is tailored so well that the pocket's hidden in the sharp folds of cotton.

They don't make clothes like this anymore, Nora. She'd said that the first time we met, when she was spinning in that red skirt of hers with the gold swirls. It had flared out around her like magic, like she was the flick of flame before an inferno, and I hadn't been able to breathe around how much I wanted her to be *something* in my future.

Just like right now. She's my present and my future, with our only weapon tucked into deceptive layers of cotton and tulle. She's already thinking this through to freedom, and it's the spark of hope I need.

I nod the slightest bit to let her know I get it. One edge of her mouth quirks up so her dimple flashes, just for a second.

Asset #1: Lighter

— 5 —

The Iris of It All

When I met her, I didn't fall for Iris Moulton like a ton of bricks.

No, I actually tripped over her, like she *was* a ton of bricks.

One weekend last year, I'd been running some files downtown for Lee, and I wasn't looking where I was going. Next thing I know, I'm falling ass over ankles, the papers are everywhere, and this girl, this freckled brunette who looks like she's cosplaying a Hitchcock movie, is tangled up with me.

It was the perfect meet-cute, except when you're a girl who likes other girls, there's this little additional dance, because what if she doesn't? So you're not looking for red flags like a girl does with a guy—you're looking for rainbow ones.

I thought we were going to be friends. And we were, at first. But I told myself that's all we could be. After everything with Wes . . . I told myself I *couldn't*. Not until I figured out how to explain everything in a way that didn't ruin everything. And I was pretty sure that was impossible, so basically, I was looking at a life of celibacy and misery and hiding.

Then there was Iris, with her poofy fifties sundresses and her wicker purse shaped like a frog and that fixation on fire that would be creepy if you didn't know she wanted to be an arson investigator.

It took months. She slow-rolled a kind of subtle romantic warfare I didn't even see coming, and then one day, I was on a date with her before I even realized what was happening. It was a whole Mr. Darcy/Elizabeth Bennet *I was in the middle before I knew I'd begun* sort of thing, where I was Darcy and she was Elizabeth, and I do not have the gravitas or snobbery to pull a Darcy, let me tell you. But apparently, I had the Darcy cluelessness, because we were halfway through dinner before I realized it was maybe a date. Partly because I kept telling myself it *couldn't* be a date.

And I wasn't completely sure until she turned to me on our way home, halfway through the crosswalk on the empty street, and just stopped. Her hand slipped around my waist and her hip brushed against mine like she belonged there, and it felt like she did, in every vital part of me. The last thing I saw before her lips met mine was the *WALK* light illuminated in her eyes, and she kissed me like I was prickly, like I was already understood, like I was worth it.

It had been *sparkly*. I hadn't even realized you could feel sparkly. I thought it was strictly a sequin-and-glitter-and-precious-gemstone thing, but then all of a sudden Iris Moulton kissed me and proved me wrong, and it was just sparkles lighting up my darkness everywhere.

I didn't fall for Iris like a ton of bricks.

I fell like I was a star and she was the end of the world. A cataclysmic crash of two people, never to be the same. Never getting back up.

Not unless we were doing it together.

6

1 lighter, no plan

"What's this?"

Gray Cap's pulled the bank bag from Iris's purse. He unzips it, inspects the thick wad of cash, and then looks at her.

"It's money we raised for the animal shelter," I say quickly. His attention slides from her to me, and the relief knocks inside my ribs like that silly, ornate bee door knocker Lee put on our front door. "We had a fundraiser. Take it. There's almost three thousand dollars."

He laughs, and it's a sound I know, just like the gun is a sight I know. It's curling in its cruelty and condescension. Designed to snake around me and make me feel even smaller than the gun does.

But I'm past the fear now. It's not gone, but it's not useful. I can only do useful right now.

"Handing over the big bucks, huh?"

The more he talks, the more I learn. So I should keep him talking. "It's what we've got."

He tosses the open bag on the table, and the money skitters out, fanning across the polished surface. "It's not what I want."

Then he grabs the table, dragging it—and all our phones—away from us.

20

What do you want? That's the question, right? My mom used to tell me: *Give a person what they want, you'll have them in the palm of your hand.* That goes double or maybe even triple for bank robbers whose plan has gone kablooey.

They want the bank manager. They can't have him. So that means they need what the bank manager would have given them.

Access to the safe-deposit boxes.

How do I give them that? Do I need to give them that? Or do I just need them to *think* I can give them that?

A plan is flitting in my brain like a bug around a porch light, but I'm not sure where all the pieces fall yet. I need more. More information. More clues. More time to understand the dynamic between these two.

But I'm not going to get it. Red Cap lets out a noise from the door, startled and worried.

"Someone's coming," he calls from his lookout spot. "Woman."

Gray Cap's focus whips from us to the door.

It's like the seven of us tense as a unit when the sound of the door rattling fills the dead-quiet bank. The sound echoes off the walls and then stops. Agonizing seconds tick by.

"She's heading back to her car."

"Keep out of sight," Gray Cap snaps.

It's a breath-holding moment, and just when they're about to let it out . . .

Feedback lances through the parking lot. You can hear it clear inside the bank before her voice booms through the walls, magnified by the megaphone:

"I'm talking to the person who's got the gun inside the bank. My name is Lee. In a few seconds, the phone in there's gonna start ringing. That'll be me calling. Pick up, we can figure out a solution to this problem you've found yourself in. Don't pick up? Well, that's a choice you can make. I don't think you want to make that choice, though."

As soon as she stops talking, I start counting.

Ten. Nine. Eight.

Red Cap scrambles away from the door, peering out the window instead.

Seven. Six. Five.

Gray Cap rounds on us, the wounded guard, the scared teller, the older lady, the three teenagers pissed off at each other, and the kid.

Four. Three. Two.

His gun's rising. Mouth's opening. Anger's coming. The dangerous kind.

One.

The phone behind the teller's booth starts to ring.

Go Time.

7

The Sister in Question

I should elaborate on my sister here. Because yes, she is the type of woman who comes equipped with a megaphone. Also a shotgun that shoots beanbag rounds instead of bullets, and the kind of fist that feels like it's full of goddamn lead even when we're just sparring.

Lee's almost twenty years older than me, so she'd gotten out before I was even born, ditching Mom a few years before then. We're not full sisters, but we're bound together by the same crooked set of con-artist genetics.

She was a kid during a time where Mom wasn't grifting. Lee's dad, he'd been a completely regular guy, but he died. And that's how Mom got into running cons: to keep the lifestyle she was used to.

It all unraveled pretty fast. When they fell, they fell from a damn tall height, so the crash was all the worse. And when they rose again, what Mom *did* to rise like that . . . Well, Lee doesn't talk about that time. Not when she's sober, at least.

I wonder if she thinks I'll judge her. I don't know how she thinks I could. She knows what I've had to do to survive.

Broken girls, both of us, growing up into women with cracks plastered rough over where smooth should be.

Me, I was born into the con. Came into the world with a lie on my lips and the ability to smile and dazzle, just like my mother. *Charm*, people call it. *Useful* is what it is. To see into the heart of someone and adjust accordingly, instantaneously, to mirror that heart? It's not a gift or a curse. It's just a tool.

I've never known a time when Mom wasn't working someone. Or what it's like to have a dad who loves you, even briefly. And I've never known a life outside of lying.

But I remember the first day I met Lee. I was six, and she was . . . *strong*. In the way she moved, how she dressed, the look she shot Mom when she started making excuses about my not going to school . . .

I'd never seen anyone who could shut Mom up. Mom was the one who bewitched people.

Lee didn't need to bewitch. She commanded.

I'd never felt more instantly connected to a person in my life. I didn't love her immediately. I was already too wary for that. But I recognized something in her, something I wanted to be but couldn't even articulate yet: *free*.

I didn't know then that she walked away from that day with a plan forming. The idea that I was out there under Mom's thumb gnawed at her. And Lee, she's the type that gnaws right back. It would take six years for her to execute her plan fully. But when she's got a mission, Lee's scary-focused. And getting me away from Mom was her mission.

Now? Getting me out of the bank is her mission. But I'm not twelve anymore, and she's not alone this time.

She's got me.

1 lighter, no plan

Gray Cap's gun is steady, but his eyes aren't. They're darting back and forth, from the seven of us to the ringing phone, then to Red Cap's position near the door. He can't decide where to pour his anger.

I can see the moment it clicks. His focus zeroes in on the teller to our left, the shotgun swinging to point at her. "Did you hit the alarm?"

I'm jammed between Iris and Wes like Nora-meat in a sandwich, so when Wes tenses and Iris's breath hitches, I don't just hear it and feel it, I'm practically absorbing their stress through my skin. Because they both know if Lee's outside, it's because *I* sounded the (metaphorical) alarm.

"No, no, I didn't!" the teller insists.

He steps forward again, into the little lobby we're crowded in, and we can't shrink away fast enough because there's nowhere to hide.

"Is she in a patrol car?" Gray Cap asks Red, who's still flattened against the wall, peering out the sliver of window available to him.

He shakes his head. "Silver truck. She's dressed normal."

"Gun?"

25

Several. But Lee won't pull them out unless she has to.

"Can't see one."

Gray Cap is just itching to shoot someone. I can see it in every line of his face. I know that look.

The phone keeps ringing. My sister's outside, a wall and who knows how many feet away. Lee's been my sense of safety forever, and I want her like I'm little again. Like I wanted her that night when everything went to hell.

I have to remind myself I'm older now. Almost a grown woman, with my shit-kicker boots and my choppy hair, and all the damage wrought on me scarred into strength. I hate the whole "what doesn't kill you makes you stronger" saying. It's bullshit. Sometimes what doesn't kill you is worse. Sometimes what kills you is preferable. Sometimes what doesn't kill you messes you up so bad it's always a fight to make it through what you're left with.

What didn't kill me didn't make me stronger; what didn't kill me made me a victim.

But I made me stronger. I made me a survivor.

Well, me and Lee and my very patient therapist.

"Maybe you should answer the phone?" The teller's voice trembles as she suggests it. "The police—they'll give you what you want, I'm sure." Her words dissolve as Gray Cap turns to stare at her, the gun swinging close.

"What's your name?" he asks.

"Olivia."

"I'm going to just get this out there," he says, leaning forward. "Whatever they've trained you to do in a robbery? Throw it away, sweetheart. I know your rules—and the cops' playbook—front to back."

"Please," she whimpers.

I'm so sure he's going to shoot her, I'm about to rise to my feet when the phone stops ringing, and the silence is so abrupt, it snatches his attention away.

Iris's shoulder twists against mine, and Gray Cap whirls at the absence of noise, too late to stop Red Cap from picking up my sister's call.

"You fucking—" he starts, and then he doesn't say anything else, running over to the phone and snatching it out of his partner's hands.

There's a split second where he hesitates. I see how his fingers curl around the receiver like he wants it to be a neck, and his shoulders tense like he wants to slam the phone down on the counter.

But then his shoulders straighten, and instead of breaking the phone, he raises it to his ear.

"You have twenty seconds."

9

Phone Transcript, Lee Ann O'Malley
Engages Hostage Taker #1 (HT1)

August 8, 9:33 a.m.

HT1: You have twenty seconds.

O'Malley: I'll get to the point, then, since I already introduced myself. What's your name?

HT1: My name doesn't matter. Ten seconds.

O'Malley: What do you want?

HT1: I have seven hostages. I want Theodore Frayn. Get him here. Now. Or I start shooting.

[Call disconnected]

9:34 a.m. (22 minutes captive)

1 lighter, no plan

"Get them up," Gray Cap orders as soon as he hangs up like a big drama king instead of actually talking to Lee. He said he knew the playbook, but he's not acting like he does. He just played his cards, tossing them out to Lee without holding anything back.

"Up! You, the boy—grab the guard." Red Cap jabs his handgun at us, and we already know how trigger-happy he is, so we scramble to obey. I go over to help Wes with the guard, and together we shuffle him down the hall as Red Cap herds us into the back of the bank, where the offices are.

"Kids in this one," Gray Cap orders, pointing to the room on the left. "Adults in that one." He points to the office across from ours.

"The kids—" Olivia, the teller, starts, her eyes widening as she looks at us.

"No arguments. Put him in the room with them," he tells Wes and me.

We lower the guard to the carpet in the office, and then Wes grabs my hand and tugs me toward the room across the hall.

"Kids, it's gonna be okay," Olivia says to all four of us, but she's so damn scared that it sounds like more of a shaky question than a reassurance, and then Gray Cap closes the door behind him and he's alone in the room with them and we can't do anything but let Red Cap herd us into our own, separate office. He rips the phone off the desk and tucks it under his arm.

Iris shifts every time he moves, sliding her body in front of the little girl.

"Stay quiet," Red Cap says. Then he leaves the room, closing the door behind him, followed by a scraping noise—he's dragging something to block it.

There's no lock, and I don't try to push it. Not yet. Red Cap might still be outside. I press my ear against it, and I think I hear the snick of the door across the hall opening, but I'm not sure. They might both be out there, and if they see the doorknob turning . . .

Iris lets out a shaky breath. The kid stifles a sob. Wes's eyes are darker than I've ever seen them.

"We need to focus," I say, and the words seem to snap the scared silence that's taken over us. "We can't fall apart." I'm not saying it to them, I'm saying it to myself, but it seems to do the same thing for me as it does for them, because the three of us take a breath. We're older and we need to be okay, because God, the kid is small and scared. Was I that small when I was that scared?

"You're right," Iris says briskly, her shoulders straightening like she's wearing armor instead of splashes of watercolor on cotton over tulle.

I turn around, scanning the room. No windows. No doors. A desk.

"I'll distract the kid," Wes mutters.

"We've got the desk," Iris replies.

Wes goes over to crouch next to the little girl, talking in a low voice as Iris and I turn to the desk. The phone is out, obviously, but maybe there's something inside that could help us.

"Check for weapons." I hurry over to it and Iris follows me, taking the left drawers as I take the right.

"They cut the cameras," Iris says in a low voice. "And they're already shooting the ones who pose the most threat."

I pause midpull. I can see sticky notes and pens in the first drawer, a stapler I suppose I could use as a club in a pinch. But for a second, all I can hear are her words.

"I know," I say, just as quiet.

She reaches out, her fingers closing over my wrist long enough to squeeze. It's not an *It'll be okay* touch, because she's just spoken the words that say it's not. It's an *I'm here* touch, and it's enough. It has to be. Because it's all we have.

She pulls away, turning back to her side of the desk, rummaging through the drawer.

"Booze," Iris reports, holding up three airplane-sized bottles of cheap vodka.

"Fire starter?"

"Possibly." She tucks them into the pocket of her dress.

Asset #2: 3 bottles of vodka

I bend back down and yank open the second drawer. It's just files, but I rake through them in case there's something hidden between the stacks of papers. There isn't.

"Scissors!" I grab them from the last drawer, but they're the big kind, and there's no way they're going to fit in Iris's pocket. Her dress is not Mary Poppins's handbag, unfortunately.

"Maybe I can . . ." She takes them from me and tries to stick them down the neck of her dress, where I know her underwear is, well, kind of delightfully complicated. Vintage lingerie is extensive, and Iris likes authenticity. But she can't find a way to get the scissors to lie flat, even with whatever antique thingamabob she's got on today.

"Let me." I take them from her when she offers, and push them into the waistband of my baggy jeans, letting my flannel drape over the handle that's peeking out from beneath my belt. I swish back and forth for a second as Iris watches. "Can you see the outline?"

She shakes her head.

"Okay. Good."

Asset #3: Scissors

"Anything else?"

I pull open the last drawer, but it's empty.

"Nothing."

Our eyes meet, a clash of her brown with my blue, and in that second, we both let the panic creep in. It's not enough. We don't have nearly enough.

And then she licks her lips and I square my shoulders and we snap to it.

"We need information," Iris says.

"I know," I answer, but I'm staring at the girl. "Where's her grown-up?" I ask suddenly.

"What?"

"She didn't go to any of the adults when they put us all together in the lobby," I say as I think back. "And none of them freaked out when they put her in here with us. Wouldn't you, being separated from your kid?"

Iris's head tilts, her eyebrows knitting together. And then without another word, she walks over to Wes and the girl, a gentle smile on her face as she bends down.

"Hey, honey," she says. "I'm Iris. What's your name?"

"Casey," the girl says. "Casey Frayn."

The bottom drops out of my stomach. The bank manager's last name. "You're here waiting for your dad, aren't you?" and my voice shakes because I know the answer even before she nods.

"He's the manager?"

She nods again.

I look up at Iris and Wes, and my face has got to be a mirror of theirs right now. All *Oh holy fuck, we're even more screwed.*

Problem #1: Bank robbery goes wrong because of
    missing bank manager.

Problem #2: Bank robbers have the ultimate leverage
    over the missing bank manager . . . They just don't
    know it.

I give her my best bullshit smile. "Casey, will you check that second drawer of the desk for me, the one with all the files? I'm worried I missed something."

"Okay."

She goes over to the desk, and Wes says, "They wanted the bank manager," as soon as she's out of earshot.

"And they haven't tried to get the teller to give them any money.

They haven't even mentioned the vault. Just the basement and the bank manager," Iris adds. "Something strange is going on. This isn't a normal *grab the cash and go* kind of robbery."

"What are we going to do?" Wes asks.

I look over my shoulder at Casey, bent down next to the desk, rummaging through the files.

"We need to learn more. They need the manager for something other than the vault if they keep asking for him."

"I don't think the bank robbers are gonna tell us their whole plan, Nora," Wes says, and the frustration that's been simmering in him since the parking lot leaches into his voice so fast it makes my cheeks heat.

Right. He's still pissed at me. Like, really, really, *really* pissed.

And he has good reason to be. Walking in on your former girlfriend making out with the girl you're both friends with is basically a fish-slap in the face when it comes to ex encounters. Even worse than that, I'd broken a promise about not lying to him anymore. He and I don't break promises to each other, not after I broke us and then we managed to painfully assemble the parts back together. *Franken-friends,* he likes to joke, and it always makes me laugh, because it's true . . . and it's edged in a dark twist of humor that the new us—the Franken-friends—needs to exist.

But there's no humor in him right now, and if my entire adrenaline system wasn't firing at the speed of light, it'd scare me. But considering I don't know if we're going to last the next five minutes, I have to put it aside. Focus.

How do you hide a girl in plain sight?

They'll want our names, eventually, if they haven't gotten them off of our IDs already. Shit. Her ID.

"Casey, did you have an ID with you?"

She looks up from the desk and shakes her head. "I left my bag at my mom's. She was mad because she didn't have time to go back and get it, she had a meeting. My phone was in there, too."

"Good," I say, and she frowns.

"Listen, if either of them out there asks, do not tell them your real name," I say. "Do not mention who your dad is. Tell them your last name is Moulton. You're Iris's cousin, okay?"

Her frown deepens. She doesn't get it, and there's not enough time to explain, because I hear the scraping outside the door. One of them is coming back.

"Casey, tell me you're on board." I'm throwing her headfirst into this, and her eyes are wide and she doesn't get it, because deception wasn't built into her blood and brain like it's been in mine.

"I—"

"Casey Moulton. Say it."

Doorknob's turning.

"Casey Moulton," she whispers.

Door swings open.

11

Rebecca: Sweet, Silent, Smiling

One of my clearest early memories is my mother standing me in front of the mirror and combing my blond hair back off my shoulders as she said, *Rebecca. Your name is Rebecca. Say it, sweetie. Rebecca Wakefield.*

My name isn't Rebecca, if you were wondering.

It's not really Nora, either. But everyone in Clear Creek knows me as Nora.

I thought it was a game. The Rebecca thing. But later Mom slaps my arm when I answer to anything but Rebecca, and I learn it isn't a game.

I learn it's my life.

Rebecca. Samantha. Haley. Katie. Ashley.

The girls I've been. The perfect daughters to the women my mother has become to con her marks.

Each girl was me, but different. *The best con has a seed of truth.* She taught me well, to take those truths and spin them into stories so believable no one would think to question them.

Rebecca wears her hair loose with an Alice band holding it back. This is when Mom stops letting me cut it beyond a trim. By the time Lee gets me out when I'm twelve, it hangs down to my hips, and people sometimes stop Mom or me to coo about how pretty it is. Rebecca wears a lot of pink. I tell Mom I don't like pink as much as purple, and she says Rebecca loves pink, that it's her favorite color . . . and then she makes me repeat it.

She makes me repeat a lot of things when we're alone. My brain is a sponge, that's what she says, and I need to learn early what the world is like. *You and me, baby. We're going to be something.*

That *something* turns out to be criminals.

Rebecca is Justine's daughter. Justine is my mother and also not her. She wears brown contacts and pencil skirts, and she calls people *sugar* with a little lilt to her voice that Mom doesn't have. Justine works as a receptionist in an insurance office, and her mark is Kenneth, the CFO. He's skimming from the company coffers—not that the insurance game isn't already a huge racket, but that's another conversation—and she's got him paying her in a blackmail scheme quicker than you can snap your fingers.

I'm little then. I'm still learning. So I don't have to do much but be cute and charming when she brings me into the office. It softens her image, and no one would ever suspect the sweet widowed receptionist with the adorable little girl.

Being Rebecca teaches me how to lie. How to look into someone's eyes while there isn't a true word coming out of your mouth, but they believe it because enough of *you* believes it. It sharpens me too soon, this power and the blurred lines between truth and lie. I'm not a cute seven-year-old lying wide-eyed and obvious about stealing a cookie. I'm manipulating people. Figuring out what actions get the desired reactions. What kind of smile gets a smile in return. What cute little twirling dance will make the older ladies at the office clap their hands and give me candy. What whimpering tantrum can work when Mom needs me to be a distraction as she slips past, papers in hand, plotting, always plotting.

Each step into Rebecca's skin is a step out of my own, but I'm expected to snap back into myself as soon as Mom says the word, as soon as we're alone, and I'm constantly reeling from the shift. Nothing's steady. There's no solid ground. I learn to dance on a tilting one instead.

Mom always knows when to pull the plug, and before Kenneth can get vengeful enough or cheap enough to come for us or use whatever he's stashed away to put a hit out on her, we're gone, ditching the town and those names. Soon, she'll be researching a new mark and standing me in front of a mirror in a new town, fixing my hair in a new way, and saying, Samantha. *Your name is Samantha.*

She chooses bad men. She says there's justice in stripping them of their money and therefore their dignity, because to men like that, money is everything, and they're not much without it.

But as the years pass and the names on my list of girls grows, the truth is hard to deny. She chooses bad men because she *likes* bad men. She's drawn to them and the risk they present, because she's all risk, full throttle, all the time. She chose this ride and put me on it with no way off, and then I grow up drawn to bad men, too, like mother, like daughter.

There's just one difference between her and me. She's drawn to bad men because deep down, she wants to love them. She needs them to love her.

I don't want to love them, and I've never needed to be loved by them.

I learned very early, the best thing you can expect from them is pain.

And the best thing you can do with a bad man is destroy him.

12

1 lighter, 3 bottles of vodka, 1 pair of scissors, no plan

This time, it's Gray Cap who comes into the office.

His knuckles are bloody. It's the first thing I notice, and it makes me want to crowd next to Casey, to hide her from him.

Who did he hurt? The guard, more? The teller, first? Or the woman who'd just cried, stone-faced, the whole time we were in the lobby?

What to do, what to do, my mind's skipping and turning, and all I know is that keeping Casey's real identity from them is the safest thing for her, so I focus on that. Hide Casey.

I have the scissors. I'll use them if I have to.

A shiver runs down my neck at the thought. I've been running from what the girls all taught me for a long time. When Lee got me out that first year, I used to whisper their names to get to sleep. *Rebecca. Samantha. Haley. Katie. Ashley.*

I haven't had to do that in a long time. I want to do it right now, but I force myself to focus. He's saying something.

"Get in the corner."

Wes plants himself in front of us in the corner as we obey, and Gray Cap's mouth twitches at the show of protectiveness.

"Go through it," he orders, and for a second I'm confused, but then Red Cap steps inside.

I watch as he searches the room and goes through the desk, tries to yank at the fake cabinets on the back wall that are sealed shut.

"Goddamn it," he says. "Nothing."

That's when I realize they're not trying to weapon-proof the room. They're looking for something.

Give the mark something they want. First step of a con. It builds trust. Find out what they want and provide it.

Red Cap stalks out of the room and Gray Cap's about to follow, so I tilt forward, trying to catch a glimpse of the hall, but it's no use. I can't see a thing.

"There's gotta be a toolbox somewhere," Red Cap mutters as the door closes behind them, and then there's just the sound of whatever they're using to block the door being dragged back into place.

I hurry over to the door and press my ear to it. Then: not voices, but sirens.

Sheriff's here. Things are moving too fast. I need time and I don't have it. I have to make some assumptions.

Assumption #1: The men out there aren't just here for money, they're here for something that only the manager has access to: the safe-deposit boxes. You need keys to get into those. Maybe even to access the vault they're in.

Assumption #2: They're trying to break into the manager's office because they need keys.

The sirens are off now, but I can hear the distant sound of the bank phones ringing in the front. They're trying to make contact again. Clock's run out. Time to move, Nora. Make a damn plan.

"Casey." I turn toward where she's sitting in the corner, slumped over and cried out. "I want you to tell me everything you know about your dad."

"My dad . . . What do you mean?"

"You said your mom dropped you off. Are they divorced?"

"Yeah, for three years now."

"Do you like your dad?"

She frowns at me like it's a ridiculous question, which tells me a lot. "Of course. I love him."

"Is he worried about money? Who wanted the divorce, him or your mom?"

"Why does that matter?"

Iris shoots me a look, then smiles reassuringly at Casey. "Honey, the guys out there? They're here for your dad. And they aren't trying to get into the cash drawers or the safe. That's . . . well, it's weird. So if you know anything, overheard anything, we don't want to get your dad in trouble. We just want to figure out what those guys want. The sooner they get what they want, the sooner we can go home."

"Are we going to get home?" she asks, and she tries not to let the tears escape, but they do, and when she wipes them away, I give her the grace of pretending not to notice. She's trying hard to be brave.

Kids like her, they're not trained for bank robberies.

Kids like her, they're trained for school shootings.

Run. Hide. Fight.

We all know the drill. We've all thought about it. We have to.

Who will you be, if it comes down to it? No shame in ____
No judgment in hiding. Nothing but fear in fighting.

But here and now, there's nowhere to run. No place to hide
really, is there a choice?

Be a viper, baby. Always be ready to bite back. That's how I was
raised. But you never know if you can do it until it happens to you.

"Yes, we are getting home," Iris says, and it sounds like she
means it even though she's just hoping. "But we need to work
together. Is there anything you can think of?"

"Dad was in Gamblers Anonymous, but he stopped going. That's
when my mom filed for divorce."

"Has anyone stopped by his place while you were there?" I ask.
"Men looking for money? Has your dad gotten hurt lately? Any
bruises? Broken bones?" Was this some sort of loan shark thing
gone wrong? Is that why they aren't wearing masks?

"No, I don't think so."

"Are there any nights he's gone?"

"I only see him three times a week," Casey says. "But . . . we
used to do Tuesday through Thursday, and now we do weekend
through Monday. I know he asked for the change, because my
mom was upset about losing our weekends. She told my aunt that
he'd probably found a new poker game."

I frown, something twisting in my brain, and when I look up at
Wes, I see his eyebrows are scrunched up, too.

"Doesn't your dad run his poker game on Thursday?" I ask Wes.

Wes nods. "When my mom stays in Chico for the opera board
meeting. He says it's just friends, but you know him."

"Oh yeah, I know him." It trips out of my mouth, all vile and dis-
gusted because I can't help myself. Mayor Prentiss hates my guts,

and the feeling is very mutual. He first hated me because Wes wasn't supposed to be dating a girl with short hair who owns more flannel than his son. It was Not Done. The horror! When we broke up, I know he thought he'd won the battle I started with him, but he's always been bad at predicting Wes's goodness; he couldn't do a thing when we stayed friends. "How much money do you think is getting tossed around those games?"

"I have no idea. It's been years since I've been in the house during a game."

"Sorry," I mutter, because this is a wound I don't like prodding, but here I am, jabbing it. "You've seen the guys who show up at the games, though, right?"

He nods.

"Anyone like Red or Gray Cap ever show up?"

"No way."

"What about a bank manager?"

"Yeah, probably, if they knew someone and had the buy-in," Wes says. "What are you thinking?"

"I don't know," I say. "The robbers know Casey's dad from somewhere. If he's a gambler, maybe he was blabbing somewhere."

"There are casinos," Wes reminds me.

"He wouldn't want to be seen," I say. "It broke up his marriage." I glance apologetically at Casey, but she just keeps watching me. "He's still respected in the community. He's trying to keep his problem quiet. A private game with the mayor . . . That has prestige and a kind of social cover that public slot machines don't have."

"So you think he's in debt to someone at my dad's poker game and they've sent thugs to rob him?" Wes asks.

"No," I say. "It's just . . . they asked Lee for the manager, and now they want a toolbox."

"Which means they didn't plan on needing tools," Iris says. "They thought the manager would be here to give them access."

"They need something in his office," I say. "Keys to downstairs, I'm thinking? His office is still locked because he had to go pick up the other teller. Olivia, the teller who's here, must not have a key. So they'll have to break in . . ."

"I don't get how that helps us," Casey says.

"If we know what they want, we can give it to them," Wes says. "It builds trust. It might buy us time."

He's echoing words I've told him, but his voice is as dead as his eyes, and he really is never going to let me live this down, is he? I pray that I live long enough to change that, but as I look up at the ceiling, trying to figure out how to pull this off, I'm starting to wonder if that's even close to possible.

My gaze snags on the air vent. In this old brick building, it's one of the big ones.

Big enough to fit into.

The manager's office is three doors down and across from this one. I saw the placard earlier. I'd have to be quiet. And quick.

There's a crashing sound through the door, and suddenly the constant telephone ringing stops. And then I hear Red Cap call my sister a name I will not repeat here.

My fingers curl into fists and I try not to wince when my nails press into my skin too hard. I keep my nails a little long, because sometimes you don't have any weapons but you.

I look back up at the air vent.

It's a bad idea.

It's a terrible beginning of a truly horrible plan.

But it's the only one I've got.

Iris sits down next to Casey on the floor and starts talking to her about school, trying to distract her from the thumping coming from outside. It's not working, but it's an effort.

I move across the room, right underneath the air vent, looking up at it.

"What are you doing?" Wes asks quietly, following me.

I point up at the vent. "Think you can boost me into there?"

"We can't get out that way."

"I don't want to get out. I want to get in."

His eyes widen. "Into the manager's office?"

"They want in, right? Red Cap was looking for tools, because if they start shooting the door, the police will come in. So if I open the door from the inside . . ."

"It's dangerous." He steps back, his arms folding, the universal sign of stubbornness, and then he does that twist of his lips that I'm so familiar with, the Wes sign of stubbornness. "You can't."

"Wes, think for a second," I say in a low voice. "Who does he remind you of?"

I don't need to clarify that it's Gray Cap I mean, not Red Cap, who's bumbling and reactive and we've both noticed.

Gray Cap's not bumbling.

Gray Cap's cruel. Wes and I both know cruel. I hate how well we know it. Wish that it was just one of us. Wish it was just me, but it's not.

There's a scar curved on the back of my hip, a crooked horse-shoe of sorts, and it doesn't match the knot of damaged tissue on

Wes's shoulder. But the first time he saw it, before we were even teenagers, he placed a hand over it and asked me, *Who kicked you?* I knew what it meant, the urgency in his voice, that he knew the shape a boot heel makes on skin so easily. And the only answer I could give in the prickle of understanding between us was to place my palm over the scar on his shoulder, the one that streaked across it in an odd, square pucker like a belt buckle, and ask, *Who hit you?*

This we share. Scars and knowledge and broken safety that was never really there in the first place, because we were born to bad apples.

The difference is, he grew far from the fruit that tree bore, while I'm rotten at the core, even if I'm good at hiding it.

"They just want what they came for," Wes says, like he wants it to be true. "If they get it . . ."

"They're not wearing masks," I say, and this time, unlike with Iris, I don't push it away. His chest hitches with the breath he takes in, because he knows. He knows what I'm going to say next.

I say it anyway. I need to make it real. Their job has gone wrong. They've already shot one person. We need to make a move.

"They are going to kill some of us," I say as quietly as possible, and he doesn't blink and I don't waver. "It's the only solid negotiation tactic they have. And you saw him in the lobby."

"He almost shot the teller."

"The one in red is stupid. But the other one . . ."

"He likes it."

Relief snaps open inside me like a trapdoor. Wes understands. He may not have had a slew of bad men in his life like mine, but Wes has had to live with his for seventeen years, and the sheer endurance it takes to survive that brings skills, too.

There won't be any heroes today. Just survivors. And I'll need him and Iris on board if we're going to survive.

"We need to be useful," I continue. "If you're useful, they don't shoot you first. If you're useful, they *listen to you.*"

"If you're useful, their *focus is on you.*"

"Exactly."

"Fuck, Nora."

He's stepping back, like I'm some toxic mold whose spores are reaching out, grabby for him. It's like the day he found out all over again, and they must be showing in my face and the light in my eyes: the girls I work so hard to keep hidden. But I need them now, all of them, with their crooked knowledge and their boot-heel scars and their Frankenstein hearts.

It's how we get through this.

"Trust me."

"You're asking me to trust a version of you I don't know," he says, and God, I hate how he just cuts to the truth sometimes. But I can, too.

"You know this version, you just don't like her. You can trust me or not, but you do know who I am, Wes. You're the only person who does. Because I laid every single secret down on the table for you to examine with a magnifying glass."

"Only because I found out."

"We are not getting into this fight again!" I hiss. "Are you going to boost me up into the vent or not?"

"Yes," he hisses back. "Of course I am!"

"Then why are you being an ass?"

"Because I'm so fucking pissed at you for lying to my face! Repeatedly!"

"Well . . . too bad!" And in the time it takes me to breathe and try to come up with a good comeback, I just deflate, and then so does he.

"Fuck, Nora," he says again, and his eyes beg me to understand. "They're gonna kill us."

"Maybe not, if we can stay one step ahead."

"You can't stay a step ahead of a guy with a gun, Nora."

I don't say anything.

Because I have, once before.

It was different then.

I was different.

But I did it.

Now I have to do it again.

13

The Making of the Franken-Friends
(aka The Destruction of WesandNora)

Let me get one thing clear, right here, right now: Wes and I didn't break up because I had a big gay epiphany. Partly because I'm not gay.

We didn't break up because I had a big bisexual epiphany, either. Even though I am bi. But we both knew that before Wes and I even got together.

We broke up because I lied. Not about my sexuality or my feelings. But about pretty much everything else, down to my name. And he found out himself—I didn't even cave and tell him, which would've been better, in his eyes . . . and worse in mine. But there was no going back after he found out. It destroyed our relationship in one gutting swoop of a day. It almost destroyed what tatters of our friendship were left after my lies punched through our sweet little world.

When Lee facilitated my escape five years ago, her side of the con and her sacrifices kept me clean legally, but I almost messed it all up. That meant there were consequences. I had to play my own game on top of the complicated chess match Lee was playing without Mom knowing.

I lost things and found others, only to lose them, too.

My sister buried her history years ago. She made a new name, a whole new identity to wrap herself in, far from Mom's reach or knowledge. She settled in a town where no one would think to look for her, and no one in Clear Creek was the wiser when she introduced herself as Lee O'Malley. She dyed her blond hair brunette faithfully, so no roots ever showed, and set up her office in town. She made "friends" with the deputies at the sheriff's department, and she never, ever slept without a knife in easy reach, because some traits you can dye away and some names you can forge fresh, but you can't hide from your true self and the lessons you learned in the dark of night.

Before she brought me home, Lee cut my blond hair that Mom had always insisted I keep long. As she dyed my hair and eyebrows brown over the motel room sink, she told me about the two-bedroom house she had on the outskirts of town, and my new room and my new school and my new backstory. By the time we walked out of that room and headed to the place I'd learn to feel like and call home, I'd shed the girl I'd been as easy as my hair . . . and Nora O'Malley was born in a flash and a few words . . . and she was supposed to be here to stay.

So I told myself that the girls I'd been before didn't matter.

I learned the hard way that I was wrong.

14

1 lighter, 3 bottles of vodka, 1 pair of scissors
Plan: Almost there

"Hey, you two." Iris snaps her fingers behind us, and we both whirl. She's staring intently, her hands on her hips, her skirt swaying in annoyance because she's tapping her foot. "Why are you arguing?"

"We're not," Wes says immediately.

"You're mad at us," Iris says. "Are we seriously going to do this now?"

"I'm trying not to," Wes grits out.

But Iris steps closer, so Casey can't hear. "What is with you?" she hisses in a low voice to him. "You told me you were completely over Nora. I would've never tried anything if . . . You were going to ask Amanda out! I had a first-date outfit planned for you. So either you changed your mind or you've gone insane and gotten all bigoted on me, and I swear to God, Wes . . ."

He goes white. "Fuck, *no*. It's not— I *am* over Nora." He looks at me. "I am *completely* over you," he says, and it's not vicious and it doesn't have any hurt buried under it. It's just . . . a statement. A fact. Something we both know. It still makes me vaguely sad, in that faded way, like a scar you press too hard on and the damaged

52

tissue remembers the wound fresh, but just for a second, and then it's gone.

"And if we get the hell out of here alive, I *am* going to ask Amanda out," Wes declares. "I'm not mad about that."

"If you're just mad we kept it from you, I don't owe you a beat-by-beat account of my love life," Iris says. "You know I'm not out to my mom yet. I have my reasons for keeping stuff under the radar."

"I'm not mad at you, Iris," Wes says. "You're right, your reasons are yours. I'm sorry I was a jerk. I shouldn't have been. You don't deserve that." He takes a deep breath, his chest rising. "But I get to be mad at her," he continues. "For my sake and your sake. Not just because she lied to my face when I told her I thought you liked her." He glares at me and I turn red, because I had been a total ass when he'd suggested it. "I get to be mad for you because she's put you in the same place I was once." His voice cracks as he stares at me, practically drilling a hole in my head with his eyes.

Iris frowns. "What are you talking about?"

"How much have you told her?" Wes asks me. "You said you'd never—"

"I said next time, I'd work my way up to it," I snap, my temper flaring red-hot in my chest, part anger, part guilt. "Excuse me if I didn't realize I was required to throw all my secrets out there three months into a new relationship. I don't owe you anything, Wes."

His eyes flare with that deep kind of hurt. "You owed it to me to not outright lie to me."

"I—" I snap my mouth shut, because I can't defend myself. I had. He'd told me last month: *I think she has a crush on you*, and he'd nudged me with his elbow in an entirely new, almost teasing way.

Wes playing matchmaker when the match was already made was bordering on rom-com territory, and I had been kissing Iris for a while at that point. It'd taken everything I had in me not to turn bright red before I shook my head and said, *You know, just because we both like girls doesn't mean we're gonna like each other* in such a bored voice he'd been the one flushing and apologizing.

I've felt like an asshole for weeks about it.

"And you owe Iris," he continues, because of course he's going to side with Iris instead of me. He used to be where she is right now: on the precarious verge of finding out the truth.

"Okay, one of you needs to stop being intense and vague right now, or I'm gonna freak out more than I already am. And we're already hostages in a bank robbery while I'm on my period, so my anxiety and desire for chocolate and revenge is kind of high right now," Iris declares with a lot more harried foot-tapping.

Both Wes and I zoom in on her like we're one person.

"Do you need to sit down?" Wes asks just as I say, "Did you take your meds? I can make them give you back your purse so you can take them."

"My meds will make me fuzzy. I'm fine. My uterus is cramping bad enough to crush a Coke can and my menstrual cup's about to overflow, but I can *deal*. As long as you two start speaking like regular people instead of talking in riddles only you two understand!" She takes a deep breath, and with a jolt, I realize how pale she is. She really should sit down. She already pushed herself yesterday for the fundraiser, and now here we are, stuck in this, when she should be resting.

I should've told her she could stay home this morning, that I had it handled. But she made me promise to not tiptoe around her endometriosis and how sometimes her pain changes our plans, so I try not to fuss when she insists she's okay. I just make sure to pack a barf bag and crackers and that extra-strong, extra-gross ginger ale she likes. And I hadn't wanted to deprive any of us of getting to deposit the money we'd raised. The photo booth at the festival with the cuddlier of the shelter animals was her and Wes's idea. They were the ones who volunteered there. I'd just been along for the ride because being with them is where I like to be most. It'd been fun. I'd been proud of how much money we'd made.

It's a distant memory now, that pride. Replaced by panic and worry and a whole lot of fear.

"Is this about your mom?" Iris asks. "I know about her mom," she says to Wes.

He raises his eyebrows at me.

I've told Iris about Mom. Kind of. I've told her that she's in prison, and that my sister lied when I moved so I wouldn't be the new kid with a felon for a mother. But I haven't told Iris who put her there. How. Why.

She doesn't know what Mom is. She doesn't know about the other girls. She thinks I'm Nora. Just Nora and I've never been Just Nora or *Just* anyone. I've always been more. Scheming and outthinking everyone because I don't know how else to be. I don't know what else to do but look for the exits and then plot how to get the mark to lead me right through them.

Iris looks from him to me, and I can see the moment it clicks in that brilliant, puzzle-loving brain of hers. "I don't know about your mom?" and the fact that her words lift in question kills me.

"You don't know everything," I say quietly.

55

"Which means she knows nothing," Wes snaps. "Fuck, Nora. I can't believe—"

"You never tried to order me around when we were together, and you certainly don't get to start now," I snarl. "If you are going to ignore the risks I'm taking here—"

"What risks?" Iris demands.

I let out a long breath, my gaze skittering toward Casey, who's pretending really hard like she's not listening. We don't have time for this. We have to make a move soon, or we're all going to end up dying in this bank.

"My mom is in prison, like I said." I can't even look at her. I'm not ashamed, but I'm furious. This isn't how I wanted to tell her. "What I didn't say was that I am the one who put her there. Because I put my stepfather in there, and he's the love of her life and she'd do anything for him, including pick him over me, which is what she did and why she's in prison, because she wouldn't take a plea deal that screwed him over. Now, if we're done spilling all my personal shit on the table, can we please hoist me up into the air vent so we can hopefully get out of here alive?"

"Air vent?" Iris echoes dazedly.

"She wants to go in the air vent and open up the manager's office from the inside for the robbers," Wes explains.

Whatever Iris was feeling about my revelation seems to disappear in a second at this information. "What? No! This is not a James Bond movie!"

"Iris, think about it," I say. "They need something in the manager's office. They've only wanted to get into the basement and the office. So we can make the assumption that there's something in the office they need *before* they get to the basement.

Considering the safe-deposit boxes are down there, what do you think it is?"

She blinks, sucking in air, and she's still reeling a little from my news, and I hate that I've dumped this on her. But it's out there now. And it's still just skating the surface of what I need to tell her.

Rebecca. Samantha. Haley. Katie. Ashley. All the girls come with stories. And they all came with consequences.

"The robbers need the keys to whatever boxes they want to open," she says. "They must be in the office."

"And if they get the keys, do you think that the one in charge is going to let the one in the red cap just go down there himself to grab whatever they came for?"

A slow smile tugs across her face. "They don't trust each other."

"We open the office, they find what they want inside, they're gonna need to *both* go down to the basement. Leaving us unguarded. It's at least an opportunity to get out."

Now she's looking up at the air vent. "We can pry this cover open, but you're going to have to bust through the one in the office. They might hear it fall. Give me the scissors."

I hand them to her, and she pulls up her skirt to expose the layers of her petticoat, cuts a long strip free, and hands it to me. "Tie that around the vent cover before you apply pressure. If it pops free, it'll dangle instead of fall."

I wrap it around my wrist like a bracelet. "Iris—"

She shakes her head, cutting me off. "It's not a great plan, but you're right. We need to give ourselves a chance."

I want to say something, but any explanation I give is going to take forever, and we don't have time. "Turn around, both of you."

Wes frowns. "Why?"

"Because it's gonna be dusty up in there, and if I don't turn my clothes inside out, it'll be immediately apparent who opened the office. We want to make them wonder."

They both turn, and so does Casey in the corner, and it takes me just a minute to get my boots off, and my pants and shirt inside out. I'll leave my flannel with Iris.

"Okay. I'm good."

"What's the plan?" Wes asks.

"I figure it'll take me at least five minutes to crawl over to the office. Keep an eye on the clock. If I'm not back in fifteen minutes, it's probably gone wrong."

Wes nods.

"Don't do anything that will draw them in here before I come back. If they know I'm loose, they'll start shooting up the ceiling."

"Be careful," he says.

I turn to Iris. She smiles, but it's shaky, and I want to lean over to kiss her because what if this is it? What if they catch me?

But if I do that, then it confirms a maybe-goodbye.

"I'll be back," I tell her. "And I'll explain. Okay? I'll explain everything."

She nods tightly, and I grab the scissors out of my waistband. Wes bends, linking his fingers into a foothold, and I step into it. He hoists me up, and using the flat end of the scissors blade, I pry the air vent cover free, place the scissors inside, and hand it down; then Wes lifts me higher. Grabbing the vent, I pull myself up and inside.

15

Abigail Deveraux, aka
the Queen of Grift (aka My Mom)

I don't even know where to start with her. My mother. Justine. Gretchen. Maya. The names go on and on . . . Who knows how many there have really been?

But her real name is Abby.

I could write novels about what she's done. The lessons I've learned. The shit she's put me through. The love I had for her. The knowledge that's so terrible it blots out that love completely.

I'd run out of ink before I even got to the rest.

I knew her, is the thing. And when you live a life like she lives, there's very few people who can say that.

I knew her, and that was not a good thing.

She wanted daughters who would grow up to be just like her. And she got Lee and me instead. Girls who were molded by her actions over her pretty words. Girls who grew up straddling this strange line between good and bad. In her work, Lee floats between the criminal world and the legal one. And me?

I don't fit anywhere. Lee pulled me out before Mom could fully get her grip in me, but Mom had too much time to get in my head to let me live a real life. I've been too many different girls to have a deep grasp on myself, and I don't know what to do with any of the parts. They're all me. They're all useful. They're all a little bit destructive . . . and that's always been my problem.

I've danced way too long on the tilted ground. I don't know what to do with myself when I'm on something steady.

Mom and I?

We have that in common.

We have too much in common.

16

~~1 lighter, 3 bottles of vodka,~~ 1 pair of scissors,
    1 strip of petticoat
Plan: In progress

The air vent is gross. Dusty and rank, and the entire time I'm breathing through my mouth as I crawl forward, stomach down, inch by inch, desperately trying to stay quiet and not sneeze.

I've left my boots behind—they'd make too much noise—and I serpentine through the cobwebs and stale air, staring down through the slats of each vent that I come across, counting. One, two, three.

I peer into the darkened room below me, and then *bam*. I hear it even in the ceiling. They're trying to ram the door open. Haven't they figured out it's not going to work? I'd be looking for a crowbar by now. Or Googling how to pick a damn lock. They've got videos online and everything.

I unwind the petticoat strip from my wrist and tie it around the vent. There's a murmur of voices I can't make out, and then the thumping stops. I can't tell if there are footsteps. I close my eyes, counting to twenty.

I scoot forward and bring my elbow down on the center of the vent's grate. It pops out easily and dangles in the air from the length of petticoat as I lower it to the ground quietly. And then I drop down, wincing as my bare feet hit the floor. I duck behind the desk, waiting.

". . . isn't working," I hear, muffled through the door. "Barely a fucking dent!"

"You're the one who pulled out the gun before you made sure Frayn was in his office," Gray Cap's rough voice shoots back. "This is *your* mess. I never should've let you in on this."

"Oh fuck you."

More pounding, frustrated this time, instead of purposeful. But each angry burst of sound sends fear spiking inside me. My back is pressed so hard up against the desk, I'm going to have the shape of the drawer handle imprinted into my rib cage forever.

"Take a break," Gray Cap orders, and then it's quiet. Blessedly quiet.

The office is dark, the only light coming from the tiny inaccessible windows set at the top of the room that aren't more than six inches wide. I peek over the edge of the desk, trying to get my eyes to adjust. I can see the shadow of a phone, and my heart slams in my chest.

When the door doesn't start thumping again, I don't know if it's because they've both left or if one of them is just outside, waiting for the other to cool down and come back.

I look at the phone again. *Risk. Reward. Risk. Reward.*

I grab it and dial Lee's cell. It rings twice, and then she picks up. "Hello?"

"It's me," I whisper, as quietly as possible.

"Nora?" Lee's voice cracks. "Are you okay? Where are you in the bank? Is Wes with you? His truck is here."

"I'm in the back, where the offices are. Wes and Iris are with me. There are two robbers. I've seen two guns. A shotgun and a semiautomatic. I don't know if they have more. They want the safe-deposit boxes. I'm trying to make it so they go down the basement together, so we can run for it."

"Nora, they've used the furniture to barricade the front," Lee says. "*Do not* try to get out the front. You might not have enough time to get it cleared before they come back. It's a dead end. We don't have a way in until SWAT gets here with the blasting equipment. The fucking building is like a brick fortress."

"How do we get out?" I whisper.

"The basement's got an exit. But we can't access it from the outside."

Of course. I close my eyes. Shit. Time to throw the basement plan out the window.

"Nora?" Lee says.

"I love you." I need to say it to her. I don't say it a lot. I should've said it more.

"*Nora.*" A warning I don't heed.

"I'll figure it out." A promise I have to make. "Just . . . I need you to pull out the megaphone. I need to be sure they're out of this hallway."

"What hallway?"

"Lee."

"Right. Megaphone. Got it."

"I gotta go."

I hang up before I can sob or whimper. I crouch in that dark office for a moment, fear battering through me like fists. And I wait.

This far away from the parking lot, her voice is faded, but Lee has a way of projecting, even without a megaphone.

"I've got some information for you about your friend Mr. Frayn. But you're not picking up my calls."

The phones start ringing again, on cue.

I strain to hear it: footsteps fading away. I think I hear it. God, please, let that be it and not just wishful thinking.

I've got no choice but to spring into action. I don't have time to be neat, so I tear through his desk like a whirlwind. Where are they? *Keys, gold, brass, silver, long, skinny, short,* I need them. I headed into this thinking I wanted to hand the keys over like a gift, and now the last thing I want is for them to get their hands near them. They get into the basement, we won't get out alive. Gray Cap is totally the kind of guy who'd use a hostage as a human shield.

There aren't any keys in any of Theodore Frayn's desk drawers. His filing cabinets don't yield anything either. I don't have much more time. The phones are still ringing. Gray Cap still hasn't picked up. *Pick up, you jerk.*

And then the ringing stops, and relief curls in my stomach. Gray Cap's engaging Lee. He's not right outside.

I push the filing cabinet drawer back, and that's when I hear the metallic *click* on the bottom. I pull it out again, tilting my head upside down, and there it is: two keys on a ring, taped underneath the drawer. One of the keys has come loose from the tape, dangling free. They're the old-fashioned ones with the box number stamped on them. They're the same kind that Lee used to open her own safe-deposit box here.

Unsticking them, I tuck them into my bra. I've been here too long. Even if there is a key to the vault around here somewhere, I don't have time to look more. I've got part of what they wanted, at least. Now it's time to set the trap.

First, I position the office chair underneath the air vent. With my escape secure, I grab a pen off the desk and the pad of sticky notes. Scrawling two words on it, I stick it to the stapler. Then I creep across the room, unlock the door, and open it a crack, slipping the stapler in the gap to keep it open.

The key is to kick the office chair to the side as I pull myself back into the vent. That way, it slides right back into place behind the desk and the entire room looks undisturbed. Except for the open door and my little note.

A total mind-fuck.

Step one of my new plan.

If you can't beat 'em, you join 'em.

Or, in this case, you con 'em.

— 17 —

Phone Transcript,
Lee Ann O'Malley Engages
Hostage Taker #1 (HT1)

August 8, 10:20 a.m.

HT1: Do you have Frayn? Is he out there with you?

O'Malley: You know, this would go easier if I had something to call you.

HT1: Fifteen seconds, Deputy.

O'Malley: I'm not a deputy. Just putting that out there. I'm a civilian, like you. Unless . . . you weren't always a civvy.

HT1: The words coming out of your mouth have nothing to do with Frayn.

O'Malley: Well, I do have a deputy here with me now. I'm sure you heard the sirens earlier. And the deputy informs me that Mr. Frayn was in a car accident this morning. He's in the hospital.

HT1: You're lying. Stalling.

O'Malley: No, I don't do that.

HT1: Well, that's unfortunate for everyone in this bank, then.

O'Malley: It does not have to be that way. I'm sure whatever you want from Mr. Frayn, I can get you.

HT1: We're done here.

O'Malley: Let's talk about—

[Call disconnected]

18

1 lighter, 3 bottles of vodka, 1 pair of scissors,
   2 safe-deposit keys
~~*Plan #1: Scrapped*~~
Plan #2: Work in progress

"Hurry, hurry," Iris whispers as I lower myself out of the vent and back down into the office with them. "One of them keeps yelling out there. He's pissed."

I roll out of the way once I hit the floor, and Wes pushes a chair under the vent.

"Okay, we need to change our plans," I say, standing as Wes scrambles up on the chair.

There's no time for modesty. Casey's turned her back politely, but Wes and Iris are busy, and honestly, the two of them have seen me in my bra, so I tear my shirt off, shake it free of as much dust as I can, and flip it back right side out.

"What happened?" Iris asks as she hands Wes the vent cover.

"I called Lee with the office phone while I was in there. They've barricaded the front," I explain as I tear off my pants. Shake them, too. Back on they go, and then I'm grabbing my boots and flannel. "We can't get out that way. The only way out is through the basement."

"The sheriff—"

"Can't make a move until SWAT shows up."

"That's gonna be hours!" Wes hisses, pushing the vent back into place and jumping down from the chair. I hand him the scissors.

"Is there dust in my hair?" I ask, bending down so Iris can look. She runs her fingers through it, getting rid of any fuzz.

"What are we going to do?" she asks.

"We need to separate them," I say. "Sow distrust."

"How?" Wes asks.

Before I can answer, I hear a loud "What the fuck?" from down the hall. And then "Check the rooms, now!"

They've discovered the open office door.

"Get in the corner," Wes says, tucking the scissors into his jeans and under his shirt. He almost picks Casey up in his haste to get her out of the line of sight. We huddle together as the screech of their makeshift blockade being dragged away fills the room. There's a pause, silence that stretches, unbearable, and then Gray Cap stalks inside, red crawling up his neck and eyes burning.

A vein pulses on his forehead. I can see it throb under the shadow of the cap. Wes breathes deep, like he's trying to take up more space to shield us, and I can feel Casey shaking, her shoulder pressed up against the back of my arm.

Gray Cap slaps the sticky note on the wall in front of us, my *You're welcome* adorned with a little star instead of an apostrophe for extra flair.

"Which one of you did this?" he demands.

No one looks at anyone. Wes and Iris don't know what to do. Casey's terrified.

I lift my chin, then I lift my hand.

And I smile.

— 19 —

Samantha: Dainty, Delicate, Demure

Being Samantha is the first time my mom pulls a long con since I was born. I'm old enough now, she tells me. I've learned enough.

I'm proud that she trusts me. I don't understand the consequences. The differences between being someone for a few weeks or months versus being someone for years.

Samantha is eight, and she wears her hair in double French braids, because mothers in the rich suburb Abby's moved us into have the time to French-braid their daughters' hair each morning. She has a tea set in her playroom and a mountain of stuffed toys. Sometimes I slip one of them into my own room and sleep with it like it's something secret and shameful. I edge away from comfort without understanding why, already drawing the line between them and me. Why would Samantha's stuffed bear soothe me when I slip free of her after the lights go out, and then it's just darkness and the girl no one is allowed to know?

She is hard to escape. She is hard to hold on to, in the dark or the day. So I hold on to the bear instead.

Samantha is a test. A soft rollout, if you will. Abby needs to make sure I can play the perfect daughter before she twists her way into the life of a man who wants one. So she doesn't target a man. Abby's mark is a woman—the woman who lives next door, a mother named Diana, who has a little girl the same age as me. Her husband died, and the money he left her is what Mom wants.

Mom is Gretchen this time, a widow like Diana, which is true, but also it's not. So many things are true, but not.

She spins a tragic story of a man who loved her, who died too soon, before he could even meet his little girl. It tugs at the heartstrings, and we slide right into place in the cookie-cutter house in the beige neighborhood, into playdates and ballet classes and fresh-baked brownies on the counter each Friday.

I go to school for the first time, and it's easier than I'd expected and more boring than I could have dreamed. I don't like it. I read under my desk, but my teacher calls me back after class when she catches me, and I know not to cause ripples like that, so I stop.

Samantha can't cause ripples. Samantha has to be perfect. Dainty, delicate, and demure.

Mom gives me three words for each girl I have to be. Rebecca had been sweet, silent, and smiling.

The quieter I am, the more they forget I'm around. And people—men, especially, I will find—say and do the most secret things out loud when they don't think you're important. When you're sweet and you fetch beers and slice limes and are never a bother. I wasn't real to any of them, and when you're not real, the things you learn are endless.

But the men are not important yet. Samantha's mark is. Because I have a bigger role to play in this con than I ever had before.

Diana has no idea what to do with her daughter and no interest in finding out how to. I walk into the house for the first playdate, and by the time I walk out, I understand why Mom dressed me in patent leather shoes and lace socks and a neat, prim dress that goes with the double French braids hanging down my back, tied with ribbons.

Diana wants a daughter like Samantha: frilly and lacy and very, very pink.

Her daughter is not like that. We spend most of our playdate bouncing on her trampoline, and she's all about the double bounce, even though we're not supposed to. Victoria is fearless and free in a way kids are supposed to be, and every second I spend around her, it sinks in how different we are. How different *I* am from Victoria and Samantha and any other kid who was raised to live childhood instead of fake it.

When Mom comes to pick me up, Diana sighs over how lovely my dress is and how she wishes she could get Victoria out of her jeans and into such a pretty dress, and Victoria rolls her eyes. I want to shoot her a smile, because I don't like the dress much either, but *Samantha* likes the dress. Samantha is perfect. The perfect daughter. Always obedient and smiling. Playing quietly in her room with her stuffed toys and her tea set, her hair angelic gold down her back. *She's so sweet. What's your secret, Gretchen?*

Samantha has no needs or wants. She exists to serve someone else's.

When we're in the safety of our own home, the expensive curtains drawn and Mom finger-combing my hair free of the tight braids, she says, *You did good, baby,* and the hot glow of pride almost blots out the twist of guilt when I think about Victoria rolling her eyes.

I sink into the role of the delicate little doll-daughter that Diana wants easily. She loves me, and she spends *so* much time hovering in the doorway, watching Victoria and me play. *You're such a good influence, Samantha,* she tells me, and I don't understand it then, what she's actually saying. I don't understand what she's afraid of.

I guess Diana would be surprised that the one dressed in frills turned out to be the one skipping down the rainbow path toward bisexual city. Though, who knows, maybe Victoria realized her mother's worst fears. I kind of hope not, because looking back, Diana seemed like the disowning *not in my house* type. Back then, I didn't know enough about it—or myself—to see the coded worry in her, but Mom does. Mom creates Samantha to stoke it. It's sick. It's twisted. It's dangerous.

It's my mother, in a nutshell.

Mom wiggles her way into Diana's life so neatly; they have coffee together most mornings, dropping Victoria and me off at school while they go off to yoga and then errands, and then one day Mom is casually mentioning this business idea she has, a knitting store, and Diana is falling, hook, line, and sinker.

Mom is good; there are inventory lists, and they tour storefronts and talk supply chains and it's so convincing and Mom's the kind of support system that Diana needs and I'm so perfect. I'm the kind of daughter she wants, the kind she imagined she'd have, who'd be soft inside and out and sew her own doll clothes and not double-bounce on the trampoline or run gleefully through the greenbelt behind our houses until the burrs stick to her jeans and I have to bend and pick each one off Victoria's cuffs because Samantha doesn't like mess.

"Why can't she just be happy?" I ask Mom, once. "Victoria's nice. She doesn't get into trouble. Why does she want someone different?"

"We're hardly ever happy with what we have," she tells me, one of her universal truths.

My stomach sinks. "Are you happy with me?"

Most mothers would rush to reassure. They wouldn't pause and contemplate.

"You're learning so fast," she says. "Faster than your sister did. Faster than I did." She leans over and smooths a hand over my hair. "You're a natural. We're gonna be something, baby."

It's not an answer, and she's honed me enough, even this young, to see that. But I'm too young to play the game she's shoved me in.

I won't be for long.

— 20 —

10:36 a.m. (84 minutes captive)

~~1 lighter, 3 bottles of vodka, 1 pair of scissors,~~
   2 safe-deposit keys
~~Plan #1: Scrapped~~
Plan #2: Maybe working

He drags me down the hall by the back of my shirt. Iris screams my name, and the sound scrapes inside me worse than my knees against the carpet.

"Stay there and watch them," he tells Red Cap, and the anger in his voice is enough to keep Red Cap from doing anything but obeying.

I go limp. I do not fight. I let him yank me like a doll across the floor and heave me into the lobby. Then I'm on the ground and my cheek's pressed against the cold tile, and I roll away and up before he tries to kick me. They always try that. It's like they can't resist. Getting to my feet hurts, but so does getting kicked in the ribs.

I hadn't expected this level of anger. What had Lee said to him? She would've known better than to antagonize him, so whatever she said, she hadn't realized it was a land mine.

That was bad. What if I stepped on it, too?

We're three feet apart, and I can see the front doors from here. They've moved the big cabinets from the back against them, blocking them completely, holing up for the long haul.

Whatever's in that safe-deposit box is important.

"You think you're smart?" he asks.

"I think I want to survive . . . and you wanted in that office."

He lets out a breath that maybe is a humorless laugh in another reality. He doesn't have the shotgun on him, I realize. There's a gun at his hip, but the shotgun's out of play.

Where is it? With Red Cap?

"I've gotta hand it to you, kid, you've got guts. No fucking sense. But guts."

"Just lending a hand."

"Mighty big of you, considering I'm gonna shoot you and your friends."

It's like a sucker punch, hearing him say that so casually. To confirm my worst fears. What I knew deep down the second I saw they weren't wearing masks.

"I'd like to avoid that, if at all possible," I say, and damn, does it come out steady.

He lets out another huff. I've snagged his interest. My gaze is unwavering. If you blink too much, they get nervous. If I show fear, he'll feed off it. He likes it. But he's interested in what doesn't fear him, because he's interested in *making* it fear him.

"Who are you?" he asks, and I know he's not asking for my name. This question is something more.

This question is *Why did you risk yourself* and *Why aren't you crying* and *Why aren't you shaking* and all the questions that really boil down to *What the fuck is your damage, Nora?* And like, dude, you have no idea. You are not even the worst thing that has happened to me and it's the only knowledge that's keeping me upright.

I've survived worse. I'm not naive enough to think just because of that, I'll survive this. But I can damn well try.

I glance over at the coffee table that still has all our purses and phones on it.

"I need my cell phone to answer that."

He looks at me through narrowed eyes for a moment, then goes over to the table where our stuff is piled.

"It's the one with the blue case."

He grabs it and brings it back over.

I hold out my finger, and he presses the screen up to it to unlock the phone. I make no effort to reach for it, so he doesn't think it's a power grab or a trick, even though it's absolutely a power grab.

"There's a file, on the second menu page. Labeled Miscellaneous. Password is TR, dollar sign, 65."

Breathing in and out, I'm praying that my heart isn't pumping the blood into my face too fast. If I go red, he'll notice.

I can see the exact moment the gallery loads. Because his brows snap together, and then his eyes snap up and then down again. Confirming that the blond girl in the pictures is the same as the dark-haired, older one in front of him.

"Yes, it's me," I say.

"And that's . . ."

"Yes, that's him," I confirm. And then I wait for the question that comes next. The one Gray Cap has to ask, because everyone knows that man's face, and no one knows mine. Lee made damn well sure I was far away, looking like another girl, before the tabloids and reporters even got wind of the FBI's arrest and the whispers of a girl who may or may not exist started.

"Why do you have a gallery of pictures with you and Raymond Keane?"

I take a breath. Not a deep one, not an obvious one, but just a beat. In my mind, I picture a mirror. *Ashley. My name is Ashley.*

"Because I'm Ashley Keane. He's my stepfather."

— 21 —

The Butcher

What can I say about Raymond Keane?

The tabloids that latched on to the story called him the Butcher of the Bayou. You'd think that'd tell you everything you need to know, but it's just the start.

He was untouchable. A businessman, a bank, a dealer—not just drugs, but secrets. He donated to the right charities, greased the right politicians' palms, knew the dirt on the right people, and climbed from the swamp he came from all the way up to a McMansion in the Keys.

When Mom met Raymond, I was ten. By then, she was feeling her age even though she didn't look it. But still, we'd had a rough time that year—she'd ditched the con on the car dealership owner—and we were both running ragged trying to get enough money to start over. I felt guilty all the time, because she'd left the last con halfway through because of me. It'd been the most motherly thing she'd ever done, and the glow of that made me weak instead of wary.

It should have made me wary. I knew better by then, but . . .

I needed a mom. But two years living with Raymond Keane drove that impulse straight out of me.

It wasn't even a con. Maybe I could've handled it if she was conning him. Maybe my well-being would've mattered more, because it had once, before.

But no, Raymond was never a mark.

Raymond was *love*. True blue, toe-curling, *I never thought I'd find him, baby* love.

I didn't have a chance. I was just the daughter. She'd already let go of one daughter with barely a thought.

They were married within six months.

Back then, it felt like it went bad in one night. But now I can see the signs of what was to come.

The first time he hurt me, it was my birthday. It came out of nowhere. He'd been building up to it for months. How can those two opposite things be true at once? I still don't know. I just know that in the during—in the enduring—it was like I couldn't get air, couldn't even breathe deep, let alone zoom out enough to see it was his hands that had been strangling me the whole time.

I guess I hadn't shown enough appreciation for the present he'd given me. He liked to make a show of things. Loved the idea of being the strong father figure. The *strict* father figure. Loved the idea of a picture-perfect, ready-made family. The beautiful wife, the pretty blond stepdaughter, both wrapped up in bows. But if you didn't react exactly how he'd pictured it in his head, those bows went bloody.

He didn't slap me or hit me. He *pushed* me. Right off the couch, right onto my knees, and my wrists would ache from the jolt into the next day. I clipped my head on the coffee table, and it took seconds or maybe minutes for me to realize that the sticky warmth chilling on my skin was blood.

When she shrieked, he hit her. The kind of punch that I didn't know then—but would learn—rattles your teeth in your head and fills your mouth with a tang that you can't spit or wash away.

And instead of doing what she *always* said she'd do if anyone hit us—packing up, leaving in a flash, starting up somewhere different, with a new mark—she just shrank.

I'd never seen my mother, in her precise manipulation and ballerina grace, ever tremble before. It scared me even more than the blood in my mouth, so when his fist came rearing back to deliver another blow . . .

I wasn't strong or brave. I had just turned eleven, and I was scared and I ran.

I left her there as I hid in my room and shook for what felt like *hours* until finally there was a knock at my door and a coaxing voice. *Baby, come out, okay? He's sorry. He didn't mean to. He wants to make it up to you.*

It was textbook. But I didn't know that then, because some level of danger in the men she brought around me was a given. It was my normal.

But her not leaving when the man becomes a threat was new. The new normal.

Because Raymond was love.

Love conquers all things, baby.

And it did—it conquered her.

But I refused to let him conquer me.

Part Two

———

Trust Is a Spear

(The Next 72 Minutes)

— 22 —

The Original

To understand Ashley, you have to know Katie. And to know Katie, you must meet Haley. And for Haley to exist, Samantha had to first, for practice, and before Samantha there was Rebecca. But before Rebecca there was . . .

A girl.

She has a name. But I was raised to keep it close, like secret treasure.

She was a daughter, once. But she got old enough, and then she was a convenient distraction. A little older, and she became a tool. Just a little older, and she was bait.

And once she was old enough? Those years down the line, that ended in eighteen candles?

The con would evolve. Perfect daughters aren't needed forever. They grow up.

Into perfect prey.

There's a choice, when you know your fate's to be hunted and gobbled up and used.

You can give in like it's inevitable or you can turn the tables.

I was raised for a kind of slaughter. But I grew into a huntress instead. One who always hits her target. No matter what.

Rebecca and Samantha, they were practice.

Haley and Katie were the real deal.

And Ashley?

Well, she was dangerous.

— 23 —

1 lighter, 3 bottles of vodka, 1 pair of scissors,
    2 safe-deposit keys
Plan #1: Scrapped
Plan #2: Maybe working

"Ashley Keane," he says. He takes me in, and I let it happen without showing the fear sparking under my skin. "Holy shit. I thought you were a goddamn myth."

"You did not."

He shrugs. "That's what everyone says."

I stare at the bit of Ace bandage peeking out underneath the edge of his shirtsleeve. "You're covering up a prison tattoo, right?"

He manages to stop himself before he reaches to grasp his biceps, but it's a close call.

"But you're not squirrelly enough to have been in recently. You've been out for a few years at least."

He just watches me. *Proceed with caution.* Who knows what set him off when Lee talked to him.

"If you were inside a few years ago . . . tough guy like you? You would've known the right people in there. So you would've heard about me," I continue. "Even all the way out here."

His mouth twitches. He can't help himself. Of course he's heard.

"There's a price on your head," he says finally.

"You can just say he put out a hit on me." I shrug. "You don't need to get all archaic and Sheriff of Nottingham about it."

"Is the quipping a nervous tic or something, kid?"

"You're the one using terms better left in the medieval times," I say. "Maybe I was wrong . . . Maybe you've been inside longer than I thought."

He rolls his eyes. "Last I heard, he wanted you delivered alive."

I smile. *Make the mark correct you. It'll make them feel smart.*

Men like him love feeling smarter than people. And they already *know* they're smarter than teenage girls, *of course*. Practically everyone thinks they're smarter than a teenage girl. It's what makes being one so powerful, if you know how to use that giant mistake of an assumption.

"I guess you're right: not a hit exactly. What it is, is a lot of money for a prolonged road trip to deliver the goods. Which is why you should stop pointing that at me." I look at the gun. "Because if you kill me and it gets back to him, he'll be pissed. Also if you kill me, you lose out on a double payday. You could rob the safe-deposit box *and* take me." I don't even mention Red Cap, because I want to see if he will. (I know he won't. I've got him pegged. He's already planning on screwing that guy over.)

Gray Cap's fingers flex on the gun, eyes dart down, then up to me again. "And you'll just come willingly?"

"If given the choice between *dead right now* and *maybe dead later*, I'm gonna choose the latter. Especially because your little robbery here has totally screwed up my summer plans."

"Oh yeah?"

"Please, do you think that money I brought in was *really* for an animal shelter?" I ask, the derision heavy in my voice. "Do I seem like the kind of girl who would spend her summer raising money for Mr. Mittens?"

He raises an eyebrow.

"The guy in there? The one I was with? His dad is rich," I say. "And his dad is sloppy when it comes to closing his safe, and now you're fucking up my summer con. I just needed to pull a few more jobs, and I was finally getting the hell out of here and away from my aunt who I've been stuck with since the whole thing with Raymond. The 'animal shelter money' was part of that, and now it's gonna get confiscated as evidence when all this is done and your partner has inevitably messed something up and gotten you shot or arrested." I roll my eyes, the mix of annoyed teenage girl and con swirling around my brain. I'm not Ashley right now. Ashley had been . . . well, Ashley had been scared. And she had been a little broken.

Then she got violent.

I don't know who this girl is. (Is this me? I banish the thought as soon as it comes.)

"So I messed up your con?" he asks, his voice dripping with condescension, and I know I was right.

He's like Raymond. The patriarchal type. He likes brats. He likes smart mouths.

He likes to shut them. He likes to make them bleed and break. And I may end up bloody by the end of this, but I won't break.

He's just another mark. And I survived all the other marks. I'll survive him. I tell myself this, right here, right now. I make a vow, because every second I'm alone with him, the more dangerous it gets.

"Yeah, you messed up my con," I say. "You could at least say sorry," I grumble, when he lets out a short laugh.

"The guy with the gun never has to say sorry," he says, and my teeth clench as he swings it forward. *Remember who's in charge.*

He may be in charge, but I'm going to end up being the one in control. It's the only way out.

"So what's in the safe-deposit box?" I ask. "It's either good enough to pair up with that genius in the red cap in there"—another twitch of his mouth—"or you're desperate enough to go with the worst of the worst of our criminal element. And I don't mean that in a good way."

"I think it's time you stopped talking."

"I've been in the basement before," I say, pushing it. I need to seed my path for the thorns to grow. "If I were you, I'd trade the best hostage you've got for a welding kit and start melting off those bars. Pry open whatever box you're looking for. Then you'll be good. Well. Better."

"Let me guess: The best hostage is you," he sneers.

"God, no," I say, and it's the total truth when I continue. "I'm *worth* something. That's why you shouldn't shoot me. Your best hostage is the kid." Another truth, but not in the way he thinks. "She's all tiny and scared and stuff. If you trade her for the welding equipment, the sheriff will think you're cooperating, and he'll give you what you want because they figure you can't get out of here. It buys them time for SWAT to show up because they've got maybe six guys out there: Budget cuts have totally gutted the sheriff's department."

"Keeping track of local law enforcement?"

"Aren't you?" Another incredulous, snotty look. He's going to want to put me in my place. Just one more push.

But before I can goad him any more, his eyes flick over my shoulder and I tense up. Footsteps. Red Cap is back.

"The girl in the dress is saying she'll throw up on me if I don't tell her what's going on," he complains to Gray Cap. "She keeps heaving. I think she's gonna do it."

Iris Moulton is a goddamn gift to the world, let me tell you. She totally *will* do it.

"Are you kidding me?"

"I have a thing about vomit!" he protests.

"Get back to watching them!" Gray Cap snaps, but then he lets out a frustrated breath and tucks his gun away and grabs my arm. I trot after him so he doesn't drag me again, because he's got six inches on me, plus the kind of muscle *and* personality you get when you're 'roiding. He snarls something at Red Cap as he yanks me past. I think it's *Fucking moron*, but I'm focused on him and his threadbare control.

Gray Cap's used to being a lone wolf.

They're dangerous, lone wolves. They'll chew off a whole leg to get free of a trap. I see that in Gray Cap, that *Don't give a fuck, I'll do whatever it takes* kind of gleam that's never good unless applied to a do-or-die situation. Except in this case, it's his doing and me and my friends dying, so we're fucked unless the seeds I planted blossom into sharp thorns disguised as tempting flowers. You pluck one, the thorn stabs you right through. He drags the table blocking the door away while still holding on to me. But he doesn't open the door. He turns back to me instead.

"No more helping," he orders. "And maybe I won't shoot you."

"Fine."

And then it happens. He looks me up and down, really taking

me in. I don't blink or falter even though my skin's crawling and my heart clamors *run* like a bell. I just let him do it before he asks the question that tells me the seeds I've planted have taken root.

"Did you really do what they say you did?"

I wait a beat. A breath. You need to pick your moment. My smile, when it comes, is slow. Sweet at first, and then on the edge of creepy, because it sharpens into something that shouldn't belong on such a pretty girl's face. He's transfixed, and his fingers tighten on my arm involuntarily. A few more seconds and he'll have goose bumps prickling across his skin.

I am that good. Or maybe I'm that dangerous.

"No," I say. "I did more."

24

The Myth vs. the Girl

This is what the regular world knows about Ashley Keane: She's a phantom. A blacked-out name on a lot of FBI files and a few legal briefs. She's a question mark that never got answered during the trials. Was there a daughter? Was she just a rumor? Another of my mother's lies? Did Ashley really exist? Did she do what they say she did?

There are websites dedicated to the mystery. Sightings. Discussions. Sketches of what she might have looked like then, who she might have aged into. So many theories, none of them even close to right.

My mother kept her mouth shut about me, the deal that Lee had made with the FBI cut us free and stealthy in all ways, and Raymond?

Raymond didn't want the FBI to know what I'd done. He didn't want anyone looking for me unless they were looking for me *for* him. Because Raymond had a new mission in his new life behind bars: Get free so he could find me and kill me.

This is what the criminal world knows about Ashley Keane: She's a snitch. A pretty little piece of jailbait turned deadly. A femme fatale, blond and sparkling and pink-lipped, who gutted Raymond Keane's operation with one beckon of her preteen finger. They sexualize her, all the men who talk and search for her. Otherwise, she scares them, because she did what they would never have the nerve to do.

Ashley Keane has a price on her head—and dear old stepdad will pay practically anything for that head. I'm not even sure he cares if it's attached to my body at this point. I know he'd prefer it, but so far—and for a lot longer than Raymond imagined—I've eluded the men who search for Ashley. So I've become an obsession: Raymond Keane needs to get the better of the girl who got the better of him.

This is what I know about Ashley Keane: She was twelve. She was scared. She was backed into a corner. And she did whatever it took to survive.

But there were consequences. And they might just kill me yet.

— 25 —

1 lighter, 3 bottles of vodka, 1 pair of scissors,
   2 safe-deposit keys
Plan #1: Scrapped
Plan #2: In progress

"What did he do to you?" Iris asks when I step back inside the office and the door swings shut. I hold out my hand and we wait a moment, the scrape of the table starting and then stopping as we're blocked in again.

"Are you okay?" Iris asks, and at the same time, Wes says, "What did you do?"

Two very different questions, from two very different people, directed at two very different girls. Wes knows the real one. Iris is about to.

My heart rattles in my rib cage at the thought. At the memory of how Wes reacted when he found out.

"You okay, Casey?" I ask, partly to distract myself from the inevitable.

She's sitting in the corner, her knees drawn up. She nods.

"Just hang tight. It's almost over."

Wes sucks in a breath. "What did you do?" he asks again, all intense and frowny. He is going to hate this, but I couldn't think of any other way.

"I made myself the most valuable thing in this bank."

He stiffens. He practically rears back from me. "You didn't."

"I had to."

"You told him?"

"He's been inside. He knows what she's worth. So I showed him proof."

Iris watches us back and forth like we're in a tennis match, but Wes only has eyes for me.

"What else was I supposed to do?" I ask him, because I don't know. I have no weapons but the truth here. I am not careful blond perfection anymore. I do not look sweet or shy like the girls I played at being. And Ashley . . . She started out small. She started out sweet. She started out another stereotype of a perfect daughter. But she's morphed into legend in the dreck. Into the stuff of certain men's nightmares.

"I don't know what you were supposed to do," Wes says. "But even I know exposing your secret identity is a bad idea."

"He is five seconds away from shooting someone," I say in a hissed whisper so Casey won't hear. "I had to throw something out there. I didn't have anything else."

"Can you two please stop the best-friend doublespeak and tell me what's going on?" Iris says.

"Fuck." It's Wes, not me, that says it, even though I'm feeling it. He rubs at his forehead like he's the one who's about to spill his deepest, darkest secrets out on the floor.

"Are you in witness protection? Is that what this is about?" Iris asks.

Wes lets out a breath that's almost a laugh, and I glare at him. I know why he's laughing.

He asked me the same exact thing.

"You are not helping," I tell him.

"Fine. You're right. I'm sorry. It's your story."

The thing is, it is my story. But it's partly his story now, too. Because I loved him. Because I still love him, just differently. Because Lee and I made him family in a way we were never supposed to. Because I didn't just tell him the truth, I embroiled him in it.

I look at Iris, and there she is and there I am, and I wanted this to be easier. Wes found out when chaos reigned around us and the sun shone red in the sky from wildfire smoke like some kind of sick warning. He found out, and we yelled and we cried and we broke into so many pieces, it took months to put us back together into Franken-friends.

I had wanted to tell Iris in a way that was the opposite of Wes finding out. I had dreamed of peace and quiet and no blood-red sun screaming *run* at me. I wanted to have found the right words and practiced them. I didn't want any more tears. I am so sick of crying over them . . . those girls and what happened to each of them. My mother and what she dragged me into . . . and how I clawed my way out.

But it was never going to be easy, and now it's here and it's in the middle of a bank robbery, because of course it is. So here we go. Buckle up, Nora.

"My mother is a con artist," I say. Short, fact-based sentences. Stick to them. Maybe my voice won't shake then. "She runs a sweetheart con. Her own spin on it. She targets men who won't go to the police because their businesses are already shady . . . and so are they."

"And you put her in jail?"

"Yes."

"Okay, so why were you talking about secret identities?" She directs this at Wes, but they both look at me. Her frown deepens. "If she's a con artist, then you . . ." She licks her lips; her gloss tastes like berries, but never a specific kind, and I'm struck with the knowledge I might never taste that mix of berry-sweet and her again.

"You're not who you say you are." She almost sighs it, and the realization in her face is like someone's taken a razor-sharp melon-baller to my stomach and started scooping.

I glance over her shoulder at Casey. I can't tell the whole story. Not with the kid in the room. Telling Iris is bad enough.

"I—" But I have to stop, because we all can hear it: voices rising in the hall.

"They're arguing," Wes says under his breath.

"That's good." Iris darts forward and presses her ear against the door, listening intently. I can make out some swearing, and then it's quiet again.

I wonder if it worked. The seeds I sowed. If it did, I need to get Casey ready. Fast.

She has to give Lee a message for me.

— 26 —

Haley: Humble, Faithful, Modest
(In Three Acts)

ACT 1: CURL YOUR FINGERS

"His name is Elijah," she tells me as she brushes my hair in front of the mirror and then glances at the website she's pulled up on her laptop. She's on a blog called *Happy Life, Happy Wife*, and it's full of pictures of beaming, long-haired girls close in age who all wear matching dresses and look like little versions of their beaming, dark-haired mother.

"And his son is Jamison," she continues as she begins to weave my hair into the half-up, half-down style of the girls on the blog. The one who's closest to my age, her smile doesn't reach her eyes like her sisters'. I find myself focusing on her instead of my mother.

"Haley? Haley!" She tugs my hair sharply.

"Ow!"

"You need to pay attention," she orders. "We'll be at his church on Sunday."

"Sorry," I mutter, turning my attention to my reflection in the mirror.

"Tell me," she prompts gently.

"Elijah Goddard," I recite from the files she had me memorize. "Forty-two. Started out as a youth pastor in a small ministry in Colorado, built it up into a million-dollar business."

"Prosperity gospel is the sweetest con." She shakes her head. "If I was a man, I would've gone into the church. Think of the money we could've made."

"You preach, in your own way," I point out, and it makes her laugh, which sets off a warm glow inside me. She hardly ever laughs genuinely. I'm used to the fake laugh: light and husky and practiced, a sound of temptation, not joy.

"Continue."

"Jamison Goddard, age eleven. His mother died in a car accident when he was five. Elijah never remarried."

"Until now." Mom smiles. "This is very straightforward—the simplest of long cons for your first real try. You'll be very sweet and polite to Elijah, but not draw too much of his attention unless I signal. *Your* job is to keep Jamison occupied."

"How do I do that?"

She bestows another smile on me; she likes it when I ask questions. She likes imparting her knowledge to me.

"Pay attention when you meet him. If he smiles at you, you'll know to play it up until he has a crush on you. If he doesn't, or if he starts acting like a little shit, then you can lean into that, too."

My eyebrows knit together. "What do you mean?"

"Every bully needs someone to bully, baby," she says. "And you're tough, aren't you? You can take anything he throws at you."

I lick my lips. My fingers rub against my thumb before I answer. Back and forth, back and forth.

"Of course," I say.

Jamison Goddard is the princeling of Mountain Peak Ministries. The apple of his father's eye. The ringleader of the youth group boys.

He's not just a little shit or a bully. He's a fucking terror.

He's never heard the word *no* without trying to push his way right through it.

He doesn't notice me immediately. Haley is supposed to be kind of meek, with her golden fall of hair and her modest dresses and the little white-gold cross she wears around her neck. So he doesn't notice me at first; girls are treated as lesser in quiet and loud ways in this kind of Christianity (in the entire world, too, let's be honest).

I do what my mother asks: I let his reaction guide my actions. I stay on the edges that first Wednesday and the Sunday that follows, watching, smiling sweetly, and speaking softly when spoken to. But the next Wednesday, I make my move. I get there early, before anyone else but Michael, the youth pastor, who has a goatee that he really needs to shave off because it does not make him look as cool as he thinks it does. But I don't tell him that. I help him set out chairs and then make sure to sit in the spot where I've seen Jamison holding court.

I've watched him; he steals pizza slices off his friends' plates and no one even blinks. He laughed twice during the last meeting: once when someone made a fart joke—my mother would say *that tells you he's a boy*—and once when Michael tripped over his chair—which tells me he's mean.

So I slide into the chair that he thinks of as *his* and wait like a canary in a mine that I already know is toxic.

He notices me the second he walks into the room. The hair rises on my arms. Something inside me whispers: *Run*.

It's the first time I ignore it.

"You're in my seat," he says.

My eyes are big already, but I make them go even bigger, doll-like. "Oh no, I'm sorry." I get up instantly, moving over a few chairs, and then to really clinch it, I hesitate in front of the new chair and look at him. "Is this one okay?" I ask, like I need his permission.

He nods, and when he turns back to his friends, I catch the smirk.

Abby is right: Every bully needs someone to bully.

So I make Haley the perfect target, and he homes right in.

The con takes forever, because Elijah's more concerned with appearances than some of the other marks. He refuses to take their relationship public—Jamison doesn't even know about it. Haley isn't supposed to know, but of course, I get a blow-by-blow account of each of their meetings and a breakdown of what Mom's done to twist further into his life.

When she sees the bruises on my wrist, she arches an eyebrow. "What a little shit," she mutters. "Can you handle him, baby?"

"It's fine." I tug the cardigan sleeve down so it covers me up properly.

It's not fine. Jamison has four inches and three years on me. And even if he didn't, I'm not allowed to fight back. Haley doesn't know how to throw a punch. A girl like her would tuck her thumb into her fist if she tried. She's a slow-moving target.

"He's gonna be mad," I warn her when she shows me the ring Elijah's finally given her.

Mom smiles. "Then we'll just use that anger, won't we?"

"You're dating *her* mom?" Jamison demands.

"Jamison, manners," Elijah scolds from across the brunch table.

"It's fine," Mom says. "I know this might come as a surprise to both of you." She takes my hand and sets it, wrapped in hers, on the table.

"We've been spending a lot of time together since Maya volunteered to take over the scheduling when Mrs. Armstrong broke her leg," Elijah says. "And we've prayed on it hard, haven't we, angel?"

Mom nods, her gaze on him soft and worshipful. She positively shines up at him. "We have."

"The Lord's spoken," Elijah tells Jamison and me. "He's worked to bring us all together."

"To be a family," Mom says, reaching over with her other hand and grasping Elijah's.

"What does she mean?" Jamison's looking hard at his father, his eyes narrowed.

"I've asked Maya to be my wife," Elijah tells him. "She's agreed."

"What do you think, baby?" she asks me.

We worked through my response the night before. Jamison is going to be the troublemaker in this scenario, which makes me what Mom calls the *golden child*.

"I want you to be happy, Momma," I tell her. "You, too, Pastor Elijah." I smile, making it tremulous, my shoulders hunched just a little. "You've helped so many people, Pastor Elijah. You deserve this."

That last sentence, the last part, is very true. He does deserve exactly what's coming to him. He's a con artist, just like us. He doesn't worship anything but money, and he doesn't speak any kind of truth, just careful words designed to strip naive people of their cash. *Love offerings*, my ass. More like *Elijah's private jet's fuel offerings*.

"This is *bullshit!*" Jamison declares, and Elijah's eyes go steely, like when he talks about the devil on that stage with his pop star mic looped around his head.

"Do not use that language, young man."

But Jamison is already up and bolting out of the restaurant. Elijah sighs and Mom looks at me, a significant look.

I know what I'm supposed to do.

I also know what happens if I chase him.

I do it anyway.

My lip's bleeding by the time Jamison stalks away, off to sulk in the car. I touch my tongue against the spot, tasting copper.

"Here." A napkin's thrust under my nose. I take it, holding it to my lip as I look up at Pastor Elijah.

"It's fine. I just bit my lip," I say, testing him.

He glances over to the parking lot where the car is and then back to me. He knows exactly why my lip is bleeding.

"I've watched you these last months," he says.

"I don't mean to draw attention."

"You're a good girl. You keep sweet, no matter what," he tells me, and I smile back at him when he smiles so approvingly, because oh, did I have him pegged right. He's sending me a message: This is what I am—just a bleeding target. He wants to make me smaller.

But I haven't been small this whole time. I've just been waiting to unfurl.

"I want to be good," I say, and it's true, in a way. I want to be great. I want to be *perfect*. Just like Mom.

"You'll be a good little sister," he tells me, and it's more of an order than a compliment.

"I hope so," I say, and that's true, too. If there's anything I want to be, other than my mother's perfect daughter, it's beloved by my sister.

"Come on," he says. "Let's go get your mother. We have a lot of plans to make."

He holds out his hand like he expects me to take it.

So I do.

It's all part of the plan.

ACT 3: AIM WHERE IT HURTS

Elijah throws a celebration each year to commemorate the day he opened the church. Apart from Easter and Christmas, it's the big payday in terms of those love offerings.

Mom has it figured out beat by beat: The service starts at 2:00 p.m., and some of the women go to cook the food in the church kitchen after, and others scatter to wrangle the kids. Elijah's moving through the sea of people, Mom by his side. She catches my eye and nods.

I move.

Haley is unobtrusive. No one really pays her any mind in the crowd. So no one notices when I slip out of the sanctuary and weave through the maze of halls that I've mapped not just in my head, but on actual paper for practice.

I grab the bag I stashed behind a stack of extra chairs, then head to the bathroom.

The bathrooms closest to the office are empty, and it takes ten minutes to clog the toilets enough so the water's sloshing onto the tile floors. I tiptoe out of the bathroom so my shoes won't leave wet marks and hum to myself as I stroll back down the hall. All that's left in my bag is a stack of Bibles. I pull them out and toss the bag in the garbage can as I pass. They get tucked under my arm neatly. Looking over my shoulder, I can see that the carpet in front of the bathroom door is getting darker.

Perfect. Right on time.

By now, Mom has made the excuse to go check on the women in the kitchen, leaving Elijah behind in the sanctuary.

He won't see her again.

Still clutching the Bibles, I knock lightly on the office door at the end of the hall, then swing it open and peek my head in before there's an answer.

Adrian, Elijah's administrative assistant, is sitting at his desk like he always does after a service. The beauty of this con is that Elijah runs a big operation, and does it in a way that's good for him financially but bad for him if he's about to get robbed, which he is. He underpays people and doesn't like shelling out for security. Adrian is a twenty-three-year-old unpaid intern from the Bible college. He shouldn't be sitting there "guarding" the safe. But Elijah doesn't trust anyone to handle—or count—the money. It all goes straight down here, completely unaccounted for until the next morning, when he's got time to deal with it. It's a terrible way of doing things, but it does make it easier for us. Because after a big day like this, that safe's going to be full. And the only thing standing in our way is Adrian, who is sweet and the kind of naive that comes from your parents sheltering you from the scary secular world and you never poking a toe out, even once.

"Adrian, I think there's a *big* problem in the bathroom," I say. "I was bringing these Bibles back to storage for my mom and there's dirty water all over the hall!"

"What?" He leaps to his feet, and I hold the door open for him as he speeds out and down the hall, turning the corner so he's out of sight. "Oh my gosh!" I hear his voice echo a little down the hall when he sees the disaster I've created.

I don't have a lot of time. My heart's in my throat as I rush to the window, unlocking it and pushing it open. Mom's there, climbing inside as soon as there's space, and I step out of the way as she slides into the room.

"You're on lookout."

My entire body feels like it's vibrating as I go to the door and crack it. I keep one eye on the hall, but every few seconds, I glance back to watch her progress.

"Took me weeks to get him to punch in the combo with me in the room," she mutters as she goes down on her knees in front of the safe and opens the expensive leather tote that all the richer moms carry. "Maybe I'm losing my touch." She keys in the number. The safe swings open.

The noise she makes is all pleased triumph. She moves faster than I can believe, and that money is all in the bag lickety-split. She swings the safe shut with a snap.

"Walk me through it," she orders.

"I'll offer to go get more help for Adrian. Then I slip out and walk across the greenbelt, where you'll be waiting in the car."

She smiles and kisses her pointer and middle finger, pressing it to my cheek. "That's my girl. Let's do it."

I grab the blanket off the couch in the office and go out the door, and she climbs through the window with the leather tote full of love offerings.

I run down the hall, exaggerating my breathlessness as I push the bathroom door open, brandishing the blanket. "I found this! To soak up the water!"

Adrian is standing in the middle of three inches of toilet water, his normally pristine button-down stained and his eyes a little wild.

"That's—That's good," he says, looking hopelessly around, because one blanket is not going to be enough. "How did this even happen?"

I look down, worrying my lower lip.

"Haley," he says, because I'm being obvious enough that even he picks up on it. "Do you know something?"

"No, I—" I stop, biting my lip again.

"You can tell me."

"It's just that I saw Jamison coming out of the bathroom. That's all. But I'm sure there's an explanation."

"Yes. I'm sure there is." He clears his throat nervously. "Why don't you run and try to find the janitor? And can you please tell Pastor Elijah what's going on? They're going to need to shut off the building's water, and he has the access keys."

"Okay. I'll go right now."

"Thank you, Haley."

"Anytime."

The excitement—the rush—is thrumming under my skin as I take to the halls again—but not toward the sanctuary. I'm heading out now.

Finally free of this place and Jamison Goddard and his pinching and slapping and bruising, that little shit. But as I make the final turn on my mental map, it's like me thinking about being free of him has conjured him up, because he's standing there in front of the vending machine that's stashed outside the break room.

Shit. It's too late to turn back. I have to keep moving. His focus is on the candy selection, but any second it's going to snap to me.

I have a split second to decide. What to do?

"Hey." The voice out of my mouth is not Haley's; she was softer and timid. This is *my* voice: lower, harsher.

My fist smashes into his face the second he turns. He staggers, falling right on his ass in front of the vending machine; it's more out of surprise than because of my strength, but it pleases me all the same.

He sputters out my name like he can't believe it.

I smile. My real smile this time, and for the first time, I don't just understand the power here, I like it, because his eyes go wide like I'm the creepiest thing he's ever seen.

"You know, you hit enough girls, eventually you'll find one who hits back."

"I'm—I'm—"

I don't even let him finish—I don't have the time. I need to go before he starts yelling or something. "Don't forget." And then

I skip off, not wanting to run but needing to get the hell away. I push through the doors beyond him and break into a run, just in case he does try to follow. But he doesn't. He's more likely to run to Daddy than chase me.

The church is spread across acres of undeveloped land, and I don't see the car for a few minutes as I swish through knee-high grass sheltered by old oak trees. I try to ignore the little spike of panic inside me, the irrational little voice that says, *She left without you.*

But then I catch a sight of blue through the trees. I pick up the pace, awkward in Haley's plaid Mary Janes that have no grip on the soles.

I slide into the car and she starts the engine, driving on the dirt road until we get to the main one, turning left and heading away from the church.

"All clear?" she asks, glancing at her rearview mirror.

"All clear."

"What did you do?" She gestures to my hand.

"Jamison was in the hall," I say as we turn onto the highway.

"I thought you said all clear."

"I did. It's fine."

She merges into the flow of traffic, taking the middle lane. She never drives too fast—it's amateur to get pulled over for something like speeding—and we'll sail over the state line toward the West Coast long before they even realize we're gone.

"But you punched him?"

"I had to get past him. It seemed like the easiest way."

She laughs.

"I thought it'd give us more time," I explain. "He'll go to his dad and cry about it. Elijah will text you. When you don't text back, he'll think it's because you're dealing with me. He might be so distracted, he won't even check the safe until tomorrow night or something. He'll probably blame Adrian before he realizes we're gone."

She's not laughing anymore. She's suddenly quiet. Have I done something wrong? I'd hoped she'd be proud.

"You thought of all that?"

"I thought about what you'd do."

"Oh, baby," she says. "You're so sweet."

It made me smile, that conversation.

It makes me smile, thinking about it now. But for very different reasons.

27

Phone Transcript, Lee Ann O'Malley
Engages Hostage Taker #1 (HT1)

August 8, 11:03 a.m.

O'Malley: Thanks for picking up. You still haven't told me your name.

HT1: You can call me Sir.

[Five-second silence]

HT1: *[laughter]* I didn't think you'd like that.

O'Malley: You sound like you're in a good mood. That's encouraging. Can you tell me if the hostages inside are okay?

HT1: They're fine. For now.

O'Malley: What can we do to bring this to a safe end for everyone?

HT1: I want to talk to Frayn.

O'Malley: Mr. Frayn is still in surgery, so I'm afraid that's not possible.

HT1: You're really keeping on this *he was in a car accident* stalling tactic?

O'Malley: It's not a stall. His car was T-boned by an F-150 that blew through a red light. If you take a beat here, you're going to realize that me keeping you from the only thing that you've expressed a want for is not to anyone's benefit. If I could get the manager here to talk to you, I would. But he's a little busy getting asphalt picked out of his crushed pelvis, so you're going to need to start thinking about what else you want besides a chat with Mr. Frayn.

HT1: You really aren't a cop, are you?

O'Malley: I'm just here to help out. What can I do?

HT1: You can tell the sheriff to back up about thirty feet. And then you can bring me a welding kit.

O'Malley: I can do that. But to get the sheriff to agree, I'm going to need to bring him some good news. If you let the hostages go . . .

HT1: You can have *one*.

O'Malley: Okay. I can do that. It'll take a while to find a kit. Can you stay on the line?

HT1: Get the kit. Move the sheriff. Then you get the girl.

[End of call]

28

1 lighter, 3 bottles of vodka, 1 pair of scissors,
2 safe-deposit keys
~~Plan #1: Scrapped~~
Plan #2: In progress

"Casey," I say. "Can you come over here?"

She gets up and walks over, looking uncertain.

"What?" she asks.

"In a few minutes, they'll come in here. They'll probably tie your hands up. Let them. They're going to trade you."

"Trade me?" Her voice shakes.

"You're getting out of here," I tell her. "They need a welding kit to get through the bars downstairs. They'll trade you for it. They'll take you through the basement exit, not the front. It'll be scary, and they'll put you in front of them, like a shield. *Let them.* Focus on your feet, on your steps. No sudden movements. Do not run away from them or toward the deputies when you see them. Just keep walking slow and steady until a deputy grabs you."

"Why aren't they letting us all go?" she asks.

I don't have time to explain the fine art of con artistry or the power of suggestion, but luckily, Wes is there with a better answer:

"You're the youngest, so you go first," he says firmly.

"Wes is right," Iris says, but she's staring hard at me. I can practically see the wheels turning in that brilliant brain of hers. Iris likes puzzles, and I've just presented her with the one that is me. I can't even imagine how many directions she's going off in right now, with the bits I've told her and what Wes has said. Plus whatever I've let slip in the last year, little things that didn't seem like anything when I was just Nora but now have got to be spinning in her head as she tries to get the clear picture.

"What about Hank?"

We all look at Casey, puzzled.

"The security guard? Shouldn't he go first?"

None of us say anything. Because we're all wondering the same thing: Is he even still alive? Gray Cap had had blood on his hands. Had he . . .

"Kids first," I say, not answering her question. It makes her go white, and I grit my teeth.

"I don't want to be alone with them. What if they . . ." She doesn't finish. It's like she can't. Her lips tremble.

Iris makes a noise in the back of her throat, pained and strangled.

"They're not going to hurt you," I say firmly. "They need equipment to get into the safe-deposit vault. The sheriff won't give them the equipment unless they give you to the sheriff."

"How do you know?"

Because I made it happen. But that'll just confuse her. "Because that's what the one in the gray cap told me he was going to do. But we need to be fast. I need paper. A pen."

Wes and Iris spring into action, and in a few seconds, I've got a sticky note and a pen. I draw a crude map on one side, detailing the hall and where they're keeping us. And on the other, I write a message.

"My sister is Lee—she's the one outside with the megaphone," I tell Casey, handing her the note. "Tuck this into your shoe. Give it to her when you're safe. And tell her something for me: Tell her that the guy in charge, the one she's talking to? Tell her he's a Raymond."

"I—"

"She'll understand what it means," I assure her. "Can you do this?"

Her eyes are huge, the pupils blown wide from fear and adrenaline, almost swallowing up the blue-flecked hazel. She takes a breath, and then gives a shaky nod.

"Great." My hands grip her shoulders a little too tight, and when she stares up at me, eyes shining with tears, I want to be the kind of person who hugs people she barely knows in a crisis. But I'm not. That's Iris. Or Wes. They're snuggly, and I'm just sharp. The kind of person who can count on one hand—on four fingers— the people she's hugged genuinely in her life.

"You're gonna do great. You'll get through this, and I promise, your mom is not going to be mad about you forgetting your bag."

That draws an almost-smile from her, but it flicks out when I continue:

"Remember: Don't run away from them. Do what they say."

"And give your sister the messages."

I squeeze her shoulders. "It's just a few minutes of walking, and then you're safe."

"Okay," she says, nodding. Then she gulps. God, this is not fair. I see myself in her. I see the steel wrapped in fear that all little girls find on the spike-strewn road to womanhood. I hate that this is where she finds it.

I look over my shoulder at Iris and Wes, and I don't even want to start to figure out what their expressions mean. "You two need to act upset when he takes her. Like you don't know why she's going."

The now-familiar scrape of the table blocking the door being drawn back creaks through the walls, and we all move back into the corner.

Red Cap comes in first, followed by Gray.

"Get her," he tells Red, and Iris lets out a cry of protest when he grabs Casey way too roughly by the arm.

"Hey!" I snap as Wes jolts forward.

"Don't touch her," he says.

"Where are you taking her?" Iris demands, but they're silent as they shuffle Casey out of the room. I fight the urge to grab Casey back, because letting her go . . . It's for the best, I remind myself. They're not going to hurt her. They need her; they just don't know why or how bad, and if I can get her out before they do, then she's safe.

Iris sags against the wall as the door closes again. Her hands are shaking. Her lip gloss is smudged. She's so pale. And the worry creeps up inside me until her eyes flash and meet mine, and there is that inferno of a girl wrapped in seventy-year-old tulle that I fell for. Her eyebrow arches and her arms cross as she keeps leaning against the wall for support.

"You made that happen," she says. It's not even remotely a question.

"Until we hear honking from the parking lot, we don't know they actually let her go," I say, because I really don't know how to *not* try to avoid this. My therapist would probably call me pathological or something, but I just call it sheer survival.

"You're a con artist," she says.

"She's not on the take anymore," Wes points out.

"*Now* you decide to defend me?" I ask him.

"I just mean, you're not going around conning old ladies out of their pensions," Wes continues, like that's going to *help*.

"I didn't con any little old ladies ever!"

This is technically true. But what's also true is that I've left behind a string of crimes. They've stacked up, and they got worse and worse. The older I got, the deeper my mother drew me in, the more girls I had to be. And all the terrible, inevitable things that you think of when you think of a little girl growing up in that kind of life? They happened. And it built and built, until that night on the beach, with Raymond pushing me forward, *Go, get it, now!* and when it exploded, the sand went bloody and I walked free, but never clear. Never clean.

It's not like I've fully given it up since moving to Clear Creek. I've just winnowed it down to the essentials.

"What did you do, then?" Iris asks. "Because from where I'm standing, you somehow mind-jacked the bank robber into giving up his best hostage for a welding machine before he realizes she's his best hostage."

"That's exactly what she did," Wes says.

"That's . . ." Her lips press together, smudging her lip gloss further. "Your name isn't even Nora O'Malley, is it?"

I shake my head.

"And that's not your natural hair color, is it?"

I have to lick my dry lips before I croak out the answer. "It's dyed." I gesture to my hair and eyebrows, and my cheeks burn. It's almost worse that this is happening in front of Wes. The one person who knows all the answers, who's been in her shoes. Maybe it's better for her, though, that she has someone who gets it.

I love her, and that means putting her first in this moment. Because I have lied like it's truth so much that the lines blur scarily even for me. And I know what it's like to love someone like that. It's too hard. You can't hold on to them. There isn't enough *them* to hold on to.

"Are your eyes even blue?" she asks, and her voice cracks and my stomach drops. I'm moving toward her before I can think it through, but she shakes her head, short and decisive, and I freeze on the spot.

"They're blue. Colored contacts make my eyes itch too much."

She blinks, absorbing the information. "So you do this a lot. Change your appearance. Your name. Your . . ." She fades off.

"Not anymore," I say, filling that dreadful, almost exhausted silence. "My mom raised me in it. But when I was twelve, I ran away," I say, and it's possibly the most understated way to put what I actually did. "Lee helped me. My mom's been in prison since then. And I've been . . ." Now I'm fading off. Not because of exhaustion, but because I don't know how to put it.

"She's been in hiding," Wes says.

Is that true, though? Have I been in hiding? Or have I been lying in wait?

"From who?" Iris asks.

"My stepfather."

"But you said he was in prison, too."

"He is. But he was powerful before prison, and just because he's inside doesn't mean he lost that power."

"He wants to kill her," Wes says.

"Wes." I glare at him. He's making it sound scary. But I guess it is, for him. And he knows it'll be scary for her, too.

I don't know if it's scary for me anymore, or just a fact of life that I can't let crush me.

"And she just told the guy out there all about it, because there's a ton of money going to anyone who brings her back to Florida."

Iris's pale face barely flushes. "What? Why would you do that?"

"Because she's completely incapable of staying safe."

"I hate you," I tell him.

"You do not," he says back.

"Okay, fine, I don't. But I *am* totally capable of staying safe. What do you think I've been doing for the past five years?"

He just shoots me one of those looks, and my love/hate relationship with his sarcastic streak swivels full into hate in that moment.

Iris rolls her eyes at us, then she zeroes back in on me. "How much are you worth?"

"The bounty's up to seven million if they bring me back to Florida alive," I say. "He adds to the pot every spring. Happy birthday to me."

Something flickers in her face as she absorbs my words. "So he's not a big fish in a little pond, your stepdad."

I bite my lip. Telling Iris this is going to change things. She reads and listens to stuff about true crime and arsonists. She'll have heard about him.

She'll have heard about Ashley. About me.

I look at Wes, and he nods encouragingly. *It's okay. I know you can do it.*

"My mother married Raymond Keane," I say. "That's who I put away."

There's a split second where the name doesn't register, but then it clicks, and her eyes widen. She says, so fast her voice cracks, "The guy who allegedly chopped off his enemies' fingers and fed them to alligators?"

"There's no allegedly about it. He did that. It's one of his favorite drinking stories."

It was one of his favorite threats. He kept an array of cleavers around, from his days as an actual butcher—the nickname didn't come out of nowhere. I didn't just wonder if he could break down a person's body like a side of beef . . . I *knew* he could. He taught me everything I know about knives. He probably regrets that now.

"Oh my God," Iris says. "I—" But before she can even articulate whatever she's feeling, I hear it: honking. It's coming from the parking lot. Three long ones, then two short ones.

My knees nearly buckle in relief. Wes lets out a smile that's a little too big for today's situation.

"Oh my God," Iris says again. "You did it. Casey's safe."

Then she promptly turns around and throws up in the trash can next to the desk.

Phone Transcript: Lee Ann O'Malley +
Clear Creek Deputies Receive Hostage #1
(Casey Frayn)

August 8, 11:25 a.m.

O'Malley: I've got the welding machine. Do you have one of the hostages?

HT1: I do. You'll find that I'm a reasonable man. I'm giving you the youngest of the group. A little girl.

O'Malley: I appreciate that. A kid has no place in something like this. Are you a parent?

HT1: Are you?

O'Malley: Oh, you know family. It's complicated. Why don't I tell you how we're going to do this?

HT1: I don't think so. Put the welding machine in front of the back door. Stay at the end of the lot.

O'Malley: That can be arranged.

HT1: Call me when it's done.

[Call disconnected]

O'Malley: We need to move to the back. He's giving up one of the kids.

Sheriff Adams: Get this machine in position!

O'Malley: We've got to play this carefully, Sheriff.

We don't want to spook him with the rest of the hostages inside.

Sheriff Adams: I've got it, Lee. Stay back here, okay?

Deputy Reynolds: Sir, she's been leading the negotiation. If he doesn't see her—

Sheriff Adams: That's an order, Reynolds. You stay back, too.

O'Malley: Like it or not, I am leading this negotiation. When this is over and everyone's out safe, you can have all the credit and the glory. But if you continue to get in my way and something happens to the hostages, *you're* going to be blamed. So you need to move back about three steps and let me take care of this for you. Do we understand each other?

[Pause]

Sheriff Adams: Yes.

O'Malley: Then I'm going to make the call.

Sheriff Adams: If this goes to hell . . .

O'Malley: It won't.

[Pause. O'Malley dials bank number. Three rings.]

HT1: Is everything in place?

O'Malley: The welding machine is ready.

HT1: I want all the cops in the front. If I see anyone but you waiting for the hostage in the back alley, we'll start shooting.

Sheriff Adams (background): Fucking A.

O'Malley: It'll just be me.

Sheriff Adams (background, muffled): Fucking madness. Fucking PIs.

HT1: Five minutes.

O'Malley: See you there.

[Call disconnected]

Sheriff Adams: Someone get O'Malley a vest! What have you got on you, O'Malley?

O'Malley: My Glock . . . and my Winchester's in the truck.

Sheriff Adams: I'd strap the rifle to my back if I were you.

O'Malley: It's a rare moment when you and I agree, Sheriff. I'm gonna take it as good luck.

Sheriff Adams: Get in that vest. And don't get shot. I'll never hear the end of it.

[Muffled noises and voices, unable to transcribe. Time passed: 3 minutes, 18 seconds. From Official Report: Deputies retreated to the front of the bank, leaving O'Malley at the back entrance.]

O'Malley: Milwaukee. Akron. Austin. San Francisco. Seattle. Rochester. Milwaukee. Akron. Austin. San Francisco. Seattle. Rochester. Milwaukee. Akron. Austin. San—

[Banging sound]

O'Malley: Hands where I can see them!

HT1: I thought we were being civilized about this.

O'Malley: Is that what you call pointing a gun at a middle-schooler?

HT1: Desperate times.

O'Malley: Let the kid come toward me, you get the welding machine pushed toward you. Deal?

HT1: Deal.

O'Malley: On three. One. Two. Three.

HT1: Go.

[From Official Report: Hostage #1 (ID: Casey Frayn, age 11) crosses the alley and into police custody. O'Malley kicks the dolly with the welding equipment toward HT1. He retreats back inside the bank.]

O'Malley: Hey, hey, you okay? Did they hurt you? What's your name? I need paramedics down here!

Casey Frayn: Are you Lee? Are you her sister?

O'Malley: Yes. Is she okay?

Casey Frayn: She told me to tell you that he's a Raymond. Do you understand that? He's gonna kill them. All of them. She didn't think I knew, but I could tell. I could feel it. She told me to . . . Here . . . I have it . . . She—

Unidentified Deputy: Ambulance will be here in two minutes.

O'Malley: Take her. Get her out of here. And for God's sake, someone call her mother.

Deputy Reynolds: What's that?

O'Malley: Nothing.

Deputy Reynolds: Lee. You just put something in your pocket.

O'Malley: No, I didn't.

Deputy Reynolds: Lee. I—

O'Malley: No. I didn't. Now let's go figure out when the hell SWAT is gonna arrive. Otherwise it'll take a miracle to get everyone safely out of the bank.

— 30 —

The Pool

Two Months Ago

When Iris and I start dating, we keep it secret. I feel guilty that I'm relieved she's not ready to be out to her mom, because I know hiding is hard. But not telling anyone makes things so much easier for me. It surrounds us in this little bubble that I don't want to pop with the real world.

I've been living in a world of truth with Wes and Lee for years now, and when I have to close shut doors I've flung open, it hurts. I'm delaying the inevitable with Wes by not telling him about Iris, and lying to Lee about certain things is just the way it is, but Iris is . . .

I have a blank slate with her, and the last time I had that, it was with Wes. I filled it with lies and thought they were written in permanent ink, but really, they were chalk, and they wore away as love and safety worked me free of them. Wes saw through them.

Iris will see through me. Maybe not today. Maybe not tomorrow. But she'll figure it out unless I figure out how to tell.

Her ponytail is silk against my arm, her head resting on my stomach. It pleases me more than I can say, getting to play with her hair. I thought it might remind me of the fall and the swing of blond against my back, the heat of it in the summer, my mother's hands weaving it into each girl's hairstyle, but it's different when it's not mine. Iris's hair smells like jasmine, like the bush that's in front of our mailbox that only blooms at night, and it reminds me of the place it took me forever to think of as *home*.

"Your phone's buzzing," she tells me, and then she reaches over to grab it from the desk set next to her bed. I take it, and see that it's Terry calling.

Terrance Emerson the Third is Wes's best guy friend since kindergarten and the heir to an almond empire. He's sweet to the point of gullible, he's stoned most of the time, and he gets into trouble constantly but never stays in trouble because of the whole heir-to-an-almond-empire thing. He'd be the easiest mark in the world, like taking candy from a very rich, very sleepy baby, but Wes loves him and he's a good guy—fun if you guard your junk food around him.

"Terry? What's up?"

"Nora? Oh thank God," Terry says. "You've gotta come."

"What's wrong?"

Iris sits up at my question.

"Wes is high. He can't go home like this."

"What?" Now I straighten up, and Iris mouths, *What's wrong?* I hold up a finger. "What did you do?"

"I didn't dose him, if that's what you're implying!" Terry says, all wounded.

"Terry . . ." I grit my teeth.

"Okay, it is kind of my fault because I had a bunch of cookies in a bag and they weren't marked."

"He ate pot cookies? Oh, shit." I start to button up my shirt. "How many?"

"He went through half the bag before I got back upstairs."

"Terry!"

"I know, I know, I'm sorry, but—" Is that off-key singing in the background? Probably. Wes gets very emotional and melodic when he's stoned.

"You know what happened last time." I want it to come out as an admonishment, but it's strangled, too thick with the memory.

"That's why I called you," he says earnestly. "I can't keep him here—when my parents come home and he's like this, it'll get back to the mayor."

"Just keep him in your room until I get there."

I hang up and Iris looks at me expectantly.

"I'm really sorry," I say. "I have to go."

"Is Wes okay?"

"How did you know I was talking about Wes?"

She arches an eyebrow. "I don't mean this in a bad way, but who else would it be? You don't really hang out with anyone else."

"I hang out with *you*."

"You know what I mean."

"I've never been the kind of person to have a ton of friends," I say, trying to make it breezy, but she stares at me in that perceptive way of hers.

"Is he okay?"

"Yeah. I just need to take him back to my house until he's normal. I don't want him to get in trouble." I keep my voice level, but my heart is beating violently against my chest like I'm fifteen again, walking up those stairs and opening the door to his

128

bathroom, knowing what I was going to find. I need to go. I need to get him.

"Can I come with you?" The way she asks is careful, and the look in her eyes is guarded, like she's almost daring me to say no.

I'm so focused on getting out of there that I don't think about it deeply. "Sure. I'll drive."

Terry answers the door with a bag of Doritos in his hands and a gazillion apologies on his lips. "I only left him alone for a few minutes," he tells me as I march up the staircase, the sound of singing getting louder and louder. Wes has a *terrible* voice. He can't carry a tune to save his life, and usually he remembers this, but when he takes a few hits, he starts acting like he's in an opera.

"I'm sure it'll be fine," Iris says reassuringly to Terry, but when he just shakes his head grimly at her, she frowns a little. Terry doesn't do grim, and it's unsettling, but he knows what'll happen if the mayor finds out.

Terry has Wes stashed in the entertainment room, and he lights up when he sees us. I can't help but smile back, because it's been a while since he's looked this unburdened.

"You guys are here!"

"I heard you ate some cookies."

"I thought they were normal."

"You should know by now that food in Terry's room is probably full of pot," I point out.

"But they had toffee chips." He actually pouts after saying this.

"Oh, well, then, you had to," I say, and he nods seriously, my sarcasm totally lost on him. "Get up. You're gonna come home with me and sleep it off."

"Lee will probably want a cookie. But I ate them all." He laughs a little too long, and I grab his arm and pull him up. I get him downstairs and into my car, though it takes him three tries to buckle his seat belt and his eyes start to droop on the drive home. He has such a shit tolerance for booze or weed.

I don't think it through before opening the door to what was once the guest room but is now understood to be Wes's room. His clothes are in the dresser and his shoes are on the floor and his laptop is on the desk, open with that screensaver of him posing with some of the shelter dogs in various costumes. He throws himself onto the bed with a sigh and pulls the rumpled blanket over himself like he's done it a hundred times, because he has.

It only hits me when I turn and see Iris standing there in the doorway, taking it in, that she has never been in here before. That the unspoken agreement that Lee and I have in this house—that Wes is welcome anytime, day or night, for as long as he needs— wasn't clear to Iris until now.

I've skirted around it. I told myself I didn't need to tell her. But now that I'm holding my secrets and Wes's secrets and some of Iris's, my loyalties are split, and I don't want them to splinter as well.

"You gonna rest?" I ask him, and he nods underneath the blankets. "Okay, we'll be out by the pool."

I keep the door open halfway and then tilt my head toward the back door. "Do you want?"

"Oh yes, I want," Iris says, and the crispness to her voice sinks to the bottom of my stomach like a rock hurled into a still pond. She's upset and she deserves to be, because it's one thing to be best friends with your ex, it's another to kind of live with him.

We go outside and I wait until she's settled on one of the chaises that Lee built from wood pallets and I found cushions for at a rummage sale.

"So," Iris says. "Are you going to say *I can explain*?"

I sit down on the edge of the second chaise, flipping the tag on the cushion back and forth between my fingers.

"I like that you two are friends," she says when I don't offer up any explanation. "I really do. But I didn't . . . Does he *live* here?"

"Not officially."

"Almost every time I'm over here, he's here, too, unless he's with Terry or at the shelter," Iris says slowly, like she's just realizing it. "Last week, Lee was helping him with a practice essay for college. There's those onion crackers he likes in the pantry, and I know you think they're gross. And he has a room in your house. Across from your room."

"Please don't say it like that."

"Like *what*?"

"Like it's sordid or something. It's not."

"Then what is it? Because I'm confused," she says, with such earnestness that it kills me. "No one at school knows why you two broke up. I asked around when I became friends with both of you. I got the same story from everyone: that one day you were together and the next, bam, broken up, no explanation, ever, and you went back to being friends like nothing happened."

"That's not how it was."

"Then how was it?" she asks. "How *is* it? Because now I'm

wondering if I've stepped into the middle of some prolonged break that'll mend someday. And I'm not doing that, Nora. I am not the bi diversion in act one of the rom-com where you end up back with the hot guy in act three."

"You aren't a diversion from anything," I say fiercely, because I don't know how to deal with hearing her fear like that. "There's nothing to be diverted from. You . . ." I let out a breath. "You terrify me," I blurt out, because that? That is the truth.

And that is probably the wrong thing to say to her, because it makes her scowl.

"That's not something you want your girlfriend to tell you."

"You make me want to tell you everything, right here, right now," I continue. "Every mistake I've made. Every secret. Every scar and bruise and thing that's hurt me. Being with you . . . I didn't know things could be like this. I am terrified of fucking it up. If I do tell you everything about me and my mistakes, I'm afraid that *will* fuck it up. But it's not because I'm pining for Wes or he's pining for me. Did you see how he was looking at Amanda giving her speech last week? *That's* what he looks like when he's pining."

"He really needs to just ask her out," Iris mutters.

"I know. She's great."

"How do you think *she'd* react to your living arrangement?" Iris asks, and God, she is sharp like a brand-new box cutter . . . the kind you have to assemble yourself and pray you don't slice your fingers in the process.

"He's my best friend," I say.

"So you both have told me."

"His dad sucks, Iris."

"I know they don't get along," she says like it's some offhand thing. "But—"

"No, Iris, listen," I say slowly, staring at her, trying to convey the truth beyond my words, because if I use my words, I'm betraying him. "His dad *sucks*. Do you understand?"

Her head tilts, her ponytail swinging free of her shoulders at the movement.

The back door bangs open before she can tell me, and we both turn at the noise just in time to see Wes streaking across the scrubby lawn and cannonballing into the pool, splashing us both with water.

Iris shrieks and jumps to her feet, and I just sputter as he bobs up out of the water, delighted.

"Wes! This belt has eighty-year-old gelatin sequins! They gum up if they get wet." Iris shakes her head, fanning her skirt in front of her to better dry it. "You're so—" She glances up, and her voice dies right out when she sees them.

He took his shirt off before he jumped into the pool. He doesn't take his shirt off in front of people. He doesn't go swimming anymore unless he's here with me and Lee. He's been careful for a long time.

But he's not careful right now, and Iris sits down hard on the yellow chaise cushions with a soft "*oh*."

He has shorts on, thank God. And he's splashing around in the water like a human-sized golden retriever, so he doesn't see or hear or realize. My eyes are on Iris as her horrified gaze fixes to his shoulders, and there's no way I can even begin to spin the truth into fiction when she finally tears herself free of the shock.

I try to see the scars through first-time eyes, but I know him and them too well. My heart has a piece of Wes wrapped around it like a bandage. My skin will hold the memory of him as permanent, because you don't forget the first person to touch you with love after life's taught you all touch is fear and pain.

I say her name, trying to break her of the spell of *Oh, God, what happened?* When she whips toward me, whatever anger there was before has flipped to concern.

"Are you okay?" I ask her. "Do you want some water or . . ."

She shakes her head, staring at the ground as she puzzles it out. Her eyebrows are drawn together so hard, I wonder if the V between them will scrunch there permanently.

"Why didn't you just say something?" she asks finally.

"He's my best friend," I say, like a broken record.

She just nods at this. A quick, decisive bob. "So he stays with you and Lee so he doesn't have to be at home."

"That's part of it," I say. I could just let her think that's all of it, but I can't let her think Wes is some sort of charity case. I don't want her to think it's like that. But I also don't want her to think it's like *that*. The idea that she's been looking over her shoulder, wondering when I'd drop her hand for his makes me sick to my stomach. That's not something I want or Wes wants, considering he's spent half of last semester staring after Amanda like her dimples hold the answers to the universe. They might; as we have covered, Amanda and her dimples are really great.

"And the other part? *Parts?*"

I sit down next to her, tilting my legs and body toward her. I fight the urge to reach out and grab her hand. I don't know if she wants me to touch her right now. I don't know anything. Is this it? I don't want it to be.

"Wes and I broke up because of me," I say. "I fucked up. We can talk about all of it someday, but it's not the kind of conversation you have after dating for a month, Iris. I'm sorry, but it's not. I'm not—"

I stare hard out at the pool. Wes has gotten hold of the unicorn floatie raft that Lee brought home one day in a rare fit of whimsy. He's sprawled across it, his eyes half closed.

"He's my family," I say finally. "I'm not going to say that he's like my brother, because that's gross. But until him, I had one person to trust. And being in love, that was just one small part of it. When that part ended—and that part has way, *way* ended— the other parts didn't."

"The Franken-friends," she says.

"He told you about that?"

"He tells me about a lot of things. Or, I guess, I thought he did." She almost smiles as she watches him hugging the unicorn floatie's neck, humming to himself, but then it flickers out. It'll come in waves, the realization of all the secrets he and I keep; she doesn't even know the half of it. I'm not sure she ever will. "God," Iris says, almost to herself. "Is everyone's dad just evil?"

That gets my attention. "What do you mean?" Had I let something slip? I'm tracing our conversations in flashes, trying to think.

"Nothing," she says. And then she follows it up with a shake of her head and another "nothing." She probably would've caught herself if she wasn't so rattled, but I can't help but notice.

I haven't let something slip. *She* has.

"I'm not sure I've heard you mention your dad," I say carefully, even though I *am* sure. I have a catalogue of knowledge about her in the back of my head, like a little Library of Iris I keep adding shelves to.

"There's nothing to say," she says, in such a clipped way that I know there's actually a wealth of shit to say, but she's not going to. "My parents are getting a divorce," she continues. "I don't see him. How long has this been going on?"

She gestures to the pool.

"It's not my story," I say. "He's gonna be embarrassed when the cookies fade and he realizes you saw."

She nods. "Right. I'll figure that out. Is he still getting hurt?"

The questions keep coming out of her like a compulsion.

"Staying out of the house works most of the time," I say carefully. "It's been a while since . . ." I pause, lick my lips. "It's been a few years."

"So he stopped," Iris says.

"Men like that don't stop," I say, and she stares me down, all questions she's not going to ask and silent answers that I don't know well enough to hear yet.

"No, they don't," she agrees quietly.

Is everyone's dad just evil? Her question circles in my head, because *evil* is a good word for the mayor, but it makes me wonder what her dad did to earn that moniker. She makes me wonder if I need to do something about it, like I did with the mayor. It clamors inside me, that wild horse of an urge that gallops out when I remember Wes's shoulders before they scarred and after; that day out in the woods, where I forced a dangerous change that could break at any moment, just to ruin us for good.

"So you and Lee and Terry know," she says.

"And you."

"And me," she agrees.

"We try to keep him safe." Does she understand what I'm saying? What I'm asking?

"I understand," she says, turning back to watch him lolling about in the pool, kicking his feet like a little kid.

"You do?"

She nods, still keeping her eyes on him. "You and I . . . we're more alike than you know," she says, and then she doesn't say any more. Her pinky brushes up against mine on the yellow cushions and hooks around it. Not a promise, but an entwining of her and me and this knowledge between us. A twisting of something much deeper than a vow, something that has rooted in me, poised to bloom.

I know it's love, but in that moment before the careful unfurling, it's simpler to pretend I don't.

But I've never been good at conning myself. Even when I want to.

31

*1 lighter, 3 bottles of vodka, 1 pair of scissors,
    2 safe-deposit keys*
Plan #1: Scrapped
Plan #2: In progress

I pull Iris's hair out of her face and the line of fire as she throws up, one hand pressed low on her belly as tears leak out of the corners of her eyes. When she straightens, her lower lip trembles and she wipes at her eyes with her knuckles. Her eye makeup hardly smears through those sad historical dramas with the corsets and the cliffs and the pacing along the cliffs she likes to watch, and it doesn't now. I'd be impressed if I wasn't so worried.

"I'm fine," she says. "It just hurts." But then she leans against the desk, her entire body curling into itself. "I wish I had some water," she adds in a smaller voice. And then she straightens, like her bones were broken glass for just a moment and now they're steel again. "Vodka isn't ideal for rinsing out your mouth."

"Not unless you're getting ready for a bender," Wes agrees, and she smiles shakily at him.

She sets the trash can in the corner, then goes over to sit next to Wes on the floor across the room. I stay near the desk, because I'm not sure I'm welcome. I am sure this isn't done. Her questions. My revelations.

But if the two robbers are distracted by the welding machine

138

and getting into the safe-deposit vault, we've probably bought ourselves enough time for SWAT to show up and actually do something.

The problem with *probably* is that it's *probably*. I can't gamble our lives on the Feds down in Sacramento being fast enough to get here in time. Middle-of-nowhere towns like Clear Creek aren't anyone's priority.

The only sure thing I have here is me. So I can either trust the Feds, which goes against everything I've been taught . . . or I can trust myself. And what can I say? I've never really respected authority. I'm more likely to come to Jesus than trust the FBI, and neither seems likely, all things considered. I'll never buckle under the authority of a deity or a parent or a government agency again.

"Is this why you two broke up?" Iris asks suddenly.

I know I have a totally spooked look on my face, because Wes's expression is a mirror of mine right now.

"You told me you were the one that fucked it up," she says to me. "I thought you meant you cheated or something."

"I kind of implied that so you wouldn't figure out the truth," I say, because honesty. It's the policy here.

"So me wondering if you're a cheater is better than me knowing the truth."

"It's called a secret identity for a reason," I say. "No one's supposed to know."

"Wes knows."

"She didn't tell me," Wes says. "I figured it out."

"Well, now I feel silly that I didn't," Iris says.

"Don't. It took me three years, a forest fire, and her pulling one fucking insane blackmail scheme for me to find out," Wes says.

"It was not insane. And if you keep talking about it, we're going to have to *talk about it*," I warn him.

But to my surprise, he shrugs. "Who cares? Look where we are. You think I don't remember? I wasn't *that* high. I know she's seen my shoulders."

"Oh, Wes," Iris says, but he shrugs again. Red stains his cheeks.

"We don't have to—" I start to say, because I want to protect him. I want to protect her. I don't know if I can do both. I know I can't protect myself. Can I protect them from me? What does that mean? What would it look like?

Me, gone, far away from them.

"What else are we going to do?" Wes asks. "You're putting it all out there. I might as well, too. What do you say, Iris? We may be dead any minute. Truth for Truth?"

Iris smooths out the skirt of her dress. "Truth for Truth," she agrees.

They look at me, expectant.

"Fine," I say. "Truth for Truth."

— 32 —

Truth for Truth

One of the first things I discover about Iris is that if you dare her to do something, she'll do it—unless it harms a person or animal. But she does not count herself in the person or animal categories. She is heedless and gleeful and has the self-preservation instincts of a moth drawn to dares *and* flames.

Which is how, after one escalating game of Truth or Dare that ends with Iris spraining her wrist because she almost falls off the roof of Terry's house when he dares her to climb the widow's walk, Wes comes up with the game Truth for Truth instead.

It's exactly what it says on the box: If you give someone a truth, they have to give you one in return. Usually it involves drinking, which makes things easier. But now it involves just us and danger and this locked room, and sure, Iris has that vodka in her pocket, but it's not time for drinking.

It's just time for the truth. For all of us.

— 33 —

The Mayor

Almost Three Years Ago

For three whole years, I do what Lee asks of me. I act normal. Like a kid, not a con artist. I still look for exits and people to talk into walking me through them. I still wake up three nights out of four fighting people who aren't there. But I go to therapy and I don't skip school. Wes and I are friends, and months, then years tick by, and we're fourteen and we're something more . . . and then we're fifteen and we're *us*.

I didn't realize what being part of an *us* was like. I didn't know what that kind of love would nurture and bloom in me. A thorny kind of plant, more thistle than flower, one that protected and pierced, that would turn to poison if threatened.

By the time we're an *us*, we've already got a routine. We're good at juggling it, his time in and out of that house. I don't think of it as *his* house. It's not—it's the mayor's. It's his little fiefdom. An ostentatious log-cabin-style lodge sitting on ten acres that he rules like a medieval lord. But we've made it so Wes is always out the door as the mayor's coming in. It's not an exact science, and it's not perfect. I can't keep him from getting hit. But I can reduce the time he's there, so his father has fewer opportunities.

There are good excuses and flimsy ones, study sessions and

late nights we just hold our breath, and there are times I think about creating an entire club that meets every day after school for hours if I have to, just to keep him out of there, to keep him away.

Lee watches. More often than not, she doesn't say anything about the boy in the guest room. She won't, unless I step over the line. Unless I really risk us.

And then, I do.

Because one day, Wes doesn't come over when he's supposed to.

One day, I have to go over there, looking for him.

I know what I'm going to find before I even slip through the back door without knocking, because three years and his love is not enough to strip me of instincts that took twelve years and six girls to warp into me.

He's shirtless on the floor of his bathroom upstairs, and there's so much blood on the bath towels, my stomach and my head swoop all at once. I have to grab the edge of the counter. The tile is cool against my fingers, grounding me enough to let me suck in a breath. His eyes are swollen; there are tear tracks down his face as he turns away from me.

I'm on my knees on the towel-heaped tile next to him, and for a terrible, too-long moment, my hands just hover. I don't know where to start. I don't know what to do. His shoulders . . .

I'm frozen; the girl who always knows what to do. I want to ask what happened. I don't know how to say it in a way that doesn't make it sound like I'm blaming him for something, because the mayor, shit, the mayor is usually smarter than this. I hate that thought more than anything, but it's the truth. He hardly ever leaves marks that won't go away.

And these won't go away.

"What do you need?" I blurt it out, because it's the thing that my therapist asks me sometimes. Need is more than want. Need is . . . I can do need. I can help him.

I have to help him. I have to stop this.

(*You could stop the mayor*, something whispers inside me, and it sounds so much like me, and not like my mother or any of the girls, that I don't know what to do but reject it.)

"You gotta go," he says. He whispers it, like he's still afraid, and that's when I realize he is, and that I've never seen him afraid before. He is strong and he is quiet until you draw him out, and then he runs his mouth in the best way, but he carries himself like he's accepted the pain of the world, not like he fears it. "He'll be back soon. If he finds you here . . ."

"I'm not leaving you," I say. "You need a hospital. Stitches."

He shakes his head. "I can't."

Of course. Why did I even say that? Why am I not thinking right?

I'm thinking like Nora. Like I'm normal. Time to stop doing that.

"Where's the first aid kit?"

"Downstairs. In the kitchen."

"I'll be right back. Keep the pressure on it." I press the towel against his shoulder, and his hand comes up to hold it, his fingers brushing against mine. "I love you," I tell him, and it's so little, it's *nothing*, but he looks at me through red-rimmed eyes like it's everything.

It takes me forever to find the first aid kit. I'm still rooting around in the bottom cupboards when I hear it: the sound of tires on gravel. Someone's coming.

I jerk up, snapping the cupboard door shut, the kit forgotten. The hairs on my arms rise as the sound grows louder, and I glance over my shoulder. The back door is right there. I could . . .

But if the mayor touches Wes again . . .

My mind's full of half-formed thoughts; I'm so rusty. It feels like the part of me that's supposed to react fast and smart is atrophied, struggling to come alive in time. But my body takes over like it knows what to do. I've set a pan on the stove before I'm even thinking of the plan. I move over to the fridge, pulling out the vegetables from the crisper and whatever was wrapped in butcher paper on the bottom shelf. *Don't rush,* I remind myself. I'll get red if I hurry, and he'll be looking at me close.

I grab the biggest butcher knife. Wes's mom likes to cook, and her knives are beautiful. Handcrafted in Japan and sharpened lovingly and expertly. It would be so easy to . . .

I could . . .

No. I couldn't.

I hear the honking sound of the mayor locking his car. He'll be inside the house any minute now. I drizzle olive oil into the pan on the stove and then turn back to the cutting board. By the time his footsteps hit the hallway, I've chopped an entire onion and dumped it into the heating pan. It sizzles. I pray that Wes stays upstairs. If he keeps out of sight, I can pull this off.

"Wes, are you cooking some—" He stops short in the kitchen when he catches sight of me.

I look up from the carrot I'm chopping and give him a casual smile. It's one of the hardest things I've ever done. I want to scream at him. I want to stab him. I want so many things, and most of them are violent and all of them are terrifying, because I'm not supposed to be like that anymore.

I'm supposed to be Nora.

But I'm not right now. I fall right back into my old ways now that I'm awake—*alive*—again, now that I've got a plan.

"Nora, what are you doing here?"

"I'm sorry, did I startle you?" I ask. "Wes wasn't feeling good, and there's that flu going around. I came by to check on him. He was already asleep, so I thought I'd make him some soup for when he wakes up. Mrs. Prentiss said it was okay to use the ingredients. I called her."

I go back to chopping the vegetables as the onions sweat on the stove. I keep an eye on him out of the corner of mine. He's trying to decide what's going on.

I sweep the carrots off the cutting board and into the pan with the flat of the knife and then go back to the counter to take care of the celery. "I'm going to make homemade noodles," I continue, filling the eerie silence that's taken over Mrs. Prentiss's cavernous kitchen. The mayor's just standing there, staring at me, wondering if I know. If I don't. What to do in both scenarios.

"I didn't realize you could cook, Nora," he finally says. He moves farther into the kitchen as he talks, closer to me. My fingers curl tighter around the handle of the knife. How many steps would it take to get to the back door? Ten? Fifteen? I should know this. I should've counted.

"I can knit, too. My mother taught me both before she passed away."

"Cooking's a good skill to have."

"Especially when you have a sister who works as much as mine. She's so busy catching criminals and helping keep us all safe. The least I can do is make dinner a few times a week."

He slows down at the mention of Lee. At the reminder: I have someone waiting for me at home. She'll hunt him down and gut him with a paper clip if he hurts me.

The celery gets added to the pan, and I stir the softening vegetables around. The mayor settles down on a stool set on the opposite side of the kitchen island, and I grit my teeth. At least if he's here with me, it means he can't be upstairs with Wes.

I unwrap the chicken from the butcher paper and set it on the cutting board. He's watching me so closely; I know if I take a deep, steeling breath like I want, he'll notice. So I take the knife and begin to break down the chicken like Raymond taught me to do. I'm good with knives and I've never been squicked by raw meat, so teaching me the basics had been his way of bonding that first year, when he was still in hard-woo mode with Mom and me.

I slice the chicken apart, separating the flesh and bone and skin with the deftness of a surgeon, and when I glance up at the mayor, he's staring down at my hands with surprising intent.

"My son told me you don't hunt," he says.

"I don't," I say, setting aside the chicken legs and wings before splitting the breast into halves. I switch to a smaller knife to trim some of the fat off.

"You sure know how to use a knife."

"I just know how to cook." And then, in direct contradiction to my statement, I twirl the little knife. It's showy and it's bitchy and I shouldn't do it, but I do. Because I want to throw him. Because I've already decided: I'm going to gut him my own way.

He gets off the stool. "I should check on Wes."

My hand closes over the butcher knife to my right before the words are completely out of his mouth. His eyes fall to my hand, and mine stay on his. I don't make a move to chop at the chicken or disguise the fact that I'm holding on, because he's right: I *do* know how to use a knife.

"That's okay," I tell him, that smile back on my face. That casual, naive smile. "You're so busy, I'm sure you want to go straight to your office to relax. I can do it."

But he pushes. Because they always do. Because you draw a line, and they'll walk right over it. *I know you*, something that's maybe purely me whispers inside. *I'll end you.*

"If he's sick—"

"I've got it, Mr. Mayor."

It's like time freezes and then backtracks between us, because the look he gives me has me feeling twelve years old again. But I don't lose hold of my knife this time. I tighten my fingers around it. And I don't run.

"I do have a lot of paperwork to get done."

"I can let you know when dinner's ready," I say, wishing I could lock him inside and get Wes out before setting this entire place on fire.

"You do that," he says, before turning and leaving the kitchen. My breath tangles in my throat, half scared he'll head right up the stairs to prove he's in charge. But his steps continue to click against the stone tile that leads to his office; there are no soft thuds up the wooden stairs, muffled by the antique runners.

I sag against the counter as the vegetables hiss and heat, on the edge of burning.

I don't let go of the knife.

It takes almost two months for Wes to heal. We try to keep everything clean and bandaged, but with just Steri-Strips to hold everything together instead of stitches and staples, it all keeps breaking open again. It heals so much rougher. His shoulders are new terrain now; the old scar that taught me we were the same is bisected with sensitive tissue that's purple-fresh and livid against his skin.

He tries to shrug it off, what happened. He tells me he doesn't want to talk about it. That he's fine, even though he spends hours alone in the not-guest room, reading whatever books Lee gives him.

His newfound reading habit gives me the time I need.

I fall out of normal so easily, it's laughable now that I ever thought it might stick. It's naive to think a few years with Lee would undo anything. I just locked it up, but now I'm free.

So I make two plans. I get leverage. But I don't lie in wait.

I go and find him.

The mayor likes to go shooting on Sunday after church. He likes to go alone. Just him and his rifle and his thoughts up in the deer blinds as he picks off Bambi—badly, because of course he's a shit hunter on top of being an abusive asshole.

Until Clear Creek, I've never lived anywhere that had forests like this. Abby preferred cities when she was free, for obvious reasons. But hiking with Wes through middle school and high school had taught me not just the beauty but the value of the woods. They're secret and silently loud, and the forgotten mining roads make the part of me born to run and hide settle sweetly. And now it's proving useful.

I feel kind of silly lurking behind the trees downhill from the deer blind, listening to the mayor's bad shots and waiting for the beer to catch up with him and open my window of opportunity. Finally, the erratic shooting ceases, and I hear the thump and creak of the ladder. He's on the move.

I move when he does, watching him disappear through the trees to go pee somewhere away from his hunting ground. I hurry up the embankment, heading toward the trees he'll pass on the way back to the blind. I tape the pictures against the trunk at eye level, where he won't be able to miss them. Then I climb up into the blind, pulling the ladder up and inside behind me.

Sitting back into the shadows, I wait, my heart ratcheting up with each moment that passes. His rifle is right there. I edge away from it. It's not that I'm scared . . . and it's not that I'm tempted.

It's that I know where things go if I touch it. So I don't.

His footsteps crunch through the underbrush, so loud they probably send any prey scattering for a half mile. My nails bite into my palms. I guess he found the photos. I hope he's terrified.

"Hey," he shouts from below.

I give myself a moment to breathe. Because a part of me is scared, but a part of me is gloriously excited. The kind of happy that little kids feel when they see their birthday cake. Gleeful in the *I'm gonna win* way, because this is what I'm good at. But I need to play it right. There's too much riding on this to mess it up.

"I know you're in there!"

I pop up into view in the doorway of the deer blind like the nastiest of surprises. "Hi, Mayor."

His jaw is probably still hurting, it drops so hard. It takes all the wind out of him, and he sags in shock, almost wheezing out my name. But in his hand is one of the photos I'd taped to the tree. It's glossy and high definition. I'd splurged on the good paper for effect. It creaks and crumples as he fists it.

"I'm gonna stay up here while we have this talk," I say, taking great care to settle myself in the doorway and letting my legs dangle along the edge.

He doesn't sputter, but he takes a good ten seconds to respond. They tick by, because ten seconds is a long time when it's just us two in the woods and there's blackmail material taped to the trees. A little drama to get his blood pumping.

"What are you doing here, Nora?" he asks, like that day in the kitchen where my hand curled around the butcher knife.

There's no running from this. I don't want to. I came here for this.

The mayor's never liked me. I've always unnerved him, and I could never tell if it was because I wasn't as girly as he'd like or if he somehow senses the grift in me.

Besides preachers, politicians are the other acceptable kind of grifters, after all. I've known from day one that the mayor's more than a little shady. And now there's proof in his hand and on a few trees he missed on his run back here to get his gun.

"Did your sister take these photos?" he demands. "Is she around here, too?" He looks over his shoulder, nervous for the first time.

"I took the photos. Lee doesn't know anything about your after-work activities. Just me."

His expression shifts, and even though I've been waiting for that, adrenaline has my heart knocking against my ribs as he steps forward, going from *I'm fucked* to *fuck her up* in a blink.

"Uh-uh." I press my thumb down on the stun gun that I take out of my pocket. Does he even recognize the jacket as Wes's? Probably not. I wore it as a reminder. I wore it for strength.

Electricity sparks, the *zap crackle* of it filling the space between us, and just like a dog brought to heel, he stops.

His eyes narrow. He's thinking it through. Putting it together. That afternoon in the kitchen when I stopped him from checking on Wes. All the little moments before that. What kind of girl would anticipate his every move? What kind of girl would do *this*? He's getting there.

"I've got backups of the photos," I continue. "I hacked into your email, so I have all of those, too. You need better answers to the security questions. Now it's all triggered to get sent to local news sources—and the sheriff—unless I enter a password every day. So you're not going to do anything stupid right now, like try to kill me and bury me in the woods."

"You're talking ridiculous, Nora. I think you've been watching too much television," he says, and the ice in his voice is all cornered politician. He'll try to wriggle out of this, but he can't.

There were a few things to choose from when it came to him. But I chose the one that would hurt him the most.

Money is power. Mrs. Prentiss inherited a lot of it last year when her father died. If there is ever a time for a woman to leave her abusive husband, it's when she has a lot of cash, right? It has to have crossed his mind.

So I went with his cheating. And let me tell you, I couldn't have come up with a better story if I'd written it myself.

"This isn't TV," I say. "This is real life."

"This is ridiculous," he declares, like it's the only word he knows.

"You know what gets me about you?" I ask, but I don't even wait for an answer, I just forge ahead. "I bet you tell yourself it's *discipline*. Am I right?"

He goes a dull, middle-aged sort of tomato red as a vein in his temple pulses, telling me I am. It's horrifying instead of satisfying. I wish he'd just have a heart attack and save me the trouble, and maybe I should be ashamed of that thought, but I'm not. Because you can't rehabilitate a man like him, steeped in his privilege and his rage and all the shit he's gotten away with for decades because *that's the way he is*.

Well, this is the way *I* am. He's going to have to deal.

"I bet you think it makes you better," I continue, wishing my words were weapons or poison or something more than just words. "But guess what? It's always been abuse. You've always been an abuser. You've just been better at hiding it than some people. But I see you."

"You do not get to tell me how to parent my son. You are a *child*," he hisses, eyes narrowed.

"I mean, I did ride my bike over here," I say, and I'm playing so brave and flippant. I sound so confident when I feel like shaking, but over the years, I've tricked my body, just like I've tricked him. "But I do get to tell you what to do now. That's why I went to all the trouble of gathering the blackmail material. Catch up."

"What do you want?" he asks. "What the fuck are you up to?"

My laugh comes harsh and hard. It echoes in the branches of the trees, and birds scatter at the soulless noise. His confusion doesn't bring me any satisfaction. It just makes me angrier.

It makes me want to kill him. It's not the first time, and it won't be the last. Because we'd be so much better off without him. But I can't be that. I won't let him be the making of me into something new.

I have become so many things for so many people. The daughter they never had. The wide-eyed adoration they always craved. The dangled temptation they didn't even try to resist because the world told them I was fodder.

I am done being fodder. I've become the cannon instead.

"I want one thing," I say. "It's simple. You ready?"

His hand twitches like he's longing to wrap it around my throat. I'm grateful the deer blind's so high up. I don't think my warning about not killing me would be enough if I was on ground level with him.

"I want you to stop beating your son."

"I do not—"

"I have photos of Wes's back." It's a complete lie. I would never do something like that. But I've been right about the mayor's secrets, and that allows me to press into the power of his belief. Into the power I'm showing him. "They would be a useful tool in court for Mrs. Prentiss if she decided to divorce your cheating ass."

"She would never."

"You'd be surprised what public humiliation and ruination does to a woman," I say. "And all of you should get tested. Your girlfriend isn't the only one wandering outside the Thompkins marriage. Pastor Thompkins has been treated for gonorrhea twice in the last year. So I hope you're practicing *safe* adulterous sex, because neither of the ladies deserve to get second- or third-hand infected with an STI."

The vein in his forehead starts throbbing again. "How—"

"I have ways," I say. "Which is why I know you made a deal with Pastor Thompkins to help with the rezoning of that land by the river he bought for his megachurch. Twenty percent of the tithe is impressive. Do you think he'd cut your percentage in half if he knew you were screwing his wife?"

The mayor says nothing. His face is like stone. No more toothpaste smile. No more political sheen. Just pure rage racing through him, telling him to hurt the thing that could ruin him: me.

"If you stop hurting Wes, this goes away."

"You'll want money next," he says.

"I don't need your money. I don't care about zoning laws or people who throw their money at the whole God con. I care about very few things, and Wes is at the top of that list. So you have my full attention . . . and I can be very creative."

I look down. Climbing down a rope ladder will put my back to him. He's big like Wes, tall and broad and powerful, but Wes doesn't lead with it. That's the only way the mayor knows how to; he muscles through life and gets his way.

I push off the doorway of the deer blind like I don't need the ladder. My hair ruffles as I land on the ground, trying to keep my body loose. I know how to fall, but hitting the ground on your feet from a deer blind is different—hit it wrong and you've got a broken ankle or leg or both. But I get it right. The impact jolts through my knees and ankles, but I bend at the right moment, using my hand on the ground to steady myself. He's just a couple feet away as I rise, and his hand is twitching again. So it's a tell. A murderous one. Did it twitch like that before he took that poker to Wes's back?

"It's simple: You leave Wes alone, I leave you alone," I tell the mayor. "Now I've got to head home before it gets too late. My sister doesn't like it when I ride my bike after dark."

"You'll regret this." He's trying to get the last word as much as he's trying to make a threat that he can't follow through on.

"No. I won't," I say. "This is the best thing I've ever done."

That was true then.

It's true now.

It'll probably be true forever, because I'm not very good. But I do love full and reckless.

There's no standing in the way of that. Of *me*.

34

11:27 a.m. (135 minutes captive)

1 lighter, 3 bottles of vodka, 1 pair of scissors,
*   2 safe-deposit keys*
Plan #1: Scrapped
Plan #2: In progress

We sit in a little triangle, one of their knees touching one of mine and vice versa. Wes hands me the scissors because they're poking him in the back. Iris leans up against the cabinets, letting them take her weight. I can feel it when she tenses up from the pain, the barely there tremors as she shifts, trying to find a position that'll give her some kind of relief.

"You okay?" Wes asks her. She gives him a tight and utterly unconvincing nod.

"Who's going to start?" she asks, arching her eyebrow, more dare in her than if she was flicking that damn lighter at me.

"I've already been pretty truthful."

"For the first time, apparently," she snaps, but then she breathes out, closing her eyes for a moment. Her lashes are dark against her skin, fanning out like spiderwebs. "That was mean," she whispers.

"I get why you're mad."

She shakes her head. "No. No. *You* do not get *anything* about this. *He* probably does." She nods at Wes.

"Most definitely," he says, and when I bump my knee against his, he says, "Hey, truth for truth."

157

"How gullible did you feel?" she asks him.

"Really fucking gullible," he answers, and five seconds into this and it's already my nightmare.

From the instant the two of them met, it was like they'd each finally found the sibling neither had. They snipe at each other and they have the most complicated in-jokes they can never explain properly because they end up laughing too hard. And now they're going to take all that camaraderie and unite to form a *Nora lied to me* support group?

And I can't do anything about it, because I did lie.

The thing about conning someone is that if you do it right, you're not around for the aftermath. The broken heart. The hurt. The betrayal. The working through all the lies. The questioning of *everything*.

But when Wes found out who I really was, I couldn't run away from it. I had to be there. For the broken heart and the hurt and the betrayal and the exposure of every single lie and the answering of every single question. That came with my own broken heart and my own guilt and my realization that this could never, ever happen again.

But now it is, because what did I expect when I fell for someone like Iris Moulton?

I know that it says something about me that I'm attracted only to people smart enough to figure me out. Maybe I just don't know how to live without the risk. Every time I skate too close to the edge of exposure, I smell my mom's Chanel No. 5 and hear the whisper of silk that always seemed to accompany her. It doesn't spur me on; it jerks me back, makes me feel young, helpless, and spinning wild again.

"Is Lee your actual sister?" Iris asks suddenly. Then she shakes her head. "She has to be. You look so much alike. Or . . . did you make yourselves look alike?"

"She's my sister. Same mom. Different dads."

"And where's your dad in all of this?"

"Where's *your* dad, Iris?" It's low. But the game is Truth *for* Truth, not just All of My Truths for No One Else's.

"Nora, come on," Wes says in such a way that has me staring at him as heat crawls across my face. Not out of guilt, but out of the horrible dawning that he *knows*. He knows whatever there is to know about her dad. She told him, but not me.

I know it makes me the biggest hypocrite in the world, but it hurts in that chest-aching way that only she can squeeze my heart into feeling. The back of my throat burns with tears I'd never dare shed.

"My dad is in Oregon," Iris says, like it's a real answer, when we all know it's not. She's playing me, and if I can't take my own game, what does that make me? She's twisted this into the ultimate dare with the same skill she applies to mending her clothes and raising money for shelter kittens and calculating probable wind patterns in a wildfire.

"I have no idea who or where my dad is," I say.

"And my dad is an asshole who Nora had to blackmail so he'd stop beating me," Wes says, and Iris's eyebrows disappear into her bangs at this information. "Everyone in this room has a fucking asshole for a dad. There's the truth."

"So do you just hop around town, doing crimes and conning people?" Iris asks me.

"I've never hopped anywhere in my life, thank you very much.

And blackmailing the mayor was a . . . coming-out-of-retirement thing."

"How can you be retired from something you're actively involved in?"

"I'm not involved in anything," I say, acutely aware of Wes at my right. He's looking down at his knees, at where they're touching Iris's, at where they're touching mine. I know without having to ask that he's trying to weigh his loyalties, because I'm bending the rules.

"You're not who you say you are. Your mother isn't dead. You have hitmen scouring the country—maybe the globe—for you. You talked that bank robber out there into handing Lee the little girl like some kind of magician. But you're not *involved* in anything? You're not Nora O'Malley!" Her voice rises too high on my name and I don't expect it and neither does she, I think; the full-bodied flinch that goes through me when those words come out of her mouth.

"What's your real name? I know it's not Ashley Keane."

My mouth goes dry. I can feel the phantom sting of rubber against my wrist. *You're Rebecca.* Snap. *You're Samantha.* Snap. *You're Haley.* Snap. *You're Katie.*

You're never, ever *her.* She was to stay locked up inside, somewhere safe, untouched. The only girl who goes untouched. The only girl who remains unknown.

I've said the name out loud only once since I left that hotel room in Florida with Lee. I whispered it in Wes's ear and I'd been scared he'd make it into a weapon, a final blow to the pieces I broke us into. But instead he'd extended the first warped and tattered piece to build the Franken-friends on. He's always had the grace I find so hard to fake.

Iris has grace, too. I think I shattered some of it today, and maybe too much.

"Right now, I have to be Ashley."

Her eyes narrow, and for a moment, I mistake it for anger. But when her gaze meets mine, there's a blazing in it that makes my stomach melt. "You listen to me, whoever you are," she says. "I will set those assholes out there on fire before I let them take you like some sort of bank robbery consolation prize/human shield."

"Iris . . ."

"No! You do not get to sigh my name and ruffle your hair and give me sad, sacrificial lamb eyes. You do not waltz into my life and run circles around me until I'm dizzy from you and then *leave* in the most horrific way possible. And you certainly do not get to serve yourself up to the bank robbers on a shiny platter with an apple in your mouth, roast-pig style."

My mouth twists with each order she issues, until I'm wound tighter than a corkscrew, and when she calls me out on my plan so easily, I can't stop myself from snapping, "Why the hell can't I?"

"Because I love you," she says, so crisp and sharp that the words will mark me for good and bad and doomed.

The tightness in my chest springs free in a second. "You . . ." And then I can't say any more. I can't even breathe. I'm dimly aware that Wes is *chuckling* next to me, like he knew it all along. Iris stares at me like it's Truth and Dare entwined. And I guess it is, because that's what loving her has been for me. I couldn't deny the truth of it, so I took on the risk.

"Yes," she says. "I love you, whoever the hell that happens to be. So no more lying. No more secrets. And no more running cons without including *both of us*." She waves at Wes, who's beaming like we don't have about ten metaphorical anvils hanging over our heads. "Deal?"

It's a fair deal, if you're trusting. I'm not, of course. You don't have to just be taught to trust, you have to grow up in a life with people who are worthy of it. And the tilting ground Mom put me on was not.

But I had to trust Lee. I chose to trust Wes.

And I risked everything to love Iris.

So I open my mouth to tell her we have a deal, because she deserves that from me, but before my lips can even form the word, a scream that starts and then cuts off in a horrible, gutted sort of way echoes across the hall. The sound sends Iris cringing back against the cupboards and Wes banging up against them just as fast, trying to shield her and grab me close at the same time. My heart doesn't thump fast this time. This time, it slows down, dread filling the agonizing space between.

I had laid a trap.

Did the wrong person get caught in it?

— 35 —

Katie (Age 10): Sweet, Spirited, Smart
(In Three Acts, Reversed)

ACT 3: SWEET
Four Hours After

It's still raining when I get back from the laundromat. The windows are dark, all the lights are shut off, and his car's not in the driveway.

I push inside the house through the back door, moving through it in the dark, my shirt dripping pink raindrops as I go. If I can just get to the money that I've got hidden in the downstairs bathroom, maybe I can run . . .

I have to pass the living room to get there. I tell myself to be ready, that I can bear it.

Blanket's big enough for two.

The blanket's gone now. So are the couch cushions. There'd been blood all over them, and now they're gone.

Just like him.

It's like nothing happened, like that moment got plucked out of time, and I stare, trying to make sense.

Come a little closer, sweetie.

Did he clean it up? He must've. But I thought . . .

There had been a lot of blood. And yelling as I ran.

I don't bite.

But he must be okay. If he could drive away.

Right?

"There you are."

I jump, so close to screaming I have to clap my hands over my mouth.

My mother looks at me from the hallway, a bottle of bleach spray in her dish-gloved hands.

I shiver, suddenly aware of the cold under her gaze.

My first instinct is to apologize. There are bruises on the insides of my knees and I've become someone different in the space of those minutes that were maybe hours, but the words on my lips are still *I'm sorry.*

It's hard and strange and churning sickly inside me to want to be wrapped in the protection of a person who I think I might need protection from.

"I'm almost done here," she says. "Then we're leaving."

I just stare, barely making sense of the words.

Where is he?

"You're going to be okay," and it's not a question or some sort of vow. It's not a blessing or a wish.

It's an order. She says it just like she says *Katie. Your name is Katie,* and it is so familiar that it almost snaps me out of the grasp of doubt.

What did she do to him? Was it worse than what I did?

"Come on," she says, holding out her hand. The red almost blots out the yellow rubber.

Where is he?

I can see it in her eyes. There's too much red on her gloves.

Gone. For good.

I'm rooted by it; the crash of it. The realization that she got back and saw what I did, all the blood and him and just . . .

God, we're exactly alike, aren't we?

She says my name. Not *Katie.* My real name. It jerks me out of the spiral that's tightening around me.

"Come on. You need to help me get rid of him."

She's still holding out her bloody hand.

I take it.

I have no other choice.

36

~~1 lighter, 3 bottles of vodka,~~ 1 pair of scissors,
2 safe-deposit keys
~~Plan #1: Scrapped~~
Plan #2: Fucked

In the wake of the scream, we're dead silent. This time, Iris is the one in the middle, Wes on one side, me on the other. No one is shaking, and all of us are tensed up. *What to do, what to do, there's nowhere to go.*

"Who . . ." she starts to say, a breathless word that's cut off by the scraping sound we all know now.

He's coming in.

It's not like before. *He's* not like before. His face is all storm, no substance. No more curiosity. And there's a lot more blood on a lot more than his hands now.

Shit. Shit. He's got a knife somewhere. I thought I'd covered all the weapons, but clearly I hadn't. That's too much blood.

I jump up, because he's reaching for me before he can even cross the room, and if I can get away from Iris and Wes, maybe I can . . .

He backhands me so fast, I don't have time to plant my feet; I just go down. My teeth clatter together as my cheek smacks the floor. Wes bellows like I haven't heard in years, and the only thing in my head is his scream and white-hot pain and ringing ears, and the only thing in my mouth is blood. I spit it out on the floor, along with a chunk of my back molar. Fuck.

"Don't move," Gray Cap says, and it takes me a confused, blinking moment to realize he's not talking to me. He's not pointing the gun at me.

He's pointing the gun at Wes. Because Wes is standing there, big and threatening and three seconds from going for him, gun or not.

Everything around me wobbles as I cough out more blood and groan, "Don't." I dig my elbows into the uncomfortable, ugly, bloodstained carpet. I have to get up. "Wes, don't. Isso okay." I slur the last words, still too much blood in my mouth.

"You . . ." Gray Cap spits, and the gun's back on me, away from both of them, thank God. When I meet his eyes, I see the burn of humiliation on his cheeks.

What happened? What did he find out? Who did he hurt across the hall?

"What do you think you're doing?" he asks me.

The one in red isn't behind him. Is he downstairs in the basement now that they have the welding machine? Does that mean we're dealing only with Gray Cap?

"Answer me!"

I have a choice. I can cringe and cry and hope he thinks that one blow is enough to put me in my place. Or I can go with my gut, because it's telling me that he's never going to believe anything I say or do again, so I might as well lean into it.

I let the blood dribble out of my mouth and down my chin. "Bleeding," I answer.

He snatches me up off the floor so hard my shoulder joints

scrape in protest. "You're going to bleed a lot more when I'm done with you."

It's a bad line, and I would tell him so, but I know what it looks like when a man wants to kill you and just needs one little push toward it.

"Don't touch her!" Wes shouts as Gray Cap tosses me into the hall. I bounce against the other wall, the picture above me rattling at the impact. I scramble down the hall on my butt as he drags the table in front of the office door to block Wes and Iris in, but he catches up with me in seconds. He scoops me up again, fingers digging painfully into my armpit, and drags me down the hall.

Back in the lobby we go. Red Cap's nowhere to be seen. He's gotta be downstairs; is it even going to matter in a few seconds? Is this it? Am I dead? He doesn't throw me on the ground this time. He keeps me close.

It scarier this time, because of that. He has a knife somewhere. That much blood on his shirt means he has a knife and he probably used it on one of the hostages across the hall. The knife scares me more than the gun right now.

What's he planning? How do I get out of it?

"You little bitch," he says in my face with such force I can feel the flecks of spit against my cheeks.

"Did you hurt the kid?" I ask, because I'm not supposed to know for sure that he's taken her out of the bank. Lee honked. That means Casey is safe. I have that, at least.

It's not enough. It's not even close. It's one speck of good in a whole world of bad. Wes and Iris are back there, and that means this can't be it.

I have to keep spinning.

Did he put the guard out of his misery? Is the scared teller dead? The older lady?

"No, I traded the kid," he says. "Just like you said." He lets out a huff of breath. It's not a laugh. It's not a growl. But it spreads anger and a bitterness in the air.

"Why would you hurt one of them when you got what you wanted?" I hate how bewildered I sound. He got what he wanted. Lee wouldn't have honked the horn otherwise.

"You think I wanted to give Frayn's kid up?" he asks, and oh, *shit*.

One of the adults. They must've blabbed without realizing they were blabbing. Had the teller asked about Casey? I couldn't blame her, but she couldn't have kept her mouth shut about the kid being related to the bank manager?

Still, I try not to feel too hostile, because if it was the teller who spilled, she's probably the hurt one.

I can't think *the dead one*. Not yet. Not without proof. Wishful thinking? Absolutely. I'm hanging on to it.

"Yeah, I figured it out," he says.

Denying it will make him angrier. I don't want that. I need to bring him down and then build him up. His ego's not just bruised; I battered it. He wants to take that out on me.

"If I say *too little, too late*, are you gonna hit me again?" I put just enough shake into my voice to make his mouth twitch.

"You conned me."

"I was very clear who I am."

His hand rises, and I jerk; it's not fake or practiced. It's one hundred percent real, and my mouth throbs at the idea of more damage. My cheek is swelling up, but luckily he got me in my lower jaw, so my vision isn't messed up. Yet.

"Who did you hurt?" I ask again.

"Why does it matter?"

I bite the inside of my swollen cheek to keep from screaming, the pain more than a little mind clearing. If he's just attacking people to blow off steam, we are so fucked. If he starts shooting, the deputies will find a way in. Or Lee will tear the bricks apart with her bare hands to get to me.

"Why do you care so much?" he persists.

"I'd like to get out of here before anyone important shows up."

"You care," he says, with the kind of stubborn awe that tells me I am fucked. "You're smooth. You didn't even try to get me to hand *you* over to the cops. You could have. But you protected the kid."

"She's a *kid*."

"Stone-cold bitch like you shouldn't mind that. You left a mess in Florida, but you got free. Why aren't you trying to get free now?"

He's skirting too close to the truth. I want to wrench away from him—he's still gripping my arm, holding me too close, and now I know why: He wants to look into my eyes. He thinks they'll tell him something.

"I don't want to get caught in the crossfire, is that so weird? It's not like the deputies out there get a ton of *storm the bank* training around here between traffic stops and busting pot grows. And your friend is trigger-happy."

"I didn't shoot anyone." The *yet* hangs there, unspoken, but so clear. I have no idea how to flip this. I gave away what he wanted. But why does he need leverage over the bank manager when he's got the welding machine?

The safe-deposit box keys. The ones I found in the manager's office. They're still tucked in my bra.

Gray Cap thinks the manager has them *on* him. He doesn't think they're in the bank. That's why he's so mad about Casey.

I lick my lips and take a step back. He doesn't let me go, but he doesn't step forward, his elbow straightening, allowing me the space. Good. Good. That's good.

"Who did you hurt?" I soften my voice. "The teller?"

"She should've *told* me who the kid belonged to." He almost smirks at his bad pun. "And you . . ." His grip tightens up again, and my teeth clench even as I try to keep my mouth soft. He wants to see pain. I'm not giving him that.

"I did you a favor," I say stubbornly. "The news that a kid was inside would've brought in the big guys from Sacramento faster. It's in your best interest to get out of here before SWAT comes."

"And you're all about my best interest?"

"Normally, no: I care about me. Unfortunately, that means I have to give a shit about you, because how did you put it? *The guy with the gun never has to say sorry.* The only reason you haven't shot me is because I'm betting you've done the math and whatever score is waiting down in the basement is not even close to the seven million my stepfather will pay if you bring me back to Florida, all alive and grown up."

"Sounds like a sweet deal," he says. "But I know you're trying to stall. It's not gonna work. We'll be out of here soon."

I know he's not talking about him and Red Cap. He knows I know he's not talking about the two of them. He's talking about him and me.

I made myself bait because that's what I was born to be, and now I've got to pay the price. At least Iris and Wes will be safe.

"You gonna fight me?" he asks.

"You gonna hit me again?"

"Depends."

"Then ditto."

He's quiet for a moment. His grip shifts on me. Changes. When his hand clenches tighter around my arm, it's nothing like before. Before was punishment.

This is violation. A prying sort of touch that sends every single sense inside me clamoring; running for cover, charging to fight, freezing in place.

"Hitting you is not the only thing I can do to make you behave," he says, and there it is, in between the lines and in the lick of his lips: the real threat.

Run. Hide. Do it. Now.

No. Calm. Breathe. He wants the fear. The gun didn't stop me. The hitting got him nowhere. So now it's this.

Breathe.

Run. Hide. Fight.

No. Swallow that fucking spit in your mouth, Nora. Speak. He can't know.

"I see we've reached the rape-threat portion of the day. Very original. Do you have some evil-dude bingo card stashed somewhere?"

I'm talking too fast. My voice rising. Shit. Shit.

Run.

He shrugs, and it's terrifying, how casual it is. And then, he gets a whole lot more terrifying, because he says, "I don't need to do anything to *you*. All I need to do is go get the girl in the poofy dress. Both you and the boy keep putting yourselves in front of her."

There is no controlling my reaction. The blood drains out of my face so fast it has him sucking a breath in with a kind of sick joy, and I am so fucking stupid. I didn't think. I didn't even *think* he'd . . .

He steps forward.

Hide.

He's too close. Too, too close.

My hand curls around the handle of the scissors tucked in the waistband of my jeans.

~~Fight.~~ *Kill.*

37

Katie (Age 10): Sweet, Spirited, Smart
(In Three Acts, Reversed)

ACT 2: SPIRITED
Forty Minutes After

My button-down is stained. I pull my jacket closer around me, trying to hide it as I pick up speed. My sneakers slap through puddles, the chill of the streets almost as bad as the late-night buzz in this part of the city. Seattle sucks in the winter and my jacket's thin, but I didn't have time to grab my winter coat.

I didn't have time to grab anything. My phone's back there, along with my warm coat and clothes that aren't rusty with blood.

I need to find a pay phone, something that's almost impossible. But I keep walking, because if I stop, I'm going to remember what happened.

No stopping. Keep moving.

I've been Katie for six months. Katie is Lucy's daughter. Katie just turned ten. She's athletic; she wears a rose-gold charm bracelet around her right wrist, little tennis rackets and hearts and the Eiffel Tower dangling from it. Katie is a country club dream; her clothes look like they're out of a Ralph Lauren for Kids catalogue, and her thick blond hair is always swinging in a ponytail. Katie is not quiet. She is not silent. She is not invisible. She is the first spitfire Mom lets me be, the closest thing to me I've been in years.

Maybe if we hadn't been so similar, this wouldn't have happened?

Don't think about it. Keep moving.

I walk for what seems like forever. I'm soaked by the time I get to the twenty-four-hour laundromat. There's only one person inside, a college-aged girl with headphones who doesn't look up when I come dripping inside.

There's a pay phone in the back, but I don't go straight to it.

I go into the dingy bathroom instead. It's trashed, like most public bathrooms. I lean against the sink anyway. My jacket gapes open. I look down at my once-pristine white button-down. The buttons are askew, off by one. I didn't notice until now.

I had to fasten on the run, my fingers slipping on the buttons as I bolted. My hands shake as I stare at my reflection in the mirror, and then I'm clawing at the shirt, frantically trying to get the buttons right. It becomes the most important thing. They *have* to be right, and then that frisson of fear and hysteria flashes wide and true. It crashes in me, and I can't stop it.

I finally get the buttons right, but it doesn't make me feel any better.

I could go back. Already, the idea is tugging at me. I want to curl up in her arms and cry. Mom will be home soon, and what she's going to find . . . She'll be worried. There might be police. She'll hate that.

I could tell her. I could trust her to be on my side.

But I don't think there is a *my side*. I think there's only a *her*

175

side. That's what being Haley taught me . . . and I have the scars to prove it.

It isn't just that I don't know if she'll believe me.

It's that I don't know if she'll believe me, and tell me to deal with it. *That's the way the world is, baby.*

How many times has she told me that? That's the way the world is. That's the way men are. That's the way it works, so make it work for you.

Would she tell me to make it work?

Can you handle this? she'd asked when I was Haley, and I'd said *yes*, and bled for it.

Had I been saying yes to everything?

To giving up everything?

To having it taken like this?

Is my mother a monster?

I don't know. *I don't know.*

This is what my sister's distress signal is for. This moment. I've understood for years now that she wants to protect me. I thought I knew from what.

I didn't know all of it until today.

Zipping up my jacket to my neck, I wash my hands in the sink and dry them before making my way out of the bathroom and through the laundromat.

I have emergency cash in my jacket, so I push five dollars into the coin machine for the phone. I've had her number memorized for years, the card she'd scribbled it on long ago disposed of so our mother would never find it.

Feeding the coins into the phone, I try not to feel like I'm betraying everything I've been taught, because maybe what I've been taught is wrong.

The phone rings for a long time. Too long. My heart rachets up with each *bring-bring* in my ear and then, *finally*: "Hello?"

It's been building in my mind, a picture forming, and for the first time, it really looks like rescue, because for the first time, I'm admitting I need to be.

It all comes crashing down when a woman who is not my sister answers the phone. Reality hits me so fast I'm shocked by the vertigo.

"Hello?" says the woman who is not my sister again. Her voice is low, husky, like she'd been woken up. "Who is this?"

"Who are you talking to?" She must have the phone on speaker, because I can hear my sister clear as day. "Wait—where did you get that?"

"Why do you have a second phone?" asks the woman.

"Give it to me," my sister demands.

"Answer me!"

"Give me the fucking phone!" She shouts it, and then there's a thump and a scuffling sound that has me gripping the pay phone like it's the only thing keeping me up.

Then, breathless and panting: "It's me. It's me. Is it you? Are you okay?"

My sister has a life. She won't talk about it with me, but I know she has one. I don't know why it never occurred to me that she might have *someone*.

I haven't seen her in a year. Mom doesn't see her when we're on the take, and Haley was the longest con we've pulled.

She could have changed her mind. She could have decided I wasn't worth it. I would mess up whatever life she's managed to build.

I mess everything up.

She says my name into the phone urgently, emotion bleeding off the syllables.

"Just say it," she whispers.

It would be so easy. *Olive.* She'll come. She'll hold my hand. She'll let me cry.

Her life would change. I'd change it.

She'd resent me. I'd owe her.

We'd be trapped. And I can't trap the freest person I've ever known.

I cup my hand around the mouth of the phone. "Sorry," I say in a low voice. "Wrong number."

I hang up before she can protest. And when the pay phone starts ringing a minute later, I force myself to walk away.

1 lighter, 3 bottles of vodka, 1 pair of scissors (currently
   stuck inside bank robber), 2 safe-deposit keys
Plan #1: Scrapped
Plan #2: Fucked
Plan #3: Stab

If you think I didn't stab that asshole, you have not been paying attention. Because that's exactly what I did.

Scissors are not great for stabbing. But you've gotta use what
you have.

"You . . . you little . . ." Gray Cap sags into himself, his hand closing around mine, then stumbles, trying to break my grip. I push
back, with my body and the scissors. I dig deep. I twist my wrist,
and warmth gushes down my skin.

He takes a step away, trying to fight the pain, and *shit*, it's anger
that he uses to power through it. It flares in his eyes a second
before he lurches toward me instead of away, and then his hand
closes around my throat.

After the initial freeze moment, it's almost impossible to resist
grabbing at someone's arms and wrists when they're choking you
out. It's instinctive: You scrabble, you claw, because if you can just
get one breath in, you can fight harder.

I can't let go of the scissors. So I yank them out instead. He
screams, his fingers tightening around my throat instead of

releasing like I'd hoped. Fuzzy dots pop along my peripheral vision, but I can't let go. My entire face pulses, the pain and the blood rush mixed together like a runaway roller coaster. The scissors are dripping, my hand shining wet in the fluorescent lights. Now he has a choice.

He pushes me back by the throat, flings me rag-doll style down on the floor, and I hit the tiles with a teeth-clattering thud just as Red Cap comes running into the lobby, bug-eyed and bellowing. The shotgun in his hands whips up, right on me.

"Drop the scissors," Gray Cap orders, and I know when I'm done, so I do.

"You okay?" Red Cap asks.

"She fucking stabbed me." His hand clutches his side, and when he pulls it away, it comes back all red.

"Shit, Duane!" Red Cap says, and *yes*, I've finally got a name. His gun swings back to me, but Gray Cap—*Duane*—grabs the stock.

"No," he says.

"She *stabbed* you!" Red Cap protests.

"*No*," Duane says.

He's protecting me—protecting his asset. The glee sparkles inside my chest even as I fight to take a full breath that doesn't feel like knives against my throat. I've got him on the hook.

"You're fucking crazy," Red Cap mutters, turning to me. "Hands where I can see them," he orders.

Duane sags against the deposit slip counter. He stares hard at me, his gasping shallower with each breath. It must hurt like hell. I hope I nicked something important when I went *snip snip* in there.

"Give me the shotgun," he tells Red Cap.

He hands it over, so trusting. So dimwitted.

"How's it going down there?" Duane asks him.

"Almost through. Another twenty minutes, I'd say."

"Good." Duane grimaces, pressing his hand harder against his side. He slides down to the ground, leaning against the counter. He's sweating. My heart leaps. Maybe I did nick something good.

Red Cap swears. "We need to get you a towel." He looks around. "You, get me something to stop the bleeding."

"Use your jacket," I say.

He shakes his head. "Your shirt." He points to my flannel. "Give it to me."

Leave it to these jerks to ruin my favorite flannel. I hand it over.

"Should I put her back with the others?" Red Cap asks Duane in a low voice.

Duane shakes his head. "I want her in sight at all times."

Red Cap looks at me expectantly. "You heard him." He bends down to help Duane up. The man leans heavily on him, but he's not beat yet. Far from it. And now he's got all the weapons. I'm not the only smooth one here.

Red Cap is such a good follower. I wonder what he'd do if someone told him why Duane wanted me around. Or what he was planning on doing to him to get out of here.

I guess I'll find out soon. It's time to sow distrust.

And they've just given me a front-row seat to do it.

— 39 —

Katie (Age 10): Sweet, Spirited, Smart
(In Three Acts, Reversed)

ACT 1: SMART
Before (After)

At first, I think Joseph's smiley in the way Elijah was—that kind of fake cheeriness that's all performance and pomp. After all, he owns a slew of car dealerships. He's a salesman, and a slick one at that. It would make sense.

Every time he looks at me, I try to pick it out in his face, in his eyes. What makes him smile. What makes him frown. How I can mold myself to make him do the first thing, and not the second.

What do you want? I can't pin it down.

(Later, I'll tell myself I was stupid. Even later, after a lot of therapy, I'll know I wasn't.)

Mom's too confident after how well conning Elijah went. She's sailing on the high of two successful jobs in a row, but I don't know then I can't trust her when it comes to picking the marks.

(I will question it forever: Did she know? How could she? How could she not?)

Joseph's on the hook too fast for someone who manipulates

for a living; he moves us into his house after just two months of dating, and Mom's smug about it and I'm so glad I'm not getting terrorized by Jamison anymore that I've left Haley and my curled-up fists behind.

I don't realize my fists should've stayed curled until it's too late.

(I have spent years talking through it in therapy. Those four months we lived with him and that one day that changed everything.)

(This is what I know:

He tried to draw me in in the way that men like him—predators, pedophiles—think is the gentle way, which is just so fucking sick, you know? Like there's anything gentle about it. Men like that want to groom you. They want you soft and scared and never knowing which way is up.

Another kind of tilted ground.)

(This is what I know:

I was not groomable. Not because I'm smarter or better. The opposite: because someone had got there first.

Abby had groomed me to become her. There was no room for outside influence. She was the weight that leveled my world.)

(This is what I know:

If they can't make you soft *and* scared, they just make you scared.)

(This is what I know:

I had no idea what *scared* meant, when it came to me. I had no idea what I'd do.

But I guess we all learned.)

40

11:44 a.m. (152 minutes captive)

~~1 lighter, 3 bottles of vodka, 1 pair of scissors,~~
    2 safe-deposit keys
~~Plan #1: Scrapped~~
Plan #2: ~~Fucked~~ Maybe not so fucked
Plan #3: Stab ✓

Red Cap makes me go first down the hall, him and Duane shuffling behind me. We pass the room Iris and Wes are in, and I croak, "Where are we going?" loud enough for them to hear I'm alive. My throat is killing me, throbbing in finger-shaped pulses against my skin, and my eyes feel like someone rubbed sandpaper over them while I was forced to watch bad cartoons for hours.

"Shut up," Duane tells me. He jerks his head to the office to my left, all the way down the hall. "In here."

Once we're in the office, they make me sit in the crappiest of the two office chairs. I slump in it, my eyes tracking across the room. It's the same setup as the one they had us in, but the desk is bigger and whoever works in here really likes plants. Maybe I could chuck one at them and run. Death by fake ficus.

There's that wishful thinking again. Gotta stop that.

Duane tries the good chair, but he's wincing and sliding onto the ground within a minute. Red Cap helps him shift so he's leaning against the wall. Maybe he'll pass out long enough for me to get the dimwit to let us go. But life isn't easy like that, and men like Duane are stubborn. They hang on. My flannel's getting rusty, but not soaked. The bleeding's slowing down, even as he's getting paler.

I should've gone for his neck.

"Get back downstairs and finish the welding job," Duane orders him.

"But—"

"I'll be fine," Duane says. "Tape up her hands and get back to work."

I fight Red Cap when he tapes my hands in front of my body instead of behind, even though I'm pleased. I can do a lot with hands taped in front, especially because I can flex all my fingers. It's still too many layers to break, but I'll find a way out, and at least he doesn't tape my feet.

Duane's starting to sweat as Red Cap bends down to check his wound. He murmurs something to him, and I can't make it out until he raises his voice—"Yes, I'm fucking sure"—in annoyance as he hands Red Cap the shotgun.

"I'll be fast," Red Cap says. "Don't try anything," he tells me.

"I was gonna pull a bank heist, but you two have that covered," I snipe back. My voice cracks in the middle, ruining the effect.

His footsteps fade down the hall, and I turn my attention back to Duane. He doesn't look great, but he doesn't seem to be at death's door, either. And the hand holding the gun on me is dead steady.

"So what's the plan?" I ask. "Are you going to kill him in the bank, or use him as a human shield when you shoot it out with the deputies? Remember: I'm too valuable to be a human shield."

"Do you *ever* shut up?"

"No. Get used to it. It's gonna be a long trip to Florida."

"One more word and I'll knock you out. When you come to, you'll be choking on exhaust fumes in the trunk of my car and you'll stay there until we get to Florida."

I make a mental note he said *car*, not truck. "Fine," I say. I stretch my legs out, folding my booted feet on top of each other. "She's not gonna let me go without a fight," I mutter.

It takes a second for it to register; I guess I have to factor in the whole blood-loss stabbed thing. "What are you talking about?"

"I thought you wanted me to stop talking." I'm full snot-monster right now, and it's working. He's getting agitated. He'll be all wound up by the time Red Cap gets back.

He glares at me, pressing my shirt harder against his side.

"What did she tell you?"

"Who . . ." His eyes narrow. He hates not being in the know, especially on his own job. I need to keep making him feel small and unsteady. It makes him dangerous because it makes him angry, but it'll make him slip up so I can slip through.

"Who did you think you've been talking to on the phone this whole time?" I tilt my head, the sarcasm grating. "Did she say she was a deputy?"

"You know her."

I settle back in the chair, all comfy and as relaxed as a girl can get with a bruised throat and mashed-up face. "Um, yeah. I live with her. She's my marshal. I lied before. I don't have an aunt here in Clear Creek. The FBI handed me over to witness protection after the whole thing with Raymond and the marshals stuck me up here with *her*. She is such a pain in the ass."

"She's a marshal?"

"You didn't smell the Fed on her? Are you sure you've been in prison?"

He shifts against the wall, wincing and pressing my flannel harder against his shirt. It's getting redder. He's bleeding again. I try to twist my wrists against the tape in a subtle way, testing my range of movement.

"I knew she wasn't a deputy. She talked too smooth."

"That's her," I say. "She's gonna chase you if you manage to get away with me. She has to. This is a shitshow for her. All she'll care about is getting me back."

He's looking for a trap in my words, but they're just the truth. There is nowhere in the world he could take me where my sister won't follow.

I need to paint a careful picture of Lee for him: the bitch of a career woman who's got tunnel vision. He'll buy that. He'll want to get away from her, and it'll make him screw up. I just need to be there when he does.

"She can't be very good at her job, if she's got a shithole posting watching a kid like you."

"You've totally ruined her day with this stunt, which normally would make me happy, but this kind of sucks for me."

Every time he blinks, it takes a little longer for his eyes to open again. He's starting to drift. The pain and blood loss and coming down from the adrenaline is getting to him. Maybe he'll slide into shock and I can get the gun off him.

"This sucks for *you*?" He laughs, a far too long, drawn-out thing that bares his teeth . . . and is that blood on his lips or just wishful thinking?

He coughs, holding his side. Then he coughs again, and crimson bubbles from his mouth. He reaches up to dab at it and his eyes widen.

"Oh no, did I snip something important?" I ask, digging my own shallow grave because I need to see how far I can push him. "Better hope it's your spleen or something you can live without. Organs are kind of hard to come by."

"You—" He lunges like he's trying to get up, and lets out a surprised grunt of pain instead. More sweat trickles down his face, but there's no more blood from his mouth. Whatever I hit, it's not slowing him down too much, but the pain's starting to kick in. If he stays still, he'll probably be fine.

Maybe I need to make him move. A lot.

I'm weighing how fast I could get to the door and out into the hall versus how fast he could raise the gun and aim well enough to hit me when the decision's taken out of my hands.

Duane tries to get to his feet again, and this time, the pain gets the better of him. He gets halfway up and then lets out a string of curses and his eyes roll back and *bam*, he's down, and suddenly, the ground's tilted back toward me.

Plan #4: Get gun. Get Iris and Wes. Get out.

41

Katie: ~~Spirited, Sweet, Smart~~
Katie: ~~Scared, Violated, Traumatized~~
Katie: Talking, Learning, Healing

Almost Four Years Ago

"How do you want to spend our time today?"

That's what Margaret always asks me first. I could lie and say I've lost count of how many times she's asked me, but she would call that not being productive and falling into bad habits. (It's eighty-nine times, because it's been ninety sessions and she didn't ask me the first session.)

Therapy didn't start well when Lee first brought me two counties away to Margaret. It wasn't even that I was resisting; it was that I had no concept of how to tell the truth about anything, especially myself. I had all the tools of a liar and nothing else.

Margaret knows a lot, but she also knows nothing. I'm an optical illusion, where one person sees the old lady and the other sees the young woman. Margaret gets to see slivers of both, but never either of them fully. She has my truths, but she doesn't have Raymond's name. She knows about my mother, but thinks she's dead. Little lies, not just to keep me safe, but Margaret, too.

Stumbling toward carefully picked-over truth into healing has taken longer than I've liked. I like being good at things. I'm not good at the truth or opening up or asking for help.

You're good at applying the help is what Margaret says when I tell her that. *Once you get over the obstacle of the asking.*

Sometimes it's so hard to ask.

"He wants to kiss me," I say, because it's been on my mind for weeks, ever since I noticed.

"Who does?"

"Wes."

Margaret looks like she's trying to suppress an indulgent smile that might come off as condescending. I'm not supposed to break her down like that; Lee told me that therapy was about listening to the therapist and puzzling out *myself*, not her.

"This is your friend?"

"My best friend." And then, digging for that truth: "Kind of my only friend."

She takes me in. "You've talked to me about other friends, too."

"It's not the same."

"Why not?"

"Wes knows. I mean, no. He doesn't *know*. He just . . ." I swallow. It's like the first few times in here with her all of a sudden, and I hate it so much, it heats my face up. "He knows I got hurt. He . . . got hurt, too." I'm betraying him, telling her. I'm betraying something else, by putting the abuse in the past instead of the present.

She can't tell anyone, I remind myself. She wouldn't.

"I'm impressed that you were able to share that with him," Margaret says. "That shows a lot of progress."

"He figured it out," I tell her, unable to take credit that isn't earned. "There are scars," I continue. "He saw them when we were swimming."

"And you didn't spin a story for him?"

"He would've seen through it."

She waits, in that maddening way of hers. She's got a whole thing about drawing me out. It didn't work for a long time, and then it did, and now we're here: surrounded by that tricky trust thing. We built it, she and I. Bit by bit, over ninety painful sessions. She helped me lay brick on the tilting ground, weighing it down so I could walk steady.

But I don't feel so steady anymore.

"I didn't want to lie to him," I finally say. "He's got scars, too. To lie about it . . ." I just shake my head. It had felt so wrong. Like stepping away from something sacred and into something sticky-hot and putrid.

"So he knows more about you than most people," Margaret says.

I nod.

"Do you want to kiss him?"

I can't look at her or move. The answer's not just yes or just no. It's just . . .

"It's okay to have a crush."

"It's not that simple," I mutter before I can stop myself, because of that tricky trust thing. I'm used to speaking about stuff in here, but I don't talk about some things out of choice rather than protection. And I've never talked about it because of that swirl of shame and the sour taste of bile that rises in my throat every time I think about it. Yet I find myself on the edge suddenly, like I'd planned to tell her today, even though I hadn't. "I'm not good with that stuff," I say, paddling desperately away from it like a kid who never learned how to swim but jumped into the deep end anyway.

"What stuff?"

"Kissing. Flirting. All that stuff."

"Well, considering you're just getting started with all that stuff, wouldn't you say that's acceptable?"

It lies there like a dead animal: assumption roadkill. And I don't know how to ask her what I want to ask. The blood is pulsing in my face, and I am lost in the wanting to know and not knowing how to ask.

How to admit it.

"I don't want to hurt him."

She's spent enough time with me—ninety sessions' worth—to see the buried truths beneath those words.

"Why do you think you'd hurt him?"

"Because I want to kiss him, too."

Her eyebrows twitch—the closest thing I'll get to a frown her placid-like-a-pond face can muster up. "You're not talking about emotional hurt, are you, Nora?"

I can't look at her, so I stare down at my hands. I rub my pointer and middle finger against the pad of my thumb, back and forth, back and forth.

The silence stretches, and she lets it. She waits in this little pocket of trust we created for me to find the words, because I'll never find the strength.

"Before my stepdad, there was a mark. Joseph. He owned a bunch of car dealerships. My mom had him moving us in two months after they met.

"He was always looking at me. And then he didn't just look, he . . ." I twist my fingers in the air, this helpless, shameful little gesture, a shrug that says what I can't. It'll take until session 117 before I can say the words *he molested me*, but I don't know that at the moment. All I know is that I can't say it, even though I need help with it, because I'm scared what it makes me. Because I am terrified of how I might react if Wes gets too close before I'm ready or prepared. "At first, I just froze. It was like it was happening to me, but not to me. I could see it, I could feel it, but I couldn't move. I couldn't scream. I was . . . not there. And then, outside, someone's car alarm went off. It was like I'd been playing dead and that sound woke me up."

Margaret waits. I still can't look at her. If I tell her, what will she think?

She's not normal. That's what the last woman exposed to the results of my fight-or-flight instincts said.

"I tried to pull away. He was too strong. My mom's knitting basket was sitting next to the couch. It was the only thing close enough to grab. I had to get him to stop."

Margaret can't keep her pond-placid mask from slipping as the realization fully grasps her. "You defended yourself with knitting needles?"

"It made him stop because he had to try to pull them out of his leg," I say, and it's a very simple, very neat way to talk about it when there had been nothing simple or neat about it. It'd been bloody, and the needles were thin because they were from Mom's delicate work, but they were still knitting needles, so they were dull and I wasn't very strong. I'd dragged them up his thigh as far as I could and hit something that had made it gush. He'd howled in pain, and I'd been so sick and scared at once, an overload of adrenaline as the shaky *run, hide, fight* got reversed to *fight then hide then run*.

Margaret's quiet, and it's not a waiting-quiet this time. I don't know if I've thrown her or if she's just adding this to her *Nora's fucked up* file.

"I know it's messed up," I say.

"What *he* did to *you* is very messed up," Margaret agrees, and when my face twists, she lets out a little sigh. "Oh." And she can't stop the sympathy leaching into it that's more like pity.

She folds her hands together, leaning toward me. She wears an oversized moss agate pendant on a long chain, the way older, elegant ladies sometimes do. It glows against her gray sweater, and I can't stop staring at it because if I don't, I have to look at her and receive a truth I'm not sure I'm ready for.

"You defended yourself, Nora," she says quietly.

"I'm violent." *She's not normal.* It echoes in my head.

"What was done to you was violence," she corrects. "You met violence with defense. There is nothing wrong with that."

When I don't say anything, she continues, "Have you ever initiated a fight? I know you've been in a few. We've talked about them in the past."

I shake my head.

"Have you ever engaged anyone that wasn't in defense of yourself or someone else?"

I shake my head again.

"And you're not going around school, conning people into throwing the first punch?"

"I mean, I could . . ."

"But you don't."

"No."

"I don't think you're violent, Nora. I think that you react a specific way when you have no way out. Some people freeze. You fight. Neither of these reactions are wrong."

I have to say it. I have to ask her. Because I'm scared. I'm scared that the flutter that I feel when Wes catches my eye for too long will turn into something else when he gets too close. When his hands slide around my waist or eventually under my shirt. I want to be able to have this. I want to have this. I want *this* to be the thing that isn't warped or taken from me because of the girls before.

"What if I react that way with Wes? What if when we kiss, my body reacts like it's bad instead of like it's good?"

"If kissing is something you and Wes both decide you want, then maybe you start slow. Holding hands. Going on a date. Or hanging out. Whatever you kids call it these days."

"We hang out all the time."

"Good. Then you can talk to him," she continues. "You said he knows you've been abused. Does he know about this part?"

I shake my head.

"Talking is important in any relationship. And you two talk a lot, right?"

"Of course."

"Maybe the best thing to do is tell him you want to kiss him, but you need to do it in your own time. That way you're not waiting for him to initiate anything and it's not a surprise. Would that take some pressure off?"

I never even thought of kissing Wes first, but now that she's suggested keeping the power in *my* hands, the possibility seizes hold of me. No breathless waiting for it to happen to me, but instead being breathless in anticipation because I could choose the moment.

"What if he laughs at me?" I don't think he will. Wes is not like that. But it's scary, thinking about being so blunt about what's been unspoken and said in glances and barely there touches and bodies that get closer and closer each week, sitting in front of the TV.

"Then you'll know he's not a boy who deserves to kiss you," Margaret says, and that makes *me* laugh, because she's the kind of honest I wish I knew how to be.

We fall into a silence that's not uncomfortable, but heavy. Like the air before a rainstorm: You can smell it on the wind, feel the possibility of the fall of water in the atmosphere, and then it just breaks and the skies open.

"How do I keep this from ruining my life?" I ask her.

"By doing exactly what we've been working for here," she says. "Look at you and how you're moving forward. That's not ruining your life, Nora. It's healing it. Seeing obstacles before they become roadblocks."

I want to believe her. That this is just an obstacle, not a roadblock.

But I have lived so many lives already. Been so many girls. I've learned things from each of them. Katie taught me fear. Not of men. I already knew to fear them, because don't all girls learn, in the end? I just learned faster and earlier than some, and later and slower than others.

Katie taught me a new fear. She taught me to fear myself.

197

Because she was the closest to me I've ever played at being until Nora, and something about that drew Joseph in, didn't it?

Once I finally find the words to ask her, Margaret tells me that nothing about it was my fault. That I didn't do anything wrong. She repeats that he was a predator. That I trusted myself. My instincts. I reacted the right way for *me*.

So why do I still feel so wrong?

(*She's not normal.*)

It's an answer I don't have. But I'm still looking.

I'll keep looking.

Part Three

———————

Freedom . . .

(The Last 45 Minutes)

42

Ashley (Age 12): How It Ends
(In Three Acts)

Five and a Half Years Ago

ACT 1: HELP

I'm in a hotel suite. My sister brought me here, through the back entrance and service elevator. The second the door shuts behind us, she shoves me into the shower, closing us into this artificial bubble of clean linens and expensive hotel smell.

"Rinse all of it off," she orders. "Wash your hair twice. Scrub yourself down three times. Use this under your nails." She gives me a toothbrush still in its plastic. "Put your clothes in here." She holds out a bag, and I'm numb enough to obey her.

But I'm not numb enough to not wait quietly until she's left the room so I can undress. I slip the thumb drive from the pocket of my sandy jeans, tucking it behind the stack of toilet paper where she won't look for it. Then the clothes go in the bag like she asked.

When I get out of the shower and into my robe, she's gone. So is the bag of my clothes. For a minute, I wonder if she's left me here. If she's finally decided it was better to just save herself, instead of both of us.

Can I blame her? I had the same thought on the beach.

But then the hotel room door swings open, and there she is

again. The relief has my knees turning watery, and I want to cling to her like I've never clung to anyone in my life, but I can't.

"It's okay. You don't have to apologize," she says, and I realize that's what's spilling from my mouth. *I'm sorry, I'm so sorry.*

"I screwed it all up. Our whole plan—"

"You got what we needed. It's okay that things got messy."

The sound I let out is hysterical, because she sounds so much like Mom right then.

"There are some new clothes in the bedroom. Go sleep. I'll take care of everything else."

"But—"

"The only way this works is if you let me be the adult," she says, in that matter-of-fact, no-bullshit way of hers, but still, it has me reeling.

"I'm not a kid," I say softly, and the truth of it is this cankerous weight between us.

"Now you get to be one. And that means that I'm in charge, not you."

"You sound like Mom," I say, because I'm hurt and raw, and I want her to sprout the same kind of wound.

"I'm not her," she says, so calmly that I know my barb failed to pierce. Then she says my name. My real one. Softly, like she wants it to be a comfort.

It's not.

"Please don't call me that."

There's an understanding in her face that I want to run from. "What should I call you?"

I have no idea. I'm not *her*. I'm not Ashley, either. I'm no one. I'm everyone. All of them, mixed together like liquor in a cocktail

202

shaker. I just jerk my head, hopeless, and then I say, "I'll go to bed."

She leaves the door open half a foot, like she needs to keep an eye on me, and I lie down on the bed.

Blood had swirled over my (Ashley's?) glitter-painted toes in the shower. Pink sudsy water, and God, I don't think I'll ever look at pink and think *happy* again. It'd taken the three scrubs she had demanded to get the water to run clear.

Is he dead by now? Did he bleed to death out there in the sand? Am I a murderer?

I turn over in the bed, away from the door, so I can stare at the wall.

Why did she come back? She could've run. She didn't sign up for this. She was just trying to get her kid sister free.

But I'm not a kid, I've never been a kid, and I never will be, will I? Not now.

It's all different. The risks . . . They're the kind even Mom wouldn't want to take on.

Act 2: Safety

There's a sharp rap on the door, and when she gets up to answer it, I take advantage of her distraction. I slip out of bed and sit in the armchair in my room instead, because it has a better view of the other room. Water drips down my back, trickling cold against skin that's still half numb. I'm done being quiet and talked about but never included. I found a way tonight, when none of them could. Didn't that earn me a place at the table?

"Yvonne, thank you for coming," she says.

"Amelia, this is not what we talked about."

I jerk a little at the sound of this stranger using my sister's real name, because it's against the rules. And that's when it hits me: There aren't any more rules.

I didn't just break them. I broke free of them. I want to hold the realization in my hands, squeeze it until I crush it, until it's embedded in the raw skin on my fingers and becomes a part of me that can't be cut out.

"I'm sorry," she says, and her voice cracks.

"Oh, Amelia." The woman reaches out and squeezes Amelia's shoulder before moving briskly into the hotel room. Her razor-sharp bob swings with each step and her suit is impeccable, even though she probably got the call long past midnight. But a good lawyer is ready at all times, and that's who this woman has to be. Amelia would've covered all the bases when engaging the FBI. She would've found the best. A shark to fight for us.

"I can make this work. Unless you've changed your mind, considering . . ." She trails off. Amelia looks down at her feet before shaking her head tightly.

"We make them stick to the original deal."

"All right. I understand," Yvonne says. "Then we're clear: We don't leave this room without the original terms we agreed upon, signed and official."

"Agreed."

"She's had a tail on me since day one," Yvonne says. "So she's waiting in the lobby."

"Of course she is."

"There are at least three undercover agents positioned downstairs. Who knows how many she put on the other floors."

"She's such a drama queen," Amelia mutters.

"I'll call her up, if you're ready."

She nods.

The click of the phone, then: "This is room 206. Can you please send my guest up? Thank you." She shoots Amelia a reassuring smile. "It will be fine. You have what they want."

Amelia nods, but it's shaky, and it makes me worried. But when there's a knock at the door a few minutes later, her shoulders square, and suddenly she's all swagger and strength again in a single breath.

"Good evening, Agent North," says Yvonne. "I'm Ms. Striker; I represent the Deveraux sisters. Would you like some coffee?"

"I'm fine," says the woman, coming in. She has short blond hair and a somber face. "Lawyering up, Amelia?"

"Do you have it?" Amelia asks, her face as blank as the agent's.

"He was where you said he'd be, if you were wondering," Agent North says. "Well, kind of. He'd dragged himself a good fifty feet down the beach, trying to find help. She did a number on him, your little sister."

Amelia's mouth twitches.

"Neither of my clients have any knowledge of what you're speaking of," Yvonne says smoothly.

"Sure," Agent North drawls sarcastically.

"My client—"

She holds her hand up. "This isn't what we talked about."

"I don't care," Amelia says. "It's your mess now."

"You're such a piece of work," Agent North says disgustedly. "Do you at least have the hard drives?"

"Do you have the immunity agreement?"

"Amelia . . ."

Amelia's up out of her chair and walking toward the door so fast, it has the woman's eyes widening. "Out, then."

"You were supposed to get your sister out next week when they went on vacation. If things had gone according to plan, she would've had a fingerprint kit and we'd be able to move in on his entire operation after a thorough vetting. Now I've got Raymond Keane in the hospital and the only other person around that night was your sister. That does not look good."

"If you would like to know the details of my evening, I'm happy to provide them," Amelia says.

"Sure, enlighten me," Agent North drawls.

"I got a call from my sister last night asking me to pick her up. Raymond and our mother had been fighting, and when my sister tried to stop him, he hit her. Again. So I came and got her. She was waiting for me in the foyer of the house. I did not go farther inside. And if you are audacious enough to make me say this in front of lawyers or a judge or even any of those other pesky agent friends of yours? I will say the same thing. Along with some other choice secrets of yours and maybe some of your higher-ups' secrets, too."

"And if we question your sister?"

"We had a deal, Marjorie. You get Raymond and Abby and the proof to lock them away, and I get my sister."

"I don't see the hard drives," Agent North says.

"You won't see the rest until I have the deal in front of me," Yvonne says.

There's a beat. A moment of showdown where someone's gotta blink.

It's Agent North. She bends down, pulls a sheaf of paper out of her briefcase, and hands it to Yvonne.

"Show her one," Yvonne says, turning to the papers, settling her glasses on her nose.

Amelia gets up, goes over to the safe, keys in the number, and pulls out one of the hard drives and a laptop. She plugs it in and boots it up, then clicks on the folder. "This one has all the video," she says. "Raymond likes to have video."

"Fuck," Agent North breathes as she watches. "You've got to be kidding me."

Amelia closes the laptop as she leans forward. "Not until Yvonne tells me that agreement is solid."

"I could just take her in right now," Agent North says, and there's a note of threat in her voice I don't like. "I have cause."

"You touch my sister and you will not make it out of this room alive," Amelia says, with such flat sincerity it sends a warm jolt of something—I don't know it then, but it's security—through me.

"Amelia," Yvonne warns. "Agent North, she didn't—"

"Yes she did," the agent says. "She meant every word."

"Yes, I did," Amelia says. The two of them stare at each other. I can see it through the gap in the door. It crackles, whatever's between them.

"I want to talk alone," Agent North says.

I don't think Amelia will agree, but to my surprise, she nods.

"Amelia, I strongly advise—" Yvonne starts to say, but she's cut off with a firm smile.

"Can you just give us a minute?" she asks her. "You can finish reading the agreement in the back room."

Yvonne gets up, and her heels click out of the room.

I watch the two of them through the crack in the door. Amelia's head is bent, her mouth tense. She's rubbing the pad of her thumb against her pointer and middle finger, back and forth, back and forth. It's what she does when she's nervous. This tic we share somehow roots me to her in a way I never could have imagined.

"I can't believe you," Agent North hisses, all professionalism melting off her. "You extracted her yourself? The plan—"

"Went to shit," Amelia finishes. "I'm sorry the murderous psychopath parenting my sister didn't adhere to your schedule."

"I can't believe you're getting snippy with me now. Now. Of all times. This is such a fuck-up," she mutters. "I sold them on an open-and-shut case. It's not anymore."

"Not my problem," Amelia says.

"The trial's going to be harder now. If we had her participation—"

"No," Amelia says.

"The marshals are excellent at their jobs—"

Amelia lunges to her feet, crossing the room fast, out of my sight, and I hear the soft rustle that can't be a punch but has to be some sort of touch, because the agent lets out a breath that is not quiet.

My eyes flick down. I feel like I'm invading all of a sudden. My cheeks heat up when I realize I must be. But I still tilt my head to see the two of them.

They're standing close, and the agent's rubbing her wrist like she's wrenched it from Amelia's grip.

"The marshals can be bought off or conned. I can't be. You

know what I've done to get to this point. Do you really want to fuck with me when I have what I've spent six years trying to get? I finally got her away, and she's not leaving my side ever again. She is my *sister*, and she's had to . . ." She stops. She shudders, like she can't even say it. I understand, because I can barely think about it.

"No witness protection," Amelia continues. "No marshals, no safe houses, no *trials* or names. We had a deal. No testifying, no mention of her part in this, no participation—in exchange for the hard drives. You're going to stick with it. Or you won't get them."

"I can just take them," she says softly, like she's breaking it to her.

Amelia smiles, and I see the cruelty in her for the first time. "You know me, Marjorie. Do you really think I'm above pinning you to the ground while my sister smashes the drives into so many pieces there's no hope of fixing them?"

Agent North gazes up at my sister like she's the moon and North is seeing her for the first time.

No. Wait. I lean forward, trying to catch her expression, to read the secrets in her fully. She's not looking at Amelia like she's seeing her for the first time.

She's drinking her in like it's the last time.

"She almost got killed getting you what you wanted." Amelia says it like a condemnation, and the agent bristles at it.

"She did not have to—"

"Fuck you," Amelia interrupts, so fiercely that it makes North jerk back. "Fuck you and your federal bullshit that allowed a little girl to be driven to this, because your people were so bad at infiltrating Keane's organization they got *four* agents killed in two years of undercover ops. You *needed* us. I made a deal that risked her because my kid sister was more competent than your agents. You'll walk away with his hard drives and a big chunk of his operation gutted and whatever promotion they throw at you, but she'll be in danger until he dies."

"Whose fault is that?" North asks. "Hers. She took *insane* risks. I had a clean extraction plan for her. If she'd just—"

"*Stop.* She's not an asset. She's not some criminal informant you turned over the course of years and a cleaned-up coke habit. She's *twelve.* She's a fucking *kid.*"

There's a long silence where North stares at her as if she's trying to weigh the worth of saying something. I slip back into the shadows; it's like I know the words that come next will slice me raw.

The truth usually does.

"Did you see what she did to him?" Agent North asks. "No tricks," she says, as Amelia just frowns. "I just . . . Did you see how she left things?"

She still says nothing. My sister trusts no one. Even this woman, who looks at my sister like there's torn-out chapters in Amelia's life story that are all about her.

"Because if you didn't see," Agent North continues, hushed now. "Maybe you haven't realized . . ." And then she holds out her phone, showing her.

I won't lie, it flashes through me, the worry. Is this it? Will she turn away now?

But it fades as fast as it comes, because my sister laughs instead of reacting like I think and the agent wants. "Are you seriously trying to make me feel bad she smashed his face in?"

"And the rest?"

Amelia doesn't miss a beat. "How the hell else was she supposed to get you your precious hard drives? Did you expect a twelve-year-old to drag an unconscious man up the beach to the house and then all the way upstairs to his safe?"

"If she'd waited for the extraction, she would've had a kit."

"But she couldn't and she didn't, yet she still got you what you needed. So the deal holds."

There's the kind of pause that has so much tension, I'm gritting my teeth against it.

"She's not normal," Agent North says slowly. "What she did . . . how she left . . . Can't you see that? She could've called you before . . ."

"If she had called me before, Raymond Keane wouldn't be alive right now," Amelia says. "He'd be gator food. All of him."

"Stop *saying* shit like that!" North's distress bleeds into her voice and her pretty green eyes.

"Stop implying my sister is dangerous."

"Isn't she?"

"My sister," Amelia says, just as slow, but twice as dangerous, "is a victim of domestic violence and sexual abuse at the hands of the men our mother brought around her. And she has been psychologically abused by the only parent she's ever known. It is my job to give her the safety and space and whatever else she needs to become a survivor. So if you continue with your victim-blaming bullshit when she let that fucker *live* after he spent the better part of two years terrorizing and beating her, I swear to God, you're gonna go back to your higher-ups with nothing. I'll take the files to the DEA and ATF instead, and you'll be left on the sidelines. Or maybe I'll just cut all you Feds out completely. Put it on the dark web for the highest bidder."

Agent North takes a deep breath. She's steeling herself to fight more, to accuse me of liking it next, probably, or that it wasn't the first time. She'd be right about the last thing and wrong about the first.

But instead of arguing, Agent North deflates. "God, Amy," she says, the nickname falling off her lips with an ease that comes only from familiarity. "I—"

"No," Amelia interrupts, chin up, arms crossed, so damn defensive. Every shield is up, and the way she's telegraphing it tells me she isn't aware she's doing it, that this woman tripped her up once before, and she can't let it happen again. "Just give me what we agreed on."

"The original deal holds," North says after a long moment when they stare at each other, hungry in a way that makes me want to look away, because it's not faked. There's no artifice . . . no calculation or prettiness. Neither of them wants to show it, but they do, because it's all raw and a pulpy mess.

"Yvonne, you can come back in here," Amelia calls.

"It's all like we agreed," Yvonne tells her.

"Let me have it, then."

Silence as she reads through it. The minutes tick by. "Does anyone have a pen?" Then: "The code to the safe is 0192."

I bite the inside of my cheek as I hear the agent punch in the code and swing the door open. "This is all of them?"

"Yes," Amelia says, because as far as she's concerned, that's true. I think about the thumb drive tucked behind the toilet paper. I'll need to move it soon.

"Let me just verify." More silence. I can barely breathe around it. Is she going to squash the deal? Will she somehow figure out what I held back? But then there's a snapping sound. "That's all, then."

"Do not come looking for me," Amelia says, and it's not just a warning; it's a plea for mercy. And North is deep enough in it still to give it to her.

"Goodbye, Amy."

My sister does not say goodbye in return. I wonder if she's not able to. If she'll break.

The door clicks shut, and North's footsteps fade.

"That's it," Yvonne says. "Are you all right?"

Amelia nods. "Thank you for everything, Yvonne."

I tilt my head farther to the side so I can see Yvonne pause at the door, worrying her lower lip. "Free advice?"

Amelia nods.

"Go deep, wherever you end up. He won't stop. A little girl cut him off at the knees, and it's not going to sit well with him or his cohorts. So get out of here. And don't come back."

After a moment, my sister says, "Thank you, Yvonne."

"I would say *anytime*, but let's be honest: I hope I never see you again."

"Me too. But I owe you. If you ever need me . . ."

"I pray I never have to collect. But I will if I have to. Try to stay safe, Amelia."

"We will."

"You're a good sister. Remember that."

I hear her heels click out the door, and then it shuts. I close my eyes when Amelia starts rustling around, and then I hear the

TV flick on. The murmur of voices fills the room, mindless non-sense I can't fully make out. I let myself drift. Just to give her some time.

ACT 3: HOME

I wait a long time before I walk out into the suite, where she's turned on an old movie and is staring at it with the kind of frown that tells me she's not seeing or hearing any of it. I drop down next to her on the couch, crisscrossing my legs. Our knees brush, and her jeans are ripped and soft, like my sister is underneath. The exhaustion pulses through me like a heartbeat, and I want to lay my head down on her leg and let her stroke my hair off my face like I've seen sisters do in the movies. The impulse is something I should fight, shed like skin and strands of hair, because comfort isn't something I deserve, is it?

"Are we leaving soon?"

"We need to get your new ID on the way out of town. I know someone."

Of course she does.

"Are we going overseas, like you said?"

Amelia shakes her head. "I'm taking you home with me."

The word echoes strangely in the room. She's never mentioned home. I don't know where she lived before we started the Florida Plan. Amelia has always been careful with the information she's given me. She had to be, because girls are supposed to choose their mothers, and what if I did, in the end?

Abby would've chosen *him*. The last two years tell me over and over again that she would've chosen him. I have to believe that. I have to understand that the second they met, her world tilted toward him, tossing me off. I could've crashed, but Amelia helped me fly.

What had she sacrificed to get here? I know some, but not all. I look at her out of the corner of my eye, thinking about how the room had crackled between her and Agent North. *You know me,* Amelia had said, and I knew what she sounded like when she was telling the truth.

"You slept with the FBI agent, didn't you?"

And for the first time since this all started, my sister lets out a laugh. "Oh fucking hell," she says, and then that laugh turns into a mockery of it.

I don't know what to say. I feel sick. What I know about sex and relationships is purely transactional and violent and violating, but I've read enough to know that that's not right. That it can be different.

Can't it?

"I've got you less than six hours and you're already picking me apart," Amelia says, shaking her head. "You are a trip."

"I'm sorry."

She reaches over and grabs my hand, squeezing it. "Don't ever apologize for being smart," she says. "You and I, we see things differently than most people. We catch the little stuff, the hidden things."

"Because of Mom."

She squeezes too tight. I don't flinch. "No, she just saw it in us. It doesn't mean it's because of her. And it doesn't mean we have to use it the way she does."

"But . . . you *did* sleep with the FBI agent," I say, because I don't want to talk about her anymore. I can't. Not yet. Maybe never again. Can I do that? Can I just hide forever?

"It's complicated," Amelia says.

My lips feel horribly dry. I lick them. "Does that mean . . . That means you did it for me."

She starts to say my name but stops, because I asked her before not to. It's enough answer.

"You conned her," I say. "She was the one who answered your cell phone when I called you in Washington. And I called late. Which means . . ."

"I—" She leans her elbows on her knees, breathing deeply. She's not elegant, my sister. But she's all raw-hewn grace and neatly pulled-back hair, cheekbones for days and big eyes full of regret. "I want you to be a kid," she says. "I want to take you home and have you go to school and live the kind of life you haven't had and I never will. And if I tell you—"

"If you tell me, I'll know what I owe," I interrupt.

That makes her straighten. "I'm going to say this once: You owe me nothing. I chose to seek you out when you were little. I chose to get you free of her. I chose to be your sister. That was all me. There is nothing owed. You and I are on even ground. Always."

"I don't know how to be on even ground." My confession, when it comes, is just as quiet as hers, but it's so shameful. I am so ashamed. Tears well in my eyes, and am I a monster, that *this* is where I cry? Not before?

The bathroom light outlines her profile, stark bones against the golden glow. We are both so tired, and there is so much still to do. There is so far to flee. But I have to know.

If she wants us on even ground, I need to know what she did for me. What my existence did to her.

So I'm honest for once and tell her that. And in turn, she is honest with me.

"I didn't find out about you until you were three," she says. "When I ran from Mom, I was determined to never come back. I ended up in LA. Disappeared into the sprawl. I worried that if I started running cons, it might get back to her somehow. So I went legit. Worked for a PI. Got my own license. I resisted looking for her for a long time, but when I finally did . . . that's how I found out about you."

"But you didn't come to see me until I was six."

"I didn't want to come at all," she says, and she can't look at me while she says it. Honesty at its most brutal. This is what I asked for. "For years, I told myself that you weren't my business. I knew if I went back, she'd just use you to pull me in."

"What changed your mind?"

"You were turning six," she says. "I was six when—" Her fingers shake as they press against her lips, like she's trying to keep the words inside. "I couldn't leave you. I had to try to get you away from her. So I made a plan."

"You came to see me."

Her fingers are still pressed against her mouth, but her lips spread, an almost-smile for the tips of her to remember. "You were so funny and smart already. But you were wary. And the second I saw that rubber band on your wrist . . ." She shakes her head.

That was one of Mom's tricks, to keep me from messing up. She'd snap it against my skin. I'll forever associate some things with the sting and the faint smell of rubber.

"I wanted to take you right then. But I knew she'd never stop searching for you. She doesn't know how to run a con without a daughter. She needs a partner."

"She gets lonely." It's automatic, the defense of her, even now.

"It's not our job to fill that in her," Amelia says.

"You sound like a shrink."

"Probably because I go to one," she says. "And so will you, when we're safe and home."

All three of those things are unfathomable: safety, therapy, and home. I want to argue, but she says, "Do you want me to finish?"

I do, so I nod.

"When I left that first time, I knew I had to find a way to make it so that once I had you with me, Mom couldn't get to you ever again. I either had to kill her or put her in prison. And since I didn't want to add matricide to my list of crimes, I chose the latter. Which meant I needed two things: I needed you to actually want to leave, and I needed an FBI agent in my pocket for the moment that happened."

"Agent North."

Amelia nods. "I knew it was going to be a long con. That it would take time to get you on my side. But I started working on North right away. She had a big case, and one of the witnesses was in the wind. So I tracked him down and brought him in. We became friends."

"Friends or *friends*?"

"Friends," she says, but I don't think I believe her. "I'd pass her tips sometimes."

"You put Abby on her radar," I say.

"The FBI already knew about Abby, but North is ambitious. And a con woman who's tangled up with all sorts of other criminal power because of the men she targets is a big get. If they managed to bring in Abby, think of all the marks she's had through the years. Think of all the dirt she's dug up. If she turned snitch, she'd be a gold mine."

"Did she know that you were Abby's kid?"

"Not until Washington."

"You played her for four whole years?"

She nods. "It blew up after that. She found out everything. And by then . . ."

"You were together," I fill in when it's clear she won't. I understand why she can't. She broke the number one rule.

She fell for the mark. I want to reach out and stroke her arm, but I'm afraid that it'll be clumsy. That it might be unwelcome.

"I couldn't find you after you and Abby left Washington. When you finally popped up, I was just going to go to Florida and take you. Fuck the plan; I'd worry about her chasing us later. But then I saw the marriage license."

"Agent North couldn't ignore you if you gave her Raymond Keane," I say, understanding now.

"So the plan was back on. And now we're here."

"I fucked it up."

"You managed," she says. "That's what matters. And in a few hours, we'll be gone."

"He'll look for me."

"We have a head start. He has to be on good behavior through the trial. Once he's put away, it'll take him a while to gather power. They'll assume you're in witness protection. Whoever he hires to come after you will focus on that angle first. We have time."

"To do what? Hide better?"

"To make backup plans. To prepare. And to *live*. That's what this is all about."

"You want me to live like a normal person." I shake my head. "Agent North is right. I'm not normal."

"There is no normal," Amelia says. "There's just a bunch of people pretending there is. There's just different levels of pain. Different stages of safe. The biggest con of all is that there's a normal. What I want for you is happiness and safety. That's what I want for myself, too."

"Were you happy with Agent North?"

When she doesn't answer, I press further.

"Did you love her?"

Still no answer.

"Because she was kind of mean," I add.

"What I did to her was more than mean," Amelia says.

"So you did love her." I pause. "*Do* love her?"

"It doesn't matter," she says, all the answer I need. I really am just a tidal wave, destroying everything in my wake.

"I'm sorry."

She reaches out again to squeeze my hand. This is something she does, I realize. Touch people genuinely. Can I tell her that I'm not used to it? That it makes me jump inside my skin almost as much as it comforts me?

"Everything that I've done is worth it to have you here safe with me," she says. "And now you get to have a brand-new life."

"Where?"

"California," she says. "Way up north." She squeezes my hand again. "It's a little town called Clear Creek."

"And you?" I ask. She looks quizzically at me. "What are you called?"

It's like the air sharpens around us, and her entire body tenses and then releases just as quickly. An ingrained response that we both have. Amelia was her touchstone, the real girl no one but the Deveraux women know. She conned Mom into thinking she was still Amelia, but she's become someone else, truly and fully.

I know my sister, but I don't. Now I get to meet the real her.

"Lee," she says. "Lee Ann O'Malley."

Lee. Short. Matter-of-fact. It suits her.

I want to be brave when I ask the next thing, but I'm not. I'm right back in front of that mirror, Mom's hands braiding my long hair as I repeat a name dutifully after her . . . and my voice shakes.

"And what am I called?"

"That's up to you," Lee says, and choosing like that is as unfathomable as *safe* and *help* and *home*. "What do you want your name to be?"

"I get to choose?"

Her thumb settles on the pulse point of my wrist. *Thump-thump. Thump-thump.*

"You get to choose."

— 43 —

1 lighter, 3 bottles of vodka, ~~1 pair of scissors,~~
    2 safe-deposit keys
~~Plan #1: Scrapped~~
Plan #2: On hold
Plan #3: Stab ✓
Plan #4: Get gun. Get free. Get Iris and Wes. Get out.

Duane slumps to the side, his hold on the pistol slackening, and I move. I don't talk myself out of it or hesitate, because who knows if he'll jerk himself conscious any second.

It's awkward with my bound hands, but I manage to pick the gun up, though I can't shoot it or hold it properly.

I set it down on the desk, turning back to him. His breathing is shallow. The blood loss got to him, maybe, but if he just passed out from the pain, he might come to fast. But I need my hands free.

I tug up his shirt with two of my fingers, exposing the waist of his jeans, and the knife is tucked against his back. I grab it, peel it open, and, with some maneuvering, manage to flip the blade to the right position and saw through the layers of tape.

The knife goes in my pocket, and the gun's back in my hand, and I can't hesitate, even though the weight of it is a free fall in my stomach, every muscle in my body telling me to put it down.

I move forward instead. Got the gun. Got free. Now I get Iris and Wes. Then we get out.

Cracking open the office door, I peer through the slit into the hall. There's no one in sight. Red Cap's still down in the basement. We might be able to avoid him altogether.

I slip out the door and into the hall, hurrying to the heavy steel table they dragged to block the office they were keeping us in. I set the gun on the table and yank the end of it.

"Stop."

I whirl, grabbing the gun as I move, and it may look confident, but I'm not. I don't want this. But I still point it at Red Cap because he's got the shotgun pointed at me.

"Put it down," he orders.

"Put yours down."

He jerks his head to the side, and when Iris steps into the hallway, all the greedy joy of slipping free fizzes out in my chest.

"Down," he insists, and I do it, because there's no other choice. The knife's still in my pocket, but if I reach for it, he'll shoot me, so I stay stock-still. Iris stares at me as he hurries over and gets the gun. "What did you do to him this time?" he demands as he hustles us into the office where Duane is slumped against the wall.

Iris's eyes widen as she sees my bloody flannel next to him.

"I didn't do anything. He passed out on his own."

Red Cap slaps Duane's face a few times, but he doesn't move. Iris looks from both of them on the ground to me, with a question on her face.

The scissors, I mouth, making a stabbing motion.

She shoots me a look that seems to be more disappointed I didn't do it properly than horrified I did it at all.

"You're lucky he's still breathing," Red Cap tells me when he finally gets up after tying my flannel against Duane's wound. "He better wake up."

Red Cap has a point, unfortunately. I kind of need Duane awake, because Red Cap is not the leader type and he'll fall to pieces if he doesn't have someone to boss him around.

"I didn't do anything," I say again, not liking how he's straightened with the kind of intent that has my fists curling.

"You stabbed him."

"Girl's got a right to protect herself."

"I am done with your shit," he tells me as his grip on the shotgun tightens.

"I have to go to the bathroom!" Iris squeaks out. We both look at her, the tension suddenly broken.

"No," he says, in such a frustrated way that I realize this is a worn-out argument between them. What has she been up to?

"I did what you told me," she says. "I sat down there in that creepy basement and breathed in welding fumes forever. You said when we came up, I could. And now you're not going to let me?"

"Just hold it," he orders.

"I can't," she says. "I don't need to pee. I need to empty my cup."

It jerks his attention back to her. It's brilliant, and I try to hide my awe as she continues. "You know, my menstrual cup?"

He starts shuffling as soon as she says the word *menstrual*. "Not gonna happen."

"You don't understand," Iris says. "I have a condition." She folds her hands together; she is so dainty and prim in her dress, and you can't think anything diabolical about her when her cheeks are pink like that and her eyes are downcast just so. "A *heavy bleeding* condition. I *need* to change my cup. I've been waiting and waiting."

"I told you, it's not gonna happen."

"Do you know how much liquid a menstrual cup holds? If it overflows, blood will be *everywhere*."

"Not my problem."

She shakes the watercolor-squiggled skirt of her dress at him. "This is a 1950s Jeanne Durrell dress!"

He rolls his eyes. "I don't care about your dress."

She looks like she's seconds away from stomping her foot. "You should, because if you don't let me empty my cup, forty milliliters of menstrual blood is going to cover my dress and run down my legs and the deputies out there are going to think you *shot me*."

He frowns.

"I just need ten or fifteen minutes in the bathroom, and my purse."

"I'm not leaving her alone with him," he says, jerking his thumb at me.

"Well, good, because I need her help in the bathroom," she says, and it makes him frown further.

"No way."

She bristles. "Do I have to go through the entire cleansing and disposal process with you?" she asks, and her voice trembles so delicately. "This is embarrassing! You're making me beg you to let me change the modern version of a *tampon*. Why do you have to do this to me?" And then, to top it off, tears begin to form in her eyes. I have no doubt they're real. She's in a lot of pain on a normal day, but especially when she's on her period, and none of this can be helping. I'd be curled up in a ball on the ground right now if I had cramps as bad as she gets.

"Why do you need her?" he asks.

"Like I said, do you need me to go through the entire process with you?" Iris asks, her eyes wide and so innocently outraged that I'm reeling. She is good at this. "Don't you have the internet? Sisters? A girlfriend? Or are you one of those guys who thinks periods are gross?" She's shooting questions at him rapid-fire and he doesn't like it, his confusion and embarrassment over her talking about menstrual blood reddening his face.

We're more alike than you know. She'd said that to me once. I'd tucked the knowledge inside me like I was a locket and she was a secret message written on a slip of paper. I'd turned it over and over in my mind like another girl would fiddle with jewelry, wondering if it was truth.

And here is the truth playing out in front of me: Iris Moulton is a natural.

Because the next thing I know, out of sheer discomfort and the desire for her to stop saying *menstrual blood* over and over, Iris's purse gets shoved in her hands after he searches it one more time, and then we're in the women's restroom in the back of the bank.

"You lock this door, I will shoot the doorknob off," he tells her.

"We'll be fast," Iris promises with a shaky smile.

"No heroics," he says to me. "No tricks. I'm blocking you in. Bang on the door when you're done."

The door closes and Iris swings toward me, and finally, agonizingly, we are alone. There is not enough time and there is so much to say and explain and ask forgiveness for and there is too much to do and we need to *move*, we need a *plan*, I need—

She kisses me. She pushes me right up against the bathroom door and cradles the unhurt side of my face against her palm and kisses me like she thought she wouldn't get to again, and I kiss her back like a last kiss is an impossibility.

Her fingers curl in the short hair at the nape of my neck, restless little circles as she pulls away just far enough to rest her forehead against mine.

"I am so mad at you," she whispers.

My eyes close against the hurt in her voice and in me. "I know."

"Is your plan working?"

I shake my head.

She lets out a breath. "Okay," she says. "Then we're going with mine."

— 44 —

Ashley: How It Begins

You can't con a con artist. Isn't that what they always say?

Once, I thought it was true. Absorbed it with all of her other teachings and my baby food. But I've proved the adage wrong, haven't I?

I learned from the best. No—not her.

Him.

Seven Years Ago

After Washington, after I have to snap out of Katie but have no new girl to step into yet, everything is rushed and weighty. We bolt—we've never had to before, and she's furious. I can feel it in her silence, in what she's not saying, in the few words she does. It's this persistent pulse inside me: *This is your fault, you shouldn't have done anything, you should've just dealt with it.*

When we arrive in Florida and she doesn't give me a new name or a new hairstyle, it feels like punishment instead of a reprieve. Like she's taken something from me, because what's left if I'm not one of them or preparing to be one? I hate the feeling; a knife's edge that's cutting shallow into my neck as she leaves me in the hotel room for long stretches.

Katie is gone, but what happened isn't, and I don't know what to do with that except try to put it all in a box somewhere deep inside me. I want to cry all the time, but I can't, because . . . am I a girl who cries? I don't know. I don't know who I'm supposed to be. She's given me nothing to grasp—no comforting hairstyle, no orderly trio of traits, no carefully chosen clothes, no mark's insecurities to build a girl to cater to.

One day stretches into night, and she's still not back. I stay awake waiting for her as long as I can, panic and sleep finally getting the better of me around 3:00 a.m. The next thing I know, something heavy's being thrown on the foot of my bed. I jerk awake just in time to see her toss another bag of clothes down.

"Up," she says. "Bathroom. We've got work to do."

I blink at the Nike bags, and then she claps sharply and I'm scrambling up—away, far away from the bags and what they represent—and toward her, because where else would I go?

She hums as I trot into the bathroom, and when she begins to brush my hair in front of the mirror, my skin crawls. It should lull me, but the last two weeks of her dodging me has made me needy, desperate for her attention, unable to settle in the scraps of her presence. And the last two months have made me skittish in a way she didn't raise me to be. I'm supposed to be accessible. My hair is hers to choose, just like my clothes, my name, and my future; nothing on my body is mine. My body doesn't belong to me.

Nothing does.

She sections off my hair, drawing a ruler-straight part down the middle of my head. She begins to braid, tight and efficient, and she won't meet my gaze in the mirror.

Can she not look at me? Am I that horrible?

Mom secures each plait with a little plastic tie, reaching forward to pluck the bobby pins from the pile on the counter. "I've reserved a court each afternoon this week at the club," she tells me as she winds the braids around my head, pinning them in place. "I haven't had the time to research any possible targets. So this will be a good lesson for you: how to spot the right one, then how to bring him to me. What do I say about hardship?"

"It makes you better, if you're smart."

She tucks the end of the braids behind the plaits, pinning them tight.

"Our last job," she says. "It was a mistake." And for a moment, my heart leaps, and then she crushes it. "You'll prove to me you've learned from your mistakes, won't you, baby?"

It hangs there: *my* mistakes.

The shame barrels out of the box I put it in, her confirmation that of course it was my fault. (It's not, it's *not*, but I don't know that then, because she tells me it is, right then and there, she cons me into thinking it because it's easier for her.)

"Yes," I croak out.

She finishes my hair, her hands settle on my shoulders, and finally, for the first time in weeks, she meets my eyes in the mirror. It makes me sick. It makes me joyful. And her next words send relief rushing inside me so fast I'm dizzy enough to grip the sink.

"Ashley," she says. "Your name is Ashley."

"Ashley," I repeat, because I have to be dutiful. Katie wasn't, and look what happened.

She smiles. "There." She smooths my too-tight braids. "Isn't that better?"

I nod. Of course I do.

I want so badly for it to be true.

I spend a whole week sweating on the tennis court at the country club she's using as her hunting ground.

She is Heidi this time, to my Ashley. My skull aches from Ashley's hair, the milkmaid braids pinned close to my scalp with too many pins. Ashley is homeschooled, all focus and drive and Nike gear. *Wimbledon by seventeen,* Heidi tells the parents at the club, even though that's ridiculous. I'm an okay tennis player, but there's only one thing I'm a prodigy at.

I perform like the dancing bear I am, my guilt that we're in this situation heavy as a rock in my belly. But every time I slam the ball over the net, my body sings like it's something close to mine. It's almost good. It's nowhere near enough. I try to pretend it is.

She sits on the sidelines with her knitting and her pristine silk shell and skirt and her sunglasses, like she always does. Men approach her on the sidelines throughout the week as I practice my volleys, introducing themselves to the fresh meat at the club. She smiles and tosses her hair, but her attention slides back to me immediately. She's not interested in the kind of man who approaches her first; she wants one whose focus is on both of us.

I'm realizing how boring all the prep work of finding someone to lay a trap for is, because I'm feeling all kinds of impatience as we head into a second week of me at the net, against that ball machine that rattles every two balls. The *swish, swish, rattle* makes me twitch. When I miss four balls in a row, I let out a frustrated noise.

"Don't let it get to you, baby," my mother calls encouragingly.

"It's annoying," I complain. "Can we see if someone can fix it?"

"Everyone's gotta push through distractions," she reminds me. "Try to make it work for you."

She shifts her sunglasses to her head before going back to her knitting. It's a signal: Someone's watching us. I need to keep on the objective. All I've been doing for the past week and a half is lifting things from people's wallets, because the cash Mom has won't last us forever. Especially with the way she spends.

I keep at my volleys, and the third time I miss in twenty minutes, I drop the racket, my mouth twisting.

"Hey now, don't pull a McEnroe on me," she calls.

"That's a super-dated reference, Mom," I inform her, and she tosses her head back and laughs in that way that tells me whoever she's got her eye on, he's watching.

"Always putting me in my place," she says, winking at me.

"Excuse me?"

I look over my shoulder to my right. He's in the court next to ours, grinning at our little display.

"The rattling throwing you off?" he asks me.

I smile. Not my smile. Ashley's smile. It's brighter, with no hesitation. Ashley doesn't know about being wary. "Totally."

"I'll see if I can talk to maintenance about looking at it later today." His eyes slide to my mother, who's watching him, then

232

back to me as he grins. "Pulling a McEnroe on the ball machine will just make it rattle more."

"Listen to the wise man, honey," Mom says, the smile in her voice more than her face. She won't give him a smile yet, not until he earns it. That's how it works. *Thank you,* she mouths at him over my head, a little secret between them, outside of me; another kind of reward.

He lifts his racket as a sort of goodbye before jogging back to the center of his own court, where his tennis partner is waiting.

I spend another twenty minutes hitting balls, trying to ignore the rattle of the machine and the gaze I can feel on both of us from time to time as he glances over between his own sets.

Mom finally checks her watch and waves me in. "I'm going to take my steam and you need to eat lunch, young lady," she tells me, plucking a stray bobby pin from my braid and sliding it back into place. "Please don't fill up on *just* garlic fries. Order a meal with a whole grain or a crunchy vegetable or maybe even *two* crunchy vegetables, please, I beg of you." She holds out her hands clasped teasingly, and I know it's for him, the man who's still watching us out of the corner of his eye, but it's like going from invisible to seen after weeks, and I can't help but want to melt into the safe glow of it.

This is what we do. I can do this. Even if I made mistakes with Katie, like she said. I can make up for it.

I have to.

"I promise," I say, packing up my tennis racket and chasing after all the stray balls with the ball basket before she slings an arm over my shoulder and we make our way to the club locker rooms.

"Ready?" she asks after I've showered and changed out of my tennis skirt and into a sundress. I nod. We split at the locker room door, me to the club restaurant and her to the bar across the way that still is a good vantage point into the restaurant. She's half hidden by the palm fronds or whatever greenery they've got stashed everywhere.

I get a table for two and order a heaping mound of garlic fries. I page through my phone—Ashley watches tennis videos on Instagram and has kitten GIFs saved to her files—until my food arrives.

I can feel eyes on me the whole time. Setting down the phone, I dip the fries into the aioli the waiter brought and munch away, waiting.

I feel him before I hear him. The barest brush of air at my right before he sits down across from me.

"I thought you weren't supposed to order just garlic fries," he says.

My eyes go big. I project my guilt, dropping the fry on the plate.

He grins, taking a fry off my plate and eating it. "These are better than whole grains," he agrees. "Not as healthy, though. You're a pretty decent tennis player."

The *bam, bam, bam* of his words is like a tennis play in itself, and it sets warning tingling down my spine. It's rapid: agreement, followed by a criticism and right into a veiled compliment.

It's a tactic Mom's taught me to use. It sets my teeth on edge instantly.

"Thank you," I say. "Are you a coach?"

He shakes his head. "I own some gyms here in Miami. Your mother..." He trails off, like even the mention of her is distracting.

"Heidi," I supply helpfully, like I'm supposed to. When the marks decide to approach her through me, it's supposed to be a cute little dance. I'm supposed to be helpful and smiling and giggle at the right moment when they fumble finding the right words.

"Heidi," he says, and the way he says it . . .

My teeth grind together so hard my jaw hurts, and I don't know . . . I don't know if it's my gut or if it's because of what happened with Katie, what I'm feeling, which is *Go, run, now*. I'm caught in the indecision, a fish in a net, unable to flop out or breathe deep.

"And you are?" he asks me.

"Oh, sorry." I hold my hand out with a little flourish. All the girls have good manners. "I'm Ashley."

He shakes it. "Raymond."

"Nice to meet you." I drop his hand as quick as I can while still being polite. "I ordered a grain bowl with extra avocado, too," I tell him, lowering my voice conspiratorially. "I wouldn't disobey her."

"You wouldn't, would you?"

"Mom knows best," I say cheerfully.

"You're very good," he says.

"I thought I was *pretty decent*." It slips out of my mouth before I can stop it, so I follow it up with a smile for softness.

"I'm not talking about your tennis game. I'm talking about how you lifted the credit card out of that golfer's wallet yesterday when you bumped into him."

I go cold as I remember the lift I made yesterday, the black card that I had already used to buy a thousand dollars' worth of gift cards, which can be better than a bank card if you don't want to be traced.

"You've got quick hands," he continues. "And you're smart with your targets: Man like that, he won't notice a missing card for a few billing cycles. Did your mother teach you?" His gaze rises over my head, scanning the room before settling back on me.

I can't freeze or flush. I *can't*. But I've never been made before. I've never had to spin out of being caught at all, let alone so fast. I skate over the possibilities like I'm on thin, dark ice. *Play dumb. Lie. Chatter. Tell the truth.*

I pop another fry into my mouth, scrunching my nose up. "Huh?" My eyes skitter to my screen, like his weirdness isn't as important as my phone.

He smiles. I catch it out of the corner of my eye. "Talent, skill, and you look just like your mother. She must be very proud. You are quite the asset."

He looks me up and down like I'm a car he's about to buy, and that clinches it for me, because it pisses me off enough to break through any numbness and fear. I don't know then that this man will make me redefine *enemy* and *father*, two things that are already purposefully entwined in my head. All I know is that I'm outnumbered. I need to get away from him.

I need my mother.

So I give him a puzzled half smile, tearing my focus from my phone completely. I let the smile hold: one count, two. And then, I let it snap off my face, quick as you please, and suddenly, we're truly eye to eye for the first time.

"Yes," I agree. "I am quite the asset. So maybe you should back off."

"You two came into my house." His head lifts again, scanning the room. He's looking for her, wondering where she is. Where is she? Hasn't she noticed how he's looking at me? Hasn't she realized he *knows*?

"Do you own the country club on top of all the gyms?" I ask innocently, even though I know what he means. This is his turf. We've trespassed. "That's very impressive."

"You're quite the Addie Loggins, aren't you?"

"I see Mom has competition with the dated references," I say before I think it through, and when his eyes flare with delight and he laughs, I realize I've made a mistake.

I've made him even more interested.

He gets up from the table. "Tell your mother that I hope she likes my gift."

Before I can do anything, he's gone, and I'm just sitting there, blood thundering in my ears and my entire body screaming *Run*. So I do. I jolt out of the chair and I spin, intent on just *going*, anywhere but here, and I get one step before I'm colliding with her.

"What's wrong?" She pushes me gently, guiding me back into the chair, and I don't try to fight her.

"Mom, he knows," I whisper. "He—" I stop. He made us because of *me*. This is my fault. *Again.* She'll be so mad. "I don't know how," I continue, half breathless from the lie, but she doesn't seem to notice. "But he knows."

Her shoulders tense, and just like he did, she starts scanning the room. But just like her, he's out of sight, if he's watching.

"What did he say?" she asks. "Christ, drink some water. You're white as a sheet. Remember what I taught you about controlling your face?"

"He knows. We have to go." My hands shake around the water glass. Her eyes widen, and then her hands cover mine.

"*Control yourself,*" she orders under her breath.

But I can't, and she ends up taking me back to the car and finally gets the story out of me in halting bursts as we drive back to the hotel.

I'm too shaken to notice the glint in her eye, or maybe I think it's anger. But when we get to the front desk and there's a bouquet waiting for her, I see what he meant by *his gift.*

He knows where we're staying. It's a threat. *Run. Run. There are no knitting needles this time, you need to run.*

She strokes one of the flowers. "When did these arrive?" she asks the concierge.

"Around eleven thirty," she says.

"Hmm." Mom plucks the envelope off the marble counter and flicks it open, pulling out the little card. I peer around her shoulder to read it.

One word: *Dinner?*

"Would you like me to have someone bring the flowers up to your suite?"

Mom shakes her head. "My daughter will take them. Thank you."

I don't want to touch them, but I do as I'm told. She's still holding the card as we get to the elevator, rubbing it between her fingers like it's something soft and secret. I press the button, waiting until the doors swish closed to turn to her.

"Why are you smiling?" I demand.

She looks over to the flowers in my hands and presses the fingers with the card still clutched in it to her lips. "They're fox-gloves," she says.

Heat crawls in my face because I feel like she's laughing at a joke I don't know. A joke *they* know.

"They mean deception." She plucks one of the flowers out of the vase. Then she laughs. And it's not a fake laugh. It's her real laugh, surprised and little wry. Like she can't believe it.

The elevator doors slide open. She sweeps forward. I stay stuck in place.

She doesn't notice she's left me behind.

12:02 p.m. (170 minutes captive)

1 lighter, 3 bottles of vodka, ~~1 pair of scissors,~~
    2 safe-deposit keys, 1 hunting knife
~~Plan #1: Scrapped~~
Plan #2: On hold
Plan #3: Stab ✓
~~Plan #4: Get gun. Get Iris and Wes. Get out.~~
Plan #5: Iris's plan
The contents of Iris's purse: 1 wallet with 23 dollars and
    a driver's license, 1 nylon scarf, 1 cotton handker-
    chief, 1 bottle hairspray, 1 plastic water bottle, 2
    tampons, 1 celluloid brooch, 6 lipsticks, a packet of
    bobby pins, 2 hair ties, 1 brownie wrapped in tinfoil,
    3 bottles of pills

Iris tries the bathroom door, and he's definitely blocked it. It won't budge. I push the two stall doors open, but there aren't any windows. We're stuck.

"I don't think he's out there," she whispers, pressing her ear against the door.

He's probably gone to check on Duane, hoping to wake him up. We need to move fast.

"Did he have you down there in the basement the whole time? Does he have Wes too?"

She shakes her head. "Just me. Wes is still in the office as far as I know."

"Are you okay?"

She nods. "He just made me sit there while he melted through the bars."

"They got through the bars? Did he get the box?"

"He got through, but didn't even go inside."

"Why wouldn't he try to get the box open?"

"I don't think he knows what box they're looking for," Iris says. "Either the one in gray didn't tell him, or . . ."

"Neither of them knows," I finish.

"Another reason why the manager not being here messed everything up."

"The more I find out about their plan, the shittier it gets," I say.

"Yet they're still winning," Iris says. She sets her purse on the sink. "I wasn't kidding when I said I need to empty my cup." She pushes past me and goes into one of the stalls.

"Look in the cupboard below the sink," she tells me from the stall, and I bend down, yanking it open.

"We've got toilet paper, a refill bag of hand soap, toilet brushes, plunger." I reach farther into the cabinet, dragging out the big bottle in the back. "Gallon bottle of hand sanitizer."

"That," she says, coming out to rinse her cup and then going back inside the stall.

"Okay." I set it to the side. "Um . . . bleach spray, two bottles of air freshener, and a bottle of Drano."

"Perfect. All of that." The stall door opens with a click and she wipes her hands on a paper towel before pumping hand sanitizer from her own purse all over them. "Sorry for being gross and not flushing the toilet. I don't want him to hear and think we're done."

"Lucky for you I'm not terrified of menstrual blood like the ass-hole out there."

"Oh, God, don't make me laugh right now," she hisses. "I need to concentrate." Then she grabs the big trash can near the door and carries it over to the sink, pulling the top off and assessing the contents with a glance. Getting on her knees next to me in front of the cabinet, she sets her purse down with us and pulls out a shiny square from it, unwrapping the tinfoil to reveal a brownie. She sets the pastry to the side and tosses the foil at me.

"I need little balls, marble sized."

She unwinds the toilet paper with the efficiency of a seasoned TP-er, which I can't imagine is the case. She dumps the loose paper into the garbage can in layers, squirting hand sanitizer and the vodka that she'd found earlier onto the mess. By the time I'm done with the balls of foil, she's filled the can.

I glance at the door and then back at her as she feeds the balls of foil into the now-empty bottle of hand sanitizer and adds the bobby pins from her purse. Then she unscrews the bottle of Drano and, with the steady hands of a girl who can victory-roll her hair, pours the liquid into the bottle, over the foil balls.

"What are you doing exactly?"

She lets out a long breath, screwing the top of the bottle tight. We kneel there, the bottle between us, and there is nothing but fear in her face when she answers.

"Building a bomb."

— 46 —

Abby: How He Hooks Her

She goes to dinner with Raymond. She dates him. She falls in love with him.

She does everything he wants, because it's the same things she wants, and what I want . . .

Well, it doesn't matter.

"I'm tired of the game, baby," she tells me one night when I'm helping her get ready. "I've been doing this a long time. And I'm not getting any younger."

She hasn't been getting any younger all my life, it seems. She's always fretted in front of the mirror, looking for lines that aren't there because Botox, and complains about flaws that have never existed in her almost-too-beautiful face.

"You're perfect," I tell her, because that's what I'm supposed to say.

I hand her the diamond earrings Raymond gave her on their third date and she fixes them in her ears. He gave her a pair for me at the same time—little studs, a rich girl's first diamonds— and Mom cooed for days about how thoughtful it was and I wondered how I'd ever thought she was smart, because this was just basic love bombing. She *taught* me this.

It's all wrong. It's been wrong since Katie, but I thought it'd get better once I proved that *I* could do better. And now I have no way to prove that, because I have no one to con.

I get a brush to stroke through her hair, trying to lose myself in the rhythm of it as she dabs perfume on her pulse points.

"I think . . ." She looks down, staring at her hands. She strokes her ring finger, starting at the top of her French tip and ending where a ring would lie. "I think this could be good for us."

"This?"

"Raymond."

"How?" It comes out of me in a disbelieving huff.

"He wants to take care of us."

"You taught me to take care of myself."

"And look where that got you," she snaps.

My hands drop from her head, my fingers curling around the brush handle.

"You need a father," she says. *"Clearly."*

I don't know want to think about what she means. So much lately, I'm half guessing, half hoping there's another meaning than the obvious—that she's mad at me for Katie. That she thinks it's my fault.

It makes me feel like something hot and heavy's pressing into my head, my neck buckling under the weight of it.

"And just think," she continues. "You've spent all this time playing at being an amazing daughter. So being one for real will be a piece of cake."

I stare, unable to wrap my head around what she's saying. "I'm already a daughter," I remind her. "I'm *your* daughter."

"Oh, baby, you know what I mean." She laughs, getting up,

her focus slipping back toward her reflection in the mirror. "Be a good girl," she says, air-kissing my cheek as she whisks past me. "Don't wait up."

I don't wait up. I also don't wait in the room for her.

I walk down to the nearest store and I use the gift cards I've been saving up to buy three prepaid cell phones, a screwdriver, and duct tape.

When I get back to the room, I don't call the number that I've had memorized for years. I stash one of the phones in the air vent and another in the mess that is my tennis bag, and the third I leave sealed in its plastic and tape to the top of the toilet tank.

Just in case, I tell myself.

Just in case.

47

1 lighter, ~~3 bottles~~ 1 bottle of vodka, ~~1 pair of scissors,~~
    2 safe-deposit keys, 1 hunting knife, 1 chemical bomb,
    giant fire starter, the contents of Iris's purse
~~Plan #1: Scrapped~~
Plan #2: On hold
Plan #3: Stab ✓
~~Plan #4: Get gun. Get Iris and Wes. Get out.~~
Plan #5: Iris's plan: Boom!

"Don't touch it," Iris warns as I stare at the bottle—the bomb—she's made.

My eyes widen. "Of course I'm not gonna touch it!" I say as quietly as I can. My eyes skitter back to the door. "How do you even know how to do this? Don't say the internet!"

"And make my search engine history all interesting to the NSA or whatever?" she scoffs. "I want to investigate arson, not *be investigated* for it. Give me my purse."

I hand it to her and she roots around, pulling out her makeup bag and digging inside that, coming up with a plastic pin with two little hearts. It's old, like almost everything she owns. From the time people actually wore brooches. The words *Kiss Timer* are written on the hearts, an hourglass sand timer set between them. She flips the hourglass, making glittery sand trickle through it. "We need at least ten minutes for the chemicals to strip the wax off the foil," she says. "I need you to pull out all the paper towels from the dispenser and start twisting them together for a fuse."

"So how does this work?" I pry open the paper towel holder and pull the stack of them out as she keeps an eye on the timer.

"Chemical reaction. The Drano reacts with the aluminum and builds pressure. When you disrupt the bottle . . ." She flicks her fingers not holding the brooch in a sort of *pow!* movement.

"And the bobby pins?"

"Shrapnel," she says grimly. "Just in case it explodes before it hits him. There's a very short window before detonation. You can blast your fingers off."

She's staring at me with a bomb and her brilliance between us, and I'm twisting a paper towel fuse with the kind of trust I didn't think I could give another person.

"And the trash can?"

She turns the hourglass. Nine minutes to go.

"The trash can's a fire starter. We need to get out of here," she says. "We need to force them out of this building. The smoke will be terrible with how we've packed it."

My fingers tighten on the paper towels I'm twisting. "Fire forces everyone out," I say, falling into her line of thinking so easily, like it's mine.

Her mouth twitches . . . an almost-smile. "Basic human instinct is to drop everything when you're on fire."

"We use the smoke as a distraction when he opens the door and nail the one in red with the Drano bomb."

She nods. "If the one in gray is still unconscious, we can get everyone out. But if he's awake, the smoke will make it harder to shoot."

She flips the pin. Another minute down. I look toward the door. No movement, still.

"So what do you want to do for the next eight minutes?" she asks.

I don't know how to answer that. Any minute, Red Cap could be coming in here too early and we'll be dead for sure. The longer Duane stays unconscious, the riskier things get.

Iris's plan is risky. Destructive. Dangerous. Maybe deadly.

That's where we are, and it makes my heart thump. Is this it? With Wes all alone and these last minutes with her?

"Truth for Truth?" I suggest, and the tightness in her mouth eases.

"Truth for Truth," she agrees, her thumb rubbing over the heart pin's point.

"I'm scared," I say softly.

Her free hand squeezes my thigh. "Me too."

"I don't know if we can get out of this," she tells me.

"We can. I've gotten out of worse."

She's quiet. The hourglass is almost empty.

"I've read about him. And about you," she says.

"You've read about Ashley."

"Isn't that the same thing?"

That's the question, isn't it?

"What do you want to know?" I ask.

I expect her to ask prying questions. Searching, digging, uncomfortable ones. Maybe she'll even ask the same thing Duane did: *Did you really do the things they say you did?*

But Iris does the thing she always does: She surprises me.

"Are you okay? After everything you had to . . . are you all right?"

Such a simple question—and it has a simple answer. It breaks me open all the same, that she asks that first. Like I come first.

She flips the heart pin. Seven minutes.

"No," I say, because she deserves the truth. "I'm not."

Maybe someday I will be.

— 48 —

Ashley: How I Choose

She marries Raymond, and I can't stop her. He moves us to his big house in the Keys, and I've got no choice but to go where they tell me.

I've gone from a partner in my mother's schemes to a bit player in her romance. I've got nothing to do. Nowhere to go. I'm not supposed to know the details of Raymond's operation—that it's a lot bigger than running a con or laundering money through the gyms and it's a lot more complicated and wide-reaching— I'm suddenly supposed to just *be*. Be a daughter. Be a normal girl. Be okay.

I'm not any of those things. Not in the way they want me to be.

He's your father now. She tears up when she tells me this, after the wedding. Like it's beautiful. It tells me how bad it is, that she thinks that'll be something comforting, instead of terrifying.

I know about being a mixed-up handful of traits designed to lure a man in. My job is to learn how each mark works: what makes him smile, which tells me about his happiness; what makes him frown, which tells me about his fears; and what he approves of, which tells me about how much control he wants.

That's what fatherhood's about, as far as I can see: control. Not just of my mind, but of my body. That's what Elijah wanted when I was Haley, with his endless cooing about keeping sweet. That's what Joseph took when I was Katie, before I made him stop.

But I can't make Raymond stop. I don't think that's how it works anymore. If he decides he's my father, I think he's my father.

He decides other things, too. He decides everything. He decides I shouldn't go to school, because boys my age have one thing on their minds and he doesn't want me anywhere near that. I get tutored instead.

He decides that Mom should dedicate herself to charity. *It's just another kind of grift, sweetheart,* he tells her, and she laughs and pets his arm.

He decides that when he's not there, when he's off on business, there are men in the house—for security, he says. We have guards, we have a driver, we have a housekeeper, we have people watching us every minute of the day.

He eradicates any reason for us to leave, any option for us to leave, any help that could let us leave, and it's shocking how fast he strips our freedom down in the name of *family* and *care* and *protection,* because his job is a dangerous one and boys my age only have one thing on their mind and *charity's just another kind of grift, sweetheart.*

And she just . . . lets it happen.

You don't grow up with my mother and not know all about power over men. How to get it. How to use it. How to keep it.

And now she hasn't even lost it, she's given it to him on a silver platter because of *love,* and I'm reeling, because it's such a con. Most of the time, we're this shiny little Stepford family veneer to hide the criminal grime. But it's like there's a net around the house, and every day, he hauls it tighter.

I tell myself, at first, that she doesn't bend; she'll find a way to break him.

But then . . .

She doesn't bend. She doesn't find a way to break him.

She just keeps breaking.

And then she does something that breaks me.

It's a normal day on the beach. Because that's what I do now. Sit out on the beach with Mom in the mornings, before my tutoring sessions, and then in the afternoons I stay in my room and read. I try to stay quiet. I try not to draw attention as I give whatever bruises I've got time to heal. It's not hard, most of the time, because they are obsessed with each other, in that gross, gooey, show-off way that Mom relishes after so many years of being unknown.

But sometimes, his schedule is different, and that day, he comes with us down to the sand. When I trot past him, he frowns, and I catch it, but he doesn't say anything, so I keep going. Maybe it'll be okay.

Mom settles under her umbrella and spears fruit from the glass container she brought, and I try not to roll my eyes when they feed each other. I lie out on my towel with my book, but it's hot out already, so I peel off my shirt and toss it to the side.

"You want some fruit, honey?"

"I'm good, thanks."

My face is buried in my book, so I don't see them at first, but I hear it, breaking through the hum of the beach and curl of the waves: a sharp whistle and *lookitthat*, three words smashed into a laughing, skin-pricking drawl as three teenage guys walk down the beach past us. I don't even look up—this shit's been happening since I was nine—I just flip to the next page.

But Raymond's head snaps up. "Did they just . . . ?"

"Oh, love, don't worry about it," Mom says. "It's part of being a woman."

I glance over my shoulder at the two of them before going back to my book.

"Ashley," he barks suddenly.

"Yes?" I learned early he doesn't like being asked *what*. He thinks young ladies should be positive. *Yes* is so much more affirmative and positive.

"Cover up, honey," he tells me.

I don't even hesitate. I just play dumb. "Don't worry, I put sunscreen on before I left the house."

My mom's eyes narrow. She knows exactly what I'm doing.

"Ashley, put on your shirt," he says, in the kind of tone that tells me bad things will happen if I don't.

I should obey. I should say *yes*. It's what he likes.

But it's hot, and it's not my fault the boys whistled at me.

"No."

"Baby," Mom says. "Do what your father says."

I turn back to my book, ignoring both of them.

When he yanks me up off the sand, it's from underneath my arm, right at the armpit, and I flinch under his hold.

"We're going to have a little talk," he says, and Mom makes a noise of protest that dies under the look he gives her.

He marches me up the beach and to the house, and right to my room.

"Sit at your desk," he directs, before swinging my closet doors open. "Christ," he mutters, like the clothes Mom bought me are an affront to him.

"What are you doing?" I ask as he starts pulling clothes out of the closet and throwing them on the bed.

"Making your wardrobe appropriate."

"Mom picks out my clothes," I say, almost numbly, because I don't *get* this. He hits me, but he keeps talking and acting like some other guy *whistling* at me is bad. I don't understand how he can't see.

He's the one I'm afraid of. I've struggled through everyone and everything else. But I don't know how to struggle through him. I can't defeat him. She'd never forgive me. She still hasn't forgiven me for last time.

"Your mother knows how to dress for one thing and one thing only," he says.

"Hey!"

"Do not talk back to me." He shakes his finger at me. It makes my mouth snap, because once the finger is out, it's almost impossible to keep him from hitting, and my hip is just healed from where he kicked me; there's a scar now. I hate seeing it in the mirror.

I watch as he gets rid of half of my clothes. All my tennis dresses and shorts, all my skinny jeans and leggings, every sundress in my closet.

He contemplates the pile, like he's deciding if he wants to set it on fire or something. I lick my lips, glancing toward the door. Is she still sitting on the beach? Did she really just let him drag me up here and not worry what he might do to me?

"Can I—" God, my lips are dry. "Can I ask what's wrong with them?"

The approval in his eyes makes the nerves uncurl a little inside. Okay. This is the way to play this.

"You're not part of one of your mother's little cons anymore," he tells me, almost patiently. "You're my daughter, and you should be dressed appropriately and doing appropriate activities. Lying out on a beach barely dressed or bouncing around a tennis court right when you start growing up is just going to do one thing: draw every boy toward you. I'll buy you a horse and you can start riding instead." He smiles at the thought. "That's much better." He praises himself. "I should've thought of this before. Stables are full of girls, and horse girls only have time for one thing: their horses. It'll be a much healthier environment for a girl who's been through what you have."

He's planning my life out loud so casually, it takes me half a second after he's finished talking to fully process everything he's said. He's still picking through my clothes on the bed and I'm staring at his hands, tripping into the horrible realization that are his words.

"What?" I have no hope to get around it, but I still say it, even though he doesn't like it, and oh God, wait, I was supposed to say *yes* instead. He likes *yes* better, but *yes* doesn't make sense here, it doesn't, because *what* is the only response. It's the only thing I can say other than screaming because she told him, she *told* him about Seattle.

"What are you two doing?" My mother's voice breaks through the numb cloud spinning in my head.

"Talking about some changes," Raymond says. "Horseback

riding instead of tennis, for instance. And no more clothes that'll make people whistle at her."

Abby smiles, fondly and indulgently at him. "Honey, she's a girl on a beach, she's gonna get catcalled, it's just—"

"Then she won't go on the fucking beach!"

Her eyes widen at the shift and rise in his voice.

"Why don't you go downstairs and make me a list of the appropriate clothes you're thinking about so I can go shopping?" she suggests softly, going into *mollify* mode, just like I did. "I'll get these ready to donate to charity and then come downstairs. Does that sound good?"

"Fine," he says. "But she's not stepping foot back on that beach without an escort."

He leaves and Mom watches him, a smile creeping back on her face, and when she turns to see the mess on my bed, she *tuts*, like it's cute that he dragged me up from the beach and tore my entire closet out onto the bed.

"Will you get me some bags?" she asks. When I don't move or speak, she looks over her shoulder at me, expectant. "Baby?"

"You told him," I say.

"I—" She frowns for a second, her hands half full of sundresses I'm not allowed to wear anymore.

"You *told* him."

She doesn't even have the grace to blink or look ashamed now. "He's my husband."

I just stare at her, unable to voice the betrayal, seconds from launching myself at her because I want to tear her fucking eyes out. I want her to hug me. I want some part of this to be okay.

Did she tell him everything? Did she tell him what *she* did?

"The past year has been difficult for me, too," she says. "I sacrificed *everything*, baby. For you. So I need you to start behaving. Stop being so sullen. I did not raise you to show this level of disrespect to your father."

"You didn't raise me to *have* a father."

Her lips press together so hard they nearly disappear. My heart thumps in my ears, but I keep going:

"You keep acting like this was the endgame all along. It wasn't. You raised me to be one thing."

"And now I'm telling you to be another! This is not hard! You are a smart girl. You are adaptable. Why can't you just . . . *adapt*? Your sister was never like this when they . . ." Her mouth clicks shut, and my eyes widen.

My entire world splinters apart in that moment, like I was in darkness and light ripped through it, seam by seam. Because my sister . . .

My sister is the strongest person I've ever met, and my mother has made it clear that strong girls don't get hurt like I did. That I should've been stronger. That I should've just dealt with it, like I did when I was Haley.

"What are you talking about?"

She holds her hand up, shaking her head, backing away from me, already heading toward the door. I scramble off my bed; I'll chase her down the hall and those death-trap marble stairs if I have to.

"I'm talking to you! Tell me what you meant!"

"This conversation is over."

"Who's *they*? What did they do to her?"

Did you kill them, too?

She lets out a frustrated breath. "Drop it."

"I won't."

"My God," she mutters, staring at the ground, gritting her teeth against me. "Fine," she says, and when she turns on me, there's a kind of cruelty in her eyes that I've only seen directed at marks. Never at me. "What happened to your sister when I was still honing the con is a lot worse than what happened to you. I tried to keep her safe. I thought I had it under control, that they'd never get close enough to . . ." She shakes her head, like she's trying to shake it off. "If you want the details, I'll give them. But all it'll do is make you damn grateful I learned from my mistakes and adjusted the con before you came along so the marks were criminals."

"Instead of what?"

She's silent.

"What were the marks before?"

But I know. I know. I don't want to, but of course I do. Her silence says it, and I feel like I might die, right there and then, like I can't exist with this knowledge.

"I'm going to kill you," I tell her. It comes spilling, automatic, out of my mouth, so I guess it's the truth and nothing but. It certainly feels like that.

She laughs. She actually laughs at me. "Baby, you are such a drama queen. You don't have to worry about your sister. She's a grown-up and she's fine. I made my mistakes with her and I paid for them, didn't I? She's not here with me like a daughter should be."

No, she's not, is she? She got away. I know why now. She's free now. The thought sparks something in me.

"I learned from my mistakes with your sister," she says.

"That's why you've had the life you do. You got to be a little girl for as long as I could give it to you. And I worked hard to give that to you. But bad things creep through in the long run, baby. That's life. You need to learn that and get over this so it won't destroy you, because you're better than that," she says, and her voice softens, but I don't. "And you need to listen to your father. He's trying to protect you. That's what fathers do."

She leaves me alone in my room, all those clothes still spread out on the bed, and I slide against my closed door to the ground because my bed feels tainted now.

I press both hands against my mouth as the tears trickle down my cheeks. I'm not holding in sobs, I'm not holding in anything; I'm just holding myself, and my mouth has always been a lot more reliable than my heart.

I think about the bloody dish gloves and her wild eyes. Did she learn from her mistakes? Or did she just learn how to bury them better?

(She killed for me.)

(She wouldn't have had to, if she hadn't chosen him.)

I think about *her*. My sister. About how strong she is and how she keeps coming back to see us, and what both those things mean now, with this new knowledge.

I think about that phone number, memorized long ago.

I think about what I want for the first time in a very long time. Maybe forever.

I take a deep breath. And another. And then maybe about fifteen hundred more before I'm ready.

But I do. Get ready. Slowly and surely, I start to make some decisions of my own, without anyone else's input.

I decide to lift the old butcher knife from the kitchen a few nights after Mom buys Raymond a new set for his birthday. He'll never miss it now that he has his shiny new toys.

I decide to steal the gun that I find tucked in the corner of one of the linen cabinets, a forgotten backup that he really should have locked in the safe. Just think of what could happen.

I decide to dig up the just-in-case box I buried under the dock the first week they brought me here.

I decide to pull out the burner cell I have stored there.

I decide to call my sister.

I decide to run. Just like her. Because now I know:

I want to be strong. I want to be free.

I want to be just like her.

— 49 —

1 lighter, ~~3 bottles~~ 1 bottle of vodka, ~~1 pair of scissors,~~
2 safe-deposit keys, 1 hunting knife, 1 chemical bomb,
1 giant fire starter, the contents of Iris's purse
~~Plan #1: Scrapped~~
Plan #2: On hold
Plan #3: Stab ✓
~~Plan #4: Get gun. Get Iris and Wes. Get out.~~
Plan #5: Iris's plan: Boom!

"I'm sorry," Iris tells me.

I shrug, because it's hard to accept some things, especially apologies for things the people who love me had nothing to do with.

"Sometimes I'm not okay, either," she says softly, her eyes on the hourglass instead of on me.

I'm quiet, waiting.

"I'm the reason my mom left my dad."

"No," I say immediately, because the idea of it is so strange. Her mom loves her. She'd never . . .

Oh. My mind catches up with my heart, because she looks so tentative when she finally glances up.

She flips the heart pin. Six minutes.

"I got strep throat last year before we moved," she tells me.

"What?"

"They put me on antibiotics. I thought I had timed it okay

with my birth control. But Rick, my ex, he always complained about wearing condoms because hello, selfish jerk, and I just . . . I thought I would be okay. It was stupid. I should not have been sleeping with a boy who complained about wearing a condom in the first place, but there I was."

"There you were," I repeat, and I think I know where she's going—no, I know where she's going, and something's rising in me.

"I got pregnant," she says, and her eyes are on me, and they're burning with the kind of fear that makes my entire body throb, not with the pain, but with the desire to touch her, to reassure her: *It's okay.* "And I am a *what-if* person, Nora. You know I am. I like plans and details and I have been making decisions about my body and especially my uterus since I was twelve and started puking from pain with every period. So I called the clinic."

I don't speak, I just wait, her truth wrapping around me like a silk slip.

"I needed money for the abortion," she continues. "So I put some of my vintage stuff online to sell, but I forgot to block my mom from seeing the posts. And when she asked me why I was selling the Lilli Ann coat that my grandma gave me, I didn't have a lie ready. She saw through me, and I broke down." She bites her lower lip. "She did everything I needed. She drove me to the clinic and she paid for it, and she held my hair back when I puked afterward, and oh God, I'm gonna leave her alone now." She presses her hand against her chest like she's trying to keep her own heart from tearing out. "She'll be alone because now I'm here and we're gonna die."

"We are *not* going to die."

Her lip trembles. She has to take in two big, shuddery breaths to hold back the tears. I know how she feels: If she thinks about her mom, she'll break down from the potential loss. I understand, because I can't think about Lee. It'll make me weak. Clumsy.

"He found out," she whispers. "My dad. And he's always been um, protective? Controlling? For our own good, of course." She stares up at the ceiling, blinking furiously. I recognize it in her: the fight against what's ingrained in you through fear and what you're starting to learn is truth now that you're free. It spins in my head: *We're more alike than you know, we're more alike than you know,* she'd told me. I don't think I heard. But I know now. We're both girls whose bones got forged from secrets instead of steel. No wonder we snapped together like magnets. We are made of the same stuff, somehow.

"He yelled. And he punched walls and stuff. But he never *ever* laid a hand on me," she continues. "Until the day he found out."

She flips the kiss timer's hourglass. Five minutes. I glance down at the bottle, trying to control the mix of rage and revenge rocking inside me.

"He just slapped me," she says, and I hate that she's still trying to lessen it, and that I recognize that, too. "But he did it in front of my mom. I've never seen anyone move so fast. She got in front of me, and they yelled, and he stormed out. She called my aunt and uncle, and it was almost like they'd been waiting for it, because they were there to pick us up in two hours. I haven't seen my father since."

My hands are curled tight around the paper towels I've twisted into a long fuse.

"I don't want to leave my mom alone," Iris whispers.

"You won't."

"You don't know that. This is so risky. This is dangerous."

"This is survival," I tell her.

She turns the pin. Four minutes. "We need to start," she says.

"What do we do?"

It takes two turns of the kiss timer—two minutes left—but we get it done. We drag the garbage can full of sanitizer-soaked toilet paper into the biggest stall, carefully feeding the paper towel fuse inside and then laying the rest of it along the floor. Then Iris soaks the fuse with the rest of the vodka.

"There's a handkerchief in my purse. Wet it down and get ready to tie it around your mouth," she directs.

I do what she says, and then she wets down the hem of her skirt to hold in front of her face. She digs in the pocket and pulls out the lighter.

"We light the fuse, we let the room fill with smoke. Then we bang on the door to let him know we're done. As soon as he opens it, I throw the bottle. It should hit him in the chest, and maybe, if we're lucky, it'll knock him down. Get his gun if you can. Then we get Wes and the rest of the hostages. Agreed?"

I walk it through my head once, and then I nod. "Agreed."

She rubs her thumb against the bottom of the lighter, one eye on the heart pin, the other on the fuse. And then, abruptly, she fixes me with a look that rivets me in place.

"Who are you, really?" she asks me. "I don't want to die not knowing your real name."

Truth for Truth. Here we are.

But I can't bring myself to speak that name, even here, thirty seconds before we set everything on fire.

But I can give her truth. My truths. The truths that have defined whoever I've become.

"I'm not her anymore. I'm not sure I ever was."

"That's not an answer," she tells me, shrewd as ever.

"I am Lee's sister," I say. "I am Wes's best friend." I hate how my voice shakes, but I force myself to continue. I owe her this. "I am someone who survives. I am a liar and I'm a thief and I'm a con artist. And I hope I'm still the girl you're in love with, because I am really, really in love with you."

"Well, fuck, Nora," she says, the sheen of tears in her eyes back. "Now we *can't* die."

My hands close over hers holding the lighter. "I told you: I'm someone who survives. We're going to survive together."

In her other hand, the last few grains of sand trickle out of the hourglass.

It's time.

— 50 —

Raymond: How I Did It
(In Four Acts)

Act 1: Spin
Five Years Ago

The night it happens, it's just us at home. Raymond dismissed everyone early for the day. *A family day just for us,* he tells Mom.

At first, she's pleased. She's trying to cater to him, squeezing lime slices down the thin necks of his Coronas, swishing her hair over her shoulder the way she does, but his mood gets darker and darker as he checks his phone. When she asks him what's wrong, he mutters something about business and *get me another beer.*

I stay in the living room because I know what happens when I leave her alone with him when he's like this. I ran away the first time, and it was not the last time. But I have nightmares the most about that first night. Nightmares where she doesn't come upstairs to persuade me to forgive him . . . because he's killed her.

I fail her again, because I fall asleep on the couch.

When I wake up, it's dark outside. I'm covered with a blanket, and neither of them are in the living room. The TV's on mute—some infomercial—and the light dances across the neat line of empty beer bottles on the coffee table.

Thud.

There's a certain sound that a fist makes against flesh. A sound that, once you learn it, you can never forget.

I'm up off the couch, the blanket falling away, and I don't know it yet, but that blanket is the last sweet thing my mother ever does for me. Raymond's house—it was never ours, never home, never anything but a McCage disguised as a McMansion—is all cool tile and long hallways and no rugs. My feet are cold as I walk toward his study, each step echoing.

The door's open a crack, and when I push it open, neither of them notices me. He's got her on the ground and there's blood already, there are tears, and she's begging—she's *begging*, and she *never* begs, even when he's hitting me.

"Raymond, can we just talk about this, please. Just give me a second. I really don't know what money you're talking about—" She's trying to talk sense into him, but there's no talking sense into a man who's always seen you as less-than.

"You're the only one who could've taken it. I've checked out everyone else. If you don't tell me the truth . . ." His hand doesn't rear back, but instead, it pushes forward.

And that's when the shadows shift, and I see he's got a gun pointed at her.

I don't know what to do. I can't think. I can't move. The fear wraps around me and squeezes until my bones feel like they're splintering, and it almost carries me away.

I almost run.

But instead, I move toward him, toward my mother, my

267

twisted constant, toward the gun I know is loaded. It's the bravest thing I've ever done. Also the stupidest. In a second, that gun's on me, and now he's got even more leverage against her.

Mom's sobbing, mascara down her cheeks, knees bruised and scraped. He must've sent her sprawling, and my fists clench even as I stand as still as I can, trying to get his wild eyes to focus on me.

"What are you doing?" I don't sound like myself. My voice is breathy. High. Am I breathing too hard? Everything feels sped up and too slow at the same time. I wonder if this is what a panic attack is like. I'm not supposed to get those. She tells me I have to be strong.

"Get out," he snarls. "This is between me and your mother."

But I don't go. She's not even looking at me. She's slumped on that floor with her bloody knees, and she looks so much like a child that for a second, I feel like the adult.

I'm not. I'm scared shitless. But in that second, I make a decision.

If she can't con her way out of this, with her manipulation and power and the way she twists people around her gold-banded fingers like it's nothing, then I will.

"She didn't take your money," I say, and now he's completely turned toward me, so she's at his back. *Move!* I think, but she doesn't. It's like she's given up.

But I can't.

"*I* took it."

I didn't. I have no idea what money he's talking about. But I don't care. Anything to get him away from her.

"Bullshit."

It's a miracle, but I keep my face bored as I shrug. "Fine. Don't believe me. I guess I'll keep the cash. It was eighty-seven thousand dollars, right?" It's foolish to throw out a number, but it's the one I overheard him saying into the phone earlier. And I need something to really clinch it after such a gamble.

So I do the thing you should never, ever do.

I turn my back on him and the gun.

"Don't walk away from me, young lady!"

Relief twines in me. Oh thank God I was right.

His voice slurs just enough to tell me he's still the careening kind of drunk. He's sloppy slow when he's like this. I just need to get him away from her.

I look over my shoulder. "I thought you wanted your money."

I tremble as I walk away, out of the office, down the hall.

But he follows.

51

Transcript: Lee Ann O'Malley + Clear Creek Deputies

August 8, 12:17 p.m.

Deputy Reynolds: Butte County deputies left their station about five minutes ago. If we can just keep everything calm until they—

O'Malley: It won't stay calm.

Deputy Reynolds: You don't know that.

O'Malley: Something's coming.

Deputy Reynolds: What's that in your hand? Is that what you were hiding earlier?

O'Malley: Nora gave the little girl a message for me.

Deputy Reynolds: And you didn't think to show it to me until now?! What does this even mean—*He has an ace up his sleeve?*

O'Malley: I don't know, Jess. That's what I'm trying to figure out.

Deputy Reynolds: I can't believe you.

O'Malley: I'm telling you now.

Deputy Reynolds: Smoke. Shit! Smoke!

O'Malley: What? Oh my God!

Deputy Reynolds: Hey! Hey! Fire! Get on the radio.

[Scuffling noises]

Deputy Reynolds: Holy shit, Lee!

O'Malley: My kids are in there!

[Scuffling]

O'Malley: Let me go, Jessie. *Let me go!*

Deputy Reynolds: You're not running into a burning building! Are you— *Oof!*

[Yelling]

Deputy Reynolds: Lee! *Lee!*

[End of transcript]

52

12:16 p.m. (184 minutes captive)

1 lighter, 3 bottles of vodka, 1 pair of scissors,
    2 safe-deposit keys, 1 hunting knife, 1 chemical bomb,
    1 giant fire starter, the contents of Iris's purse
Plan #1: Scrapped
Plan #2: On hold
Plan #3: Stab ✓
Plan #4: Get gun. Get Iris and Wes. Get out.
Plan #5: Iris's plan: Boom!

At first, it works exactly like Iris says it will. She lights the fuse and the flame travels up to the garbage-can fire starter. It flares up. The sanitizer-soaked toilet paper fills the room with so much acrid black smoke, I'm choking underneath the hand-kerchief. I bang on the door. Fifteen or twenty heart-stopping, hard-to-breathe seconds later, I hear him start to move whatever's blocking the door away.

Iris picks up the bottle bomb and shakes it vigorously. The plastic starts to swell under her hands, the chemicals building up the pressure, but she still holds on.

The door swings open, the smoke billows out, and Red Cap starts coughing. Iris chucks the bottle right at the sound, there's a yell, a *fitz*-ing sound, and then *bam!* It explodes, in a forced projectile *zing*, spraying more smoke.

His scream is hellish—nails on a chalkboard have nothing

on it—but I don't let it stop me. I plunge forward into the smoke; it's still pouring out of the bathroom, and Red Cap is on the floor, three feet down the hall, and it's bad. It looks like it got him right in the stomach, and his hands aren't just bloody; they're raw, like the skin's been stripped from them.

Where's the gun? On him? He had the shotgun last time I saw him. Is it on the floor? Smoke pulses out behind me, and I cough. My eyes water, trying to wash away the feeling, and I turn to find Iris.

All I see is smoke and flame. Shit. *Shit.* The fire's leapt from the fire barrel to the ceiling.

"Iris!" I run forward through the chaos and smack into her. She sags against me, coughing violently.

"The ceiling tiles!" she gasps out. "They're old. Asbestos, maybe. I didn't think—"

"Go!"

I push her forward, still searching for the gun on the ground. Where is it? It's gotta be on him.

"Go!" I say again, even as I bend down on the ground next to Red Cap's moaning body. His jacket's zipped up tight. He's gotta have the pistol tucked inside . . .

Iris's little gasp and the *thump* is the only warning I get. I glance up and see him through the smoke, bloody and angry. Then the butt of the shotgun is zooming toward my face, and I think with sudden, belated clarity: *I should've gone first.*

— 53 —

Raymond: How I Did It
(In Four Acts)

ACT 2: BANG
Five Years Ago

I have nowhere to go. If Raymond starts thinking it through, he's going to realize there's no way I could've taken whatever money he's mad about. So I just keep moving, my mind latching on to the only thing I can: my just-in-case box. I don't want to be here, having to use it.

Oh God, am I going to have to use it?

"Where are we going?" he asks sharply as I lead him farther away from Mom, through the kitchen and toward the back door that leads to the deck, with stairs down to the beach.

It's one of the hardest things to do, to just keep moving, my hand turning on the doorknob like he doesn't have a gun on me. Something's building inside, this kind of reckless scream that can't come out. He'll know then.

"I buried it—duh," I say, and I am *never* rude. The girls are not supposed to be rude. Perfect daughters don't edge into that kind of real territory.

But I'm not perfect, am I? Or maybe I'm perfect at *this*.

I cross the deck and take the sand-coated steps carefully. He keeps following. That's good. I need to keep moving him away from her.

"Where?" he asks me when we get onto the beach, struggling through the sand. The wind whips at my double braids, unpinned and unkempt for once. Ashley has gone wild; he just doesn't know it yet.

I point down the beach to the docks.

"Under the dock."

"I'm punishing you for this," he tells me. "Come on. Let's go get it."

He grabs me underneath my arm—What is it about men and that spot, that painful spot that they just seem to know to grab and drag you by? Is there a class, or are they just born knowing it?—and tugs me down the beach. He's talking now, angry and distracted, about how he thought I was a good girl, how I was so tough, how disappointed he was, he gave me everything I wanted, why would I do this?

I don't answer, and he doesn't notice because he's not really talking to me, just like he never sees me. He sees a target.

I see a target, too.

We get to the dock and he bends down, frowning at the space between the sand and wood. He won't be able to fit.

"I'll get it," I say, like it's an imposition. I'm finding myself here in the sand . . . in this moment. He can't see it, I'm too scared to admit it, but there it is. There I am.

I wiggle underneath the dock, the sand tickling my stomach where my shirt hikes up, and I feel safe under here. He can't follow me.

But the storm's brewing, and for better or worse, I am the kind of girl who comes prepared.

"Hurry up," Raymond says, his voice echoing through the wooden slats.

I push forward on my elbows, heart hammering in my ears. I wish I could just stay under the dock forever, but then my searching fingers brush up against the hard edge of a box buried in the sand, and I know I can't.

I dig it out with my hands—it's harder than I thought; I used a spade to sink it in there—and sweat crawls down my chest and drips onto the sand before I finally wrench it out.

I flip the box open, praying it won't creak, and thank God it doesn't. I take it out, every muscle in my arm tense in an effort to keep my hand from shaking.

Use it. You have to.

I slither out from underneath the dock, box in my hands, and I scramble to my feet and away from him as soon as I'm in the open air again.

"Give it to me," he says, pointing to the box. The gun's in his belt instead of his hand . . . He's that assured. "No games."

"No games," I agree. And I am perfect then. Perfect in my delivery, in my never-wavering voice. My entire life has led up to this moment, and I am the picture of fearful promise, my mother's pretty protégé: *Don't blink—smile, and sell it.*

He reaches out for the box.

I move forward, like I'm going to give it to him.

Use it.

But at the last second, I drop the box and shoot him.

You had to.

— 54 —

Transcript: Lee Ann O'Malley + Clear Creek Deputies

August 8, 12:25 p.m.

Deputy Reynolds: I can't believe you hit me.

O'Malley: Get me out of these cuffs. I swear to God, Jessie . . .

Deputy Reynolds: Stop threatening me. Sheriff Adams already wants to charge you for assaulting a deputy.

O'Malley: Take these cuffs off. Right now. My kids are in that building. It is on fire. Give me the fucking keys!

Deputy Reynolds: The fire department's on the way. Calm down.

O'Malley: I'm going to kill you.

Deputy Reynolds: Lee, I know you're upset, but you need to *stop it*.

O'Malley: I—

[Shouting]

Deputy Reynolds: Shit.

O'Malley: Uncuff me! Someone's coming out!

Deputy Reynolds: I'm to stay with you. Sheriff's orders.

O'Malley: Jessie—

[Screaming]

O'Malley: That's Nora.

[Scuffling]

Deputy Reynolds: Do not make me pull my gun on you!

[Indiscernible yelling]

Deputy Reynolds: Did she just say . . . ?

O'Malley: Jessie! *Uncuff me!*

[End of transcript]

— 55 —

1 lighter, ~~3 bottles of vodka, 1 pair of scissors,~~
    2 safe-deposit keys, 1 hunting knife, ~~1 chemical bomb~~
    (detonated), ~~1 giant fire starter~~ (on fire), ~~the contents~~
    ~~of Iris's purse~~ (also on fire)

~~Plan #1: Scrapped~~
Plan #2: On hold
Plan #3: Stab ✓
~~Plan #4: Get gun. Get Iris and Wes. Get out.~~
Plan #5: Iris's plan: Boom! ✓

Third time is not lucky as he drags me down the hall again. I'm dazed, not knocked out but throbbing-hazy, the smoke and the smack to the head not helping. I fight him this time; I've got nothing to lose, I've got everything to lose. Iris. Where is she? I can't see her. She went down. He brought her down, somewhere near the door he popped out of like a murderous jack-in-the-box. He's not bleeding anymore. Red Cap must've woken him and patched him up. Stupid, stupid, *stupid* man.

The fire. It's spreading. I can hear the *crackle crackle roar* of it, see the smoke belching out of the bathroom. The paint's bubbling up the walls, and the heat's swirling. It'll reach the hall soon. We need to stop it. Wes is trapped.

I scream his name and hear banging on the wall. Fists hammering on the door and muffled words I can't make out. I scream to get low. I scream about blocking the crack in the door and all the other fire safety stuff that is *nonsense* when you're trapped. He's trapped. He can't be trapped. This can't be it. Not fire. Not like this. Not after everything.

I fight against Duane's grip on my wrists as he drags me past Red Cap, who's still a moaning, Drano-burnt mess. He dumps me at the end of the hall, much too close to the fire, and turns back to Red Cap. I struggle to my feet, staggering backward into the pocket of air that's near to searing.

It's lickety-split fast, and I saw it coming from the first time I watched them interact, but you can't steel yourself for seeing it up close. One second, Red Cap's raw and groaning, and two quick shots later, there's nothing, because he's not anything anymore.

I huff out a breath. I need to keep screaming. Wes. Iris. I need—

Oh God, he's really, *really* dead. The entire world swoops in the smoke.

"Stay there," Duane growls. He turns, and the smoke is choking-thick and acrid. My skin pinks up from the heat as the flames crawl closer to the bathroom doorway. I need to get up. No . . . *crawl*. I need to crawl. Stay low. Get to the table blocking the office Wes is in. Get him. Get Iris. Get out.

Before I can move, Duane's back, and he's got Iris slung over his shoulder in a fireman's carry.

"Did you . . ." The question dies in my throat. I can't say it. I can't breathe. No. No. No.

"I just knocked her out." He laughs. "She makes a good human shield, all these layers." He flicks the edge of her skirt and petticoat at me through the smoke.

I flush hotter than the fire, fist-curling against the need to hurt him.

"Come on." He gestures with the gun.

"No. Not without the boy." Leaving the rest of them behind is monstrous. I don't care, in that moment. I've got Iris in my line of sight. I need Wes, and then I'll go. I'll leave them. I left my own mother, after all. Leaving is what I'm built for.

Duane's eyes dart over my shoulder. The flames must be growing. I plant my feet. I can wait him out. I can play chicken.

"Now," he says.

I shake my head.

He shoots. Just like that. The plaster above my head splatters everywhere, a chunk of it hits my arm.

"Move, or she's next."

I have to move to survive. I'll die if I leave him behind. I have to protect Iris. I can't protect Wes. The thoughts misfire in my panicked head as he pushes me forward.

I have no way to spin this, and if you asked me who I am right now, I would tell you: *scared, scared, scared.*

Duane has two-thirds of everything I care about in this world in his hands, actually and metaphorically. He knows it now and he'll use it.

The basement smells metallic and charred from the welding equipment scattered near the hole in the bars Red Cap made, all for nothing. Duane doesn't even look toward the safe-deposit boxes; he's got another prize now—he just needs to get away with me.

This is not how my plan was supposed to end. This is not how it was supposed to happen. Iris isn't supposed to be draped over him, rag-doll limp, her curls and feet dangling. Wes isn't supposed to be upstairs, all alone, huddling away from the smoke pouring in. Oh God, he's all alone. He can't. Not like this. Not like *this*.

I'm screaming as Duane pushes me out of the bank. I've gone feral, every tool and clever trick chased from my head in a flood of smoke and *trapped, Wes is trapped in there*.

He has Iris slung half across him like the human version of Kevlar, and me in front, the shotgun pressed against my back, but it doesn't stop me. I keep screaming Wes's name, and *Get him, go get him* at the scrambling deputies. But they stay crouched behind their patrol cars, guns aimed, and I can see it in their faces: There's no clear shot. I don't see Lee. *Where is Lee?*

It's a blur as the smoke rises and Duane pushes me forward. The barrel digs into my back and there's no way out or back or forward. There is no spinning away from this. Someone's going to take the first shot, and then . . .

My eyes snag on the edge of his jacket, and then my mind snags on it half a second later. The jacket. He wasn't wearing a jacket earlier.

He's wearing Red Cap's jacket. Why?

It clicks together like Newton's Cradle, one thought hitting another like those little silver balls, the connection snapping through me, cause and effect.

Red Cap kept handing over the weapons, both of them, like it was nothing. I thought it was trust. I thought it was stupidity.

It wasn't.

He was armed the entire time.

He has an ace up his sleeve. That's what I'd scribbled on my note to

Lee. The most useful thing I could think to give her: my gut feeling about this man. I hadn't realized how literal I was being.

He reaches into the jacket pocket. My mind races, ticking balls hitting each other, back and forth, back and forth. Small. Portable. With enough effect to facilitate escape.

My mouth opens to scream it before he even pulls it out.

"GRENADE!"

— 56 —

1 lighter, 3 bottles of vodka, 1 pair of scissors,
  2 safe-deposit keys, 1 hunting knife, 1 chemical bomb
  (detonated), 1 giant fire starter (on fire), the contents
  of Iris's purse (also on fire)
Plan #1: Scrapped
Plan #2: Working a little too well
Plan #3: Stab ✓
Plan #4: Get gun. Get Iris and Wes. Get out.
Plan #5: Iris's plan: Boom! ✓
Plan #6: Don't die.

I'm too late. He's too fast. They're too slow.

He doesn't throw it through the air, there's no graceful arc. He chucks it underhand with the kind of slow roll that makes it skitter-soar right under the middle squad car.

They scatter like spiders, but not far enough. *Boom.* The car goes flying up and then back, and he grabs my arm, pulling so hard that this time I'm yelling from pain.

It's all smoke and fire and confused shouts, and he shoves me and Iris into the back seat of some car parked behind the bank. We squeal out of the parking lot before the deputies can recover.

He whoops as he zooms down the ranchland highway, no one following us yet. His elation is thick in the air and it just spells death for me, but why should he care? He's nearly home free.

His smile turns mean when he catches my eye in the rearview mirror. My hand tightens around Iris's arm, hoping it'll wake her up. But she's still slumped; there's a bruise on her forehead that doesn't look good, but at least she's not bleeding. That's good. Right? Unless it means she's bleeding inside.

"Finally quiet, huh?" he asks me.

I've got nothing left and nowhere to go. I've got the knife in my pocket, but I can't stab him, driving at this speed. He might shoot me or Iris. He's already proven too fucking hardy for my own good, since stabbing him the first time didn't stop him.

I'm racing through it, the anatomy I need to hit, and I'll need to go for the neck, right? But then he might slam on the brakes by instinct. This fast, the car might flip. It's old. There aren't airbags. We're not even belted in.

The world blurs and my mind turns and turns, trying to find a solution, because there's no sound of sirens behind us or even in the distance. They're not coming. They're too busy back there.

He's slowing down. My body goes alert, *find an exit, con your way through it*, and my hand tightens around Iris's wrist. I need her to wake up, but she's not. How hard did he hit her?

We're turning, off the two-lane highway and onto one of the offshoot roads that litter this stretch of outskirts. Gravel crunches under the tires as he speeds down the road, acres of rolling hills and scrub oaks for as far as the eye can see. Where is he going?

The gravel road curves and I spot it: the barn. He's going to hide the car. They'll never find us. He'll kill Iris. Wait until night and take me out of the state. They can't set up checkpoints everywhere. There are back roads that are a tangle of logging and mining trails that no one bothers with, but you can get all the way to the coast if you take the right ones.

I have to make a move. Now.

I look at Iris. I can't leave her. I have to. If we're going to have any chance, I have to get him away from her. Take away the leverage. He'll follow me. He'll leave her behind. He'll have to.

I'm the only valuable thing he's got at the end of this shitshow. He needs me.

The barn's getting closer and closer. He's driving too fast down the road.

Now or never.

I jerk the car door open and pitch myself out of it, and let me tell you, I could've really used my damn flannel at that point, because rolling out of a car and onto gravel tears the hell out of your T-shirt and your skin. Pain peppers my arms and shoulders like buckshot, but I force myself to get up as I hear him swear and yell and jerk the car to a stop.

Yes. Yes. The car's still out in the open. If they get a chopper in the air, they'll spot it. Go. Run. Make him chase you before he kills Iris.

I run toward the barn, because maybe there's a weapon, maybe there's a pitchfork, maybe there's a tractor I can run him over with. I don't care. I'll find it. I'll use it. I'll kill him if I have to.

I think I'm going to have to.

57

Raymond: How I Did It
(In Four Acts)

ACT 3: SLICE
Five Years Ago

Shooting Raymond didn't kill him. Obviously.

I could spin this. I could say that I never wanted him dead. That I'd aimed for his leg on purpose.

I'd be lying. My hands were shaking and it was dark, and I was just a bad shot. (I'm not anymore.)

Sometimes I still regret not pulling the trigger a second time and finishing it.

Sometimes I wonder where I'd be if I'd just walked off that beach and kept going, leaving him in the sand and Mom in the McMansion . . . and just fading into the world, where no one would find me.

I know how to disappear. Mom raised girls who could go invisible, ciphers who could turn into someone else with a bottle of drugstore hair dye and a smile in the mirror as they repeat names like a magic spell as they are born anew.

I made a different choice. To stop running. To be visible. To stand still.

To learn how to be someone real instead of a juggled handful of hurt and cons and hunger.

Things happen fast after I squeeze the trigger. He falls, but he doesn't pass out. He reaches for me, and I react, just like before. Like I know what to do now. This time, I don't miss, but my weapon is different. I clock him with the edge of the metal box, right on the temple, and he goes facedown on the sand, but he's still not out. So I hit him again. And again.

And then I'm still, the box raised high, poised for another blow, and he's finally limp. My heartbeat's roaring in my ears louder than the waves, and I want to run.

But I can't. Because I'm not done.

There's a plan in place. My sister's getting me out. It was just eight days away, and now . . .

Plans change. Oh, God, look how I've changed them.

I stand there on the beach; my feet are bare, and sand grits between my toes. I know how the world works; I especially know how turning snitch works. That's what I'm supposed to be doing. Turning snitch, so the FBI puts my mother and Raymond away. So we'll be safe. But the FBI needs hard proof. That was the deal my sister made with them. I get them the proof and I'm out of reach for good.

I need leverage. I need to get in Raymond's safe.

My hands curl around the box. Along with the gun, two other things are inside it: the burner cell my sister uses to contact me. And a knife.

Raymond's safe is biometric. It needs a fingerprint. My sister is supposed to get me a kit to take the print. But I've fucked everything up and now I'm here, with too many bruises and too little time and absolutely no fucking calm, because I *shot him*. I shot him and I knocked him out, so there's no taking it back and I've got a metal lunch box with a knife in it, and we all know where this is going, right?

There's no taking it back. There's only moving forward.

I need in his safe.

So I set the lunch box down on the ground and I get the knife.

58

Transcript: Lee Ann O'Malley + Deputy Jessica Reynolds Pursue the Hostage Taker

August 8, 12:30 p.m.

Deputy Reynolds: Go! Go!

O'Malley: Do you see him?

Deputy Reynolds: This is Deputy Reynolds. I need someone to get the hospital chopper or the fire chopper on Highway 3, heading north and looking for a white four-door. We need to set up roadblocks on the 3 and the 5 immediately.

[Recording cuts out for 3 minutes, 56 seconds. Please refer to Sheriff's Report Part 3A for the dispatch transcript.]

Deputy Reynolds: We've got the hospital chopper scanning the area.

O'Malley: They need to hurry.

[4-minute, 21-second silence]

[Voices over police radio, indiscernible]

Deputy Reynolds: Okay! Okay. I need all available officers in the area. This is Deputy Reynolds. The white sedan we're in pursuit of has been spotted at the abandoned Williams Farm, 1723 Castella Road. Hostage taker is armed and dangerous. He has two teenage girls as hostages. Proceed with extreme caution.

O'Malley: *Go.*

Deputy Reynolds: Lee, we need to talk about what happens when we get there.

O'Malley: You uncuffed me.

Deputy Reynolds: You punched me.

O'Malley: If I say I'm sorry, will you give me a damn gun and let me have your back?

Deputy Reynolds: Are you gonna follow my orders?

O'Malley: I'll have your back.

Deputy Reynolds: That's not an answer, Lee.

[Distortion for 2 minutes, 16 seconds]

[Car door slamming]

[Transcript ends]

— 59 —

2 safe-deposit keys, 1 hunting knife
Plan #6: Don't die.

I ran from Duane's car. Now it's time to hide.

I dart through the barn doors and slam them shut. But there's nothing I can see that'll block the doors from the inside, and I don't want him to lose interest and go back to Iris. I watch him walking toward the building through the slats in the door, my blood screaming at me to keep running. He's not moving fast; the stab wound's still bothering him, even if the initial pain's faded. He'll want to be careful. He needs to be in the best shape he can, to get me across the country. He can't put me on a plane, and he might be the kind of guy who knows someone with a boat who'll smuggle me, but does he have that kind of money?

My gut tells me no. Because he pulled this shitshow of a job with Red Cap. Duane's desperate and broke and he's going to try to hang on to me, risky as it is, because it's the best payday he has now.

The barn's dark, there are tarp-covered machines in the stalls that used to house horses. I tilt my head up; there's a loft and a ladder, but the ladder's wood and heavy. I wouldn't be able to pull it up.

But I might be able to trap him up there. I just need to draw this out long enough for the car to be found. That's all.

I'm trying to fool myself. It's not working. But I keep going. I bend down and grab a handful of dirt from the ground before I clamber up the ladder. The hayloft is large, flat and wide across half of the barn, looking out over the stalls and the entryway, sunlight streaming in from a big window in the back.

I look around, desperate for some kind of long-range weapon. I've got very little hope against him with a knife, as I know too well. I'll get one good stab in and then he'll grab me. I need something bigger. A rake or shovel or something farmer-y and lethal.

The barn door creaks open, and I freeze in the loft.

It's completely silent. He doesn't talk. He doesn't taunt. I think it'd be better with his bullshit chatter, because I've gotten used to it, and the silence is . . .

Scary. Really fucking scary.

It's just his footsteps and my heartbeat and the knowledge that I'm probably a couple of breaths from something painful. That's what he wants. He wants me to rot in it.

He still hasn't figured out who I am.

I guess that makes two of us, but at least I know what I'm capable of. I warned him, but he didn't listen, so now I'll make him hear.

Shuffling forward to the edge of the hayloft railing, I watch as he walks farther into the barn, waiting until he passes the farthest stall. Then I drop the handful of dirt right on the tarp, ducking backward before the spray of soil hits the plastic with a *rustle-ping*.

I'm already moving as he whirls toward the sound, crossing the loft as I search for something . . . anything . . .

There's a broom. The bristles are rotted and the broom part's just a stubby suggestion, but it's a staff. Something to hit with. If

I can daze him first, break it across his face or something, then maybe I can use the knife and run. Maybe he won't follow this time. Maybe he won't be able to if I yank the ladder down and trap him in the loft.

It's an awful plan and it's the only one I've got. My hand tightens around the broom handle as the ladder to the loft squeaks.

I hide as far back into the shadows I can, retreating from the sun spilling from the big window, but it's not enough. His head crests the floor of the loft and he spots me immediately.

I wait until he's stepped onto the hayloft floor, away from the ladder, and it's a mistake, I realize it too late, because there's not enough time to charge. I feint to the right, but he's moving with so much purpose and that purpose is to hurt me enough to get me to finally break. Not just my bones. All of me.

Never going to happen.

Swinging the broom handle, I aim high, but he blocks it. The old wood snaps in half against his arm, and he howls because I got his elbow at least. I have just enough time to back up a few steps, out of snatching reach, and pull the knife out. I flick it open, putting it between us, and it's déjà vu; here I am again, a girl and a blade and a bad man. It never seems to change, but I do.

I take two steps to the right. If I can just get to the ladder . . .

But he lunges and I slash out, not instinctual; practiced. You have to put your weight into it, using a knife. You have to be strong. And quick. I'm not right now. The knife catches messily against his forearm, jagged and long, not deep. He yelps, batting my arm away so hard the knife goes clattering. He closes his hand over his bleeding arm, hissing between his teeth, and the knife's too far away and this may be my only chance, this little window of pain I've caused, so I bolt.

I'm halfway down the ladder when he grabs it, jerking it forward so it flings me backward like an old-fashioned flip toy. I have one second to decide: *head or back, head or back,* and then I tuck my knees up and try to twist in the air as my hands come up to shield my skull. The road rash from my jump out of the car slows my reaction time, and I slam awkwardly into the barn floor with a horrible crunch, but my head doesn't smack, thank God. Then it radiates down, the shock of the impact, catching up to my brain and heart, and then I'm sucking in air that's not there anymore as my entire body seizes against the pain.

My lungs shudder, and for a second I'm not sure if it's because the fall knocked the wind out of me or there's a rib sticking through my lung or something. It certainly feels like the last thing, not the first one. I'm afraid to move, not just because it'll hurt, but I'm afraid I won't be able to. I stare at the barn ceiling, blinking slowly. I know I need to get up. He's going to come down from the loft now. He'll hurt me.

I can't move. I can't even focus. My fractured mind's skimming over memories like a mosquito hawk across a puddle.

Wes and a bully's black eye and my fist; the day we met, *that was a good punch*; his hand on my arm . . . the first time in forever I hadn't flinched.

Iris and gold swirls on her skirt; her twirl on the sidewalk, *they don't make clothes like this anymore, Nora* . . . her smile catching mine, lighting up my entire world.

Lee. Her hair honey blond instead of deep brown. Bending

down to meet the same blue eyes. A smile too sad at the edges. *I'm your sister.*

Lee. A scrap of paper. A scribbled number. A hand held out. *You can always use it.*

Lee. A code word. A promise whispered. A truth acknowledged. *Mom won't have your back.*

Lee. Late night. Scared girl. Bloody sand. *I'm on my way.*

Lee. Lee. Lee.

She's like a heartbeat inside me, my sister. The person who taught me what strong was.

What free looked like.

She saved me before. I'm not sure she can pull it off this time. I don't think I can, either.

But I gotta try.

I wiggle my toes. Then I turn my ankles. Good start.

Thunk, thunk, thunk. He's coming down the ladder.

It's time to get up.

Time to make her proud.

Raymond: How I Did It
(In Four Acts)

ACT 4: RUN

It's still dark inside when I get back to the house. I don't flip on the lights. I've already done the hard part, so I just go upstairs to his safe and get what I need to earn my freedom.

I put them on ice when I'm done with them. I don't know why in the moment. But I'll spend hours thinking about it later. I wish I could say it was a *fuck you* to him, because of his favorite drinking story. But the truth is, it's plain shock and horror and gore running through me and all over me.

It's because I'm scared of what he might do to me if he comes back and they're gone for good.

Even after all of it, I operate like he's going to step through the back door and grab my arm with his good hand.

So I put them on ice because I'm scared, still, and then I go into his office, because I can't be scared still. I have to keep moving. She's on the ground. Right where he left her.

"Mom, come on, get up."

She bats my hands away. Her skinned knees have made little full moons of blood on the carpet.

She's in my way. I only have so much time.

"Where is he?" And she's not asking because she's scared, but because she wants him. She wants to be comforted by him after he does this to her. I will never understand it. I will always hate it.

But I guess I'm done with it now.

"Come on." I pull her up, gentle as I can, and I get her upstairs to bed. She asks again where he is.

I don't answer.

Leaving her should be hard.

But it's not.

I walk downstairs, and it's like a dream. I have only so much time. His office is dark, and I leave it that way as I set the hard drives I took from his bedroom safe on his desk. I pull out the burner phone and dial her number as I plug in the first drive to his computer and turn it on.

It rings twice. Her voice crackles in my ear. "Hello?"

Say it. Do it. You have to.

"Olive."

My sister's breath hitches. "I'm on my way."

I don't say goodbye. I hang up like she told me to.

There's only so much time.

I check each drive—the four big ones are password-encrypted. But when I plug in the thumb drive I almost missed, tucked in the back of the safe, lines of code appear across the screen. When the code finally stops scrolling, a red cursor blinks. I'm supposed to enter something.

I stare at the thumb drive and then press Escape, pulling it out and tucking it into my pocket. I put the big drives in the lunch box.

The burner phone buzzes. My sister's outside. This is it.

I don't know how I get to the door. I don't realize how bad I must look until I open the door and see her face.

"You've got blood all over," she says, reaching toward me.

I back away. I can't be touched. Not now. Not ever? I don't know anymore. "It's not mine." Not most of it.

Her face changes again, so fast it'd have me reeling, but I'm numb, I'm so numb. I did the job. I got the drives. And now I'm fading. I'm not me. I'm not Ashley.

Who am I now?

What am I?

Ashley. I'm Ashley. I'm supposed to be Ashley.

A perfect daughter wouldn't have shot her stepfather. A perfect daughter wouldn't have reached for that knife, wouldn't have known how. A perfect daughter would've given him what he needed; she would've just let him kill her.

"What happened? Where is she? Where is he?"

"She's upstairs. He's . . . he's . . ." The world's spinning. Lock your knees.

"Look at me." My chin's between her fingers, my gaze forced to meet hers. The spinning stops. I breathe. Little puffs right into her face. I wonder if my breath smells. "What did you do?"

I can answer that. I know what I did. "I shot him. I had to. He pulled a gun on her. So I got him away and I shot him."

"Focus." She snaps her fingers in front of my face. I'm swaying again. "Where is he?"

Good. Another question I know the answer to. I like those. "I dragged him under the dock."

"Is he dead?"

I shake my head. "I got him in the leg."

Her entire body changes, the angles of her shoulders sharpen, alert and on edge. "Where's the gun?"

I hold up the box.

She nods. "We're going," she says. "Now. You're not coming back."

I don't protest. I don't try to grab my things. I don't try to say goodbye. And I don't ask if we can take Mom with us.

I just follow her. Like it's easy.

And it is. Because what's waiting behind me? It's nothing good. And what's waiting in front of me? Is everything I want.

She presses her hand between my shoulders, and I move, one step, then two, three, four. I lose track after that. Then we're in her car, and then we're driving down the street, away, and the beach is fading and her hands are tight around the steering wheel, and mine are tight around the box.

"Are you okay?" she asks, finally, after long pulls of silence.

"I got the drives," I say, instead of answering. "All four of them."

Something purrs approval under my skin as I lie. The secret thumb drive in my pocket burns. My leverage. My new just-in-case box.

I love my sister and I trust her. But only so far. And this life has taught me that *only so far* ends eventually.

My sister's lips press together. "Good job," she says, and the words, she has no idea what they mean to me. Someday I might try to tell her.

But I just stare out the window, my eyes blurring, the stained and sandy clothes on my back the only things I own, and the freedom on my tongue tastes like blood and salt.

— 61 —

2 safe-deposit keys
Plan #6: Don't die.

"You're definitely going in the trunk," Duane tells me, stepping off the last ladder rung with a little groan to his breath I can't miss.

"Scared I'll stab you again?" As I struggle to straighten, my body would very much like me to stop, but I ignore it. Gotta keep going until I can't anymore. Otherwise I end up in the trunk.

I step back, toward the barn doors, and he makes a noise, pulling the gun out of his waistband.

"Remember, I'm worth a lot more alive than dead."

"Now that I've met you, I have a feeling your stepfather wouldn't mind if I brought you back dead. He'd probably sympathize with me once I told him what trouble you were."

"You don't know him like I do. That's definitely not what he wants."

I'm so focused on him and any way to escape, I almost don't catch it, the movement up in the hayloft. I think it's wishful thinking, because there's really no way out here, but then my thinking's not wishful, because Iris Moulton is creeping across that hayloft, her giant-ass petticoat stripped from underneath her skirt and clutched in her hand like a weapon. My entire stomach flips like

301

I've been double-bounced on a trampoline because holy shit, I am the damsel in distress and I might just be getting saved. She's got her lighter in her other hand, and I understand instantly what she's got planned. It's perfect. She's perfect, and I can't even savor how much I love her in that moment because of that asshole and the danger.

"Are you going to be quiet now?" he asks me, and his voice trembles. It doesn't shake. I've snotted off to him and outwitted him and stabbed him, and he is finally where I want him to be: at the end of his rope.

She's at the railing. He doesn't see her; all his focus and rage and frustration is on me.

"Just one last thing," I say, drowning out the *snick* of the lighter as Iris lights her petticoat on fire. "You might want to look up."

He laughs. He does not look up. "Do you think I'm gonna fall for that?"

"No." I shake my head as Iris lets go of the tulle and the petticoat falls in a whoosh of fire and lace. "But I do think my girlfriend's better dressed than you," I add.

I catch just the barest twitch of his confused frown at my words before the flaming tulle envelops him. Layers upon layers of it fall over his head, the flames greedily eating up the fabric. He screams, animal instinct taking over, just like she said in the bathroom. He drops the gun as he tries to pull the petticoat off, but it's roaring around his shoulders and he has to fall to the ground, rolling in the dirt, all cool gone as *survive* kicks in.

The gun clatters to the floor and *get it, hurry, fuck, fuck*, my knees scrabble across hard dirt, and when my hand closes around it, I want to cry. I want to drop it. I want to not be here.

I don't want to be her again, but I make sure the safety's off, and I point it at him and Ashley hums under my skin like a bad habit, trigger-happy and oh so broken and way too jumpy.

He rolls in the dirt and the flames die out. Pulling frantically, he manages to tear most of what's left off him, but there's a big shiny patch of lace melted into the skin of his cheek. He lies there, finally defeated, breathing these angry little moans and wincing every time the burn on his face twitches.

I level the gun at him with hands that do not shake. "That's why you don't fuck with the girl in the poofy dress, Duane," I tell him as Iris scrambles down the ladder and veers around him. I don't relax until she's next to me.

"Are you—" she pants.

"Yeah. You?"

She nods.

"How did you—"

"There's a ladder out back." She points. "The lock on the window was broken."

"That was . . ." I can't even think of a word. "That was incredible. I can't . . . You saved me."

"I told you I'd set them on fire if they tried to take you," she says. "I meant it."

"Fucking bitches," he groans, just for the hell of it, I guess.

"You shut up!" Iris snaps. Then she bursts into tears, which makes him laugh and makes me want to shoot him. I should shoot him.

Ashley would. Rebecca wouldn't know how. Samantha would maybe consider it. Haley would for sure. Katie showed me first what I was capable of.

So where does that leave me?

"Iris," I say, because I don't know where to go after that. I'm pointing a gun at someone. Today is terrible. I don't know if Wes is okay. Iris made a bomb and melted a guy's face with a petticoat. She loves me. She's perfect. I'll love her forever. She looks how I feel: like she's about to keel over. I am not capable of much else but her name at this point.

Iris sniffs, wiping at her cheeks and letting out a shudder when she gets too close to the purple bruise spreading down her forehead. Duane doesn't move, but he watches me, just in case there's an opening.

I won't give him one.

"Do you hear that?" Iris's head snaps up toward the roof. "Helicopter."

I want to burst into tears then, too. Help. It's coming.

My fingers tighten on the gun. Punishment. It's already here.

"They'll be on the road soon," I say to Iris. "Can you get out there to flag them down?"

"I don't want to leave you," Iris insists.

"I've got him," I tell her.

Still, she hesitates.

"Iris, I don't want them to miss us," I stress, even though I know they'll spot the car.

"Okay. I'll be right back."

He starts laughing after she's gone. Blood carves out the lines between his teeth, the white washed pink.

"God, you're good," he says as the sirens wail in the distance.

"She doesn't need to be here for this."

That makes him laugh more.

"I should've shot you when I had the chance," he tells me.

"Hindsight and all that." My finger rests right next to the trigger, but not on it. Not yet.

"Do you have it in you?"

And here's the thing: I think I do. Don't I? The smart thing to do would be to shoot him. He knows. He'll tell.

It's why I sent Iris away, isn't it?

But my finger doesn't move toward the trigger. I hear sirens in the distance. Any minute now.

His smile widens despite the burn. "You're gonna let them take me in," he breathes. He gloats it out like a banshee cackle and I hate that he's right. "Stupid kid. Lucky me."

"You're not worth the bullet." It's weakness and truth wrapped together. I'm choosing something I'm not ready to name over what I know is the surest survival route.

The sirens get louder.

"You hid good," he says. "But you won't be able to hide anymore. I know it all. What you look like, where you live, who you care about. He'll know, too." His grin stretches the lace-melted burn, ghastly wide and gaping. "He's going to find you."

He says it like it's a revelation instead of the guiding truth of my life, and then I'm the one laughing.

"He was always going to find me," I say. "But today was the day I learned I was ready for anything. Even him. So thanks. I've been feeling kind of insecure. But now I know: It wasn't just luck last time. I'm good." I smile, one of those sharp almost-snarl smiles I know creeps him out. "I'm great."

"You're dead," he says, but there's a thread of defeat as sirens wail and the spray of gravel kicks up against the barn wall, brakes squealing to a halt.

I shake my head. "No. I'm just getting started." They come bursting in then. Jessie and Lee, who has the kind of wild eyes I haven't seen in five years.

Safe.

The relief sucks all the fight out of me, and I've got to dig my heels into the ground to fight the undertow. More deputies arrive and it's a blur of noise and action, my ears fading in and out, blood trickling down my side from the road rash. I hand the gun to Jessie as the sheriff snaps handcuffs onto Duane and then Lee is blotting out my view.

"Where's Wes?" I demand.

"He's okay," she says. "He helped get everyone out. They're all okay."

My eyes almost roll back in my head in relief. I sag against her, my knees liquid for a second before I'm straightening again, searching for Iris. I don't see her.

Duane's still laughing as they lead him away, the sound floating up to hook around the barn beams like cracked horseshoes, the worst kind of luck.

Lee's arms wrap around me so tight I yelp because it *hurts*. And then she's yelling for paramedics and snapping her fingers at people with one hand while the other keeps hold of me and shakes so minutely I can't see it, but I can feel it.

"Iris," I say, but I get flanked by Jessie and Lee, half supported, half walked out of the barn. The ambulance lights are flashing in the distance, and I come to a total stop when I see the stretcher the EMTs are wheeling toward us.

"No way," I say.

"No arguing," Lee says back, and she pushes me on the stretcher and I go, even though I was planning on protesting more. I fall back like I need to, and who knew my legs were that numb? I didn't.

The world swoops and fades a little, but I can hear Lee the whole time, so I know it's safe. I close my eyes. Just for a second. Then I'll sit up and pay attention.

But I don't sit up. I fade out completely, because I know Lee will be there. And Iris. And Wes. Everyone's safe.

I know that when the world sharpens again, I'll have to face the truth I've been running from: that I was never safe.

That I'll never be safe.

Not until I tilt the ground back to me . . . for good this time.

Part Four

—————

...it's just
another thing
to lose.

(August 8–30)

— 62 —

2 safe-deposit keys (hidden in jeans pocket)

I come back to earth fast when the nurses at the hospital start cleaning out the road rash. Even with the lidocaine, it stings and throbs. They dig bits of gravel and dirt and debris out of my shoulders and side, and Lee keeps trying to hold my hand while I keep telling her to go check on Iris and Wes: *Go find them, go check on them, please, Lee, please.* I need to know where they are.

"Please," I beg, but she shakes her head, just as stubborn.

"I'm gonna find them, then," I threaten, but when I try to resist the nurse, she pins me to the bed, not with her body, but with a look that could have been honed only by an emergency room full of that particular Northern California flavor of people.

"You want this to get infected?" the nurse asks me.

"I want my friends," I say, not to her, but to Lee.

"She always this way?" the nurse asks Lee.

"She's a tough one," Lee says, a note of pride sparkling in her voice.

"She's right here and doesn't need to be talked about like she isn't," I say grumpily.

"Sorry, hon," the nurse says with a smile. "You did a great job today. Heard the deputies talking about it."

"Please go find Wes and Iris," I say to Lee.

"Drop it, Nora," she says, and my mouth shuts with an annoyed click, because she never uses that line unless she means it. She's stark white still, like she's just figured out how to breathe again.

"Are you okay? Should they check you out?" I ask, and oh, that was *so* the wrong thing to say. The sarcastic eyebrow arch I get back is so quelling that I almost fall into line then and there.

"I'm going to grab some more gauze," the nurse says, and as soon as she leaves the room, Lee's shoulders set.

"Do we need to go?" she asks me.

She keeps rubbing her fingers against her thumb, skittish in a way she rarely is. One wrong word from me, and I'm going to end up across the ocean before I can talk my way out of it.

I shake my head. "We're good. It's all good."

She sags in relief, and I should feel terrible, shouldn't I?

All I feel is a different kind of relief, even though adding to the pile of secrets I've kept from her is not ideal. She'll catch me someday, and it's going to be a reckoning I'll never be ready for.

Just as long as it's not today. Today has been bad enough. I want to sleep for a month. I want to never wake up. And I really, really want my mouth and shoulder to stop hurting.

"Will you go and check on Wes and Iris for me now?" I ask.

"Nora," she says, and it's just my name, but then she starts *crying*, and it's the most surprising thing that has happened all day. That's when it hits me: She hasn't been refusing to find Wes and Iris so she could stay with me. She's been refusing because someone's hurt. Wes. Wes is hurt, and this is when she's going to tell me. When we're alone and I'm already sitting down and my entire vision tunnels like there's no light left in the world, and I'm trying

312

to breathe, trying to steel myself to hear it for real, but she just keeps *crying and not talking and I really need her to talk now*.

"Oh, God, what did you do to her?"

I croak out his name.

He's standing in the doorway, and even from here, I can smell the smoke on his skin and clothes. There's a bandage on his arm, but that's it. I start to scramble out of the hospital bed, but I'm yanked back by the IV. I feel sick and reeling, from *Wes is trapped* to *Wes is okay* to *worst-case scenario*. Because it's almost always the worst-case scenario. But not today.

"I just got away from my mom and checked on Iris," he says. "She's good. They just need to do a few more tests. Um, Lee?"

Lee is trying her hardest to sniff back the tears, and failing.

"Nora?" he asks, needing a life raft when it comes to my crying sister because, well, it isn't really a sight anyone has seen, in, you know, *ever*.

I shake my aching head and try really hard to hold it back.

But the tears trickle down my cheeks all the same, and instead of running away—which, let's be honest, is what I would've done if confronted with two people in tears—Wes walks into the room. He sits down on the edge of the bed and he curls his hand around my foot like it's the one place he's sure I'm not hurt, and the three of us sit there, a broke-then-taped-together little unit we've somehow formed through love and movie nights and hikes through the woods, patched-up wounds and shared books and blackmail schemes I will never regret. A family reunited when I was sure we wouldn't be again.

The world outside of this is harsh, and so am I. But here, with them, it is safe to cry.

3:00 p.m. (138 minutes free)

2 safe-deposit keys (hidden in jeans pocket)

After they've cleaned all the gunk out of my shoulder and side and made sure I'm not gonna slip into a coma, they finally let me see Iris. Then they release me, and the doctor gives me the number of a dentist—I have an emergency appointment tomorrow morning with her to fix that back molar.

Lee agrees to go downstairs to get my antibiotics at the pharmacy while I sit with Iris, and Wes has to go appease his own parents, so it's just me, hovering in her doorway.

She's repurposed her hospital gown as a robe over her pink rayon slip. I know the little blue flowers embroidered along the neck very well . . . or my fingers do. Getting through all Iris's layers—metaphorical and decorative—is a slow and careful practice.

At first, I think she's sleeping, but the second I step into the room, her eyes fly open.

"Nora," she breathes.

"Hey." I shuffle closer. My side is throbbing, and I don't think that's gonna change anytime soon, so I'm trying to ignore it.

"Are you okay? I saw Wes—"

"Me too. I'm fine. Lee's just getting the meds for me. Are *you* okay?"

Apparently the hospital is the place for crying, because her eyes well up.

"Please get me out of this hospital," she says, her brown eyes getting so big and liquid and miserable, they're bordering into Bambi-after-his-mother-was-shot territory. "Please. I hate hospitals. They said my head was fine. They gave me painkillers. They're just not letting me go because my mom's still in New York."

"Did you get ahold of her?"

She nods and then winces, her hand flying up to touch the huge bump on her forehead. It's a deeper purple than before. She looks awful, pale and bruised and smoke-smudged. She looks beautiful, alive and breathing and as much mine as I am hers. I want to crawl into that bed and curl around her and take every inch of her pain away.

"She's flying home. But she won't get back until tomorrow morning. I don't want to stay here. Please. I want out of here and a heating pad and a silly movie to zone out in front of. Nora. *Please.*"

She grabs my hand and she squeezes almost harder than she did in the bank.

"Okay," I say, because the way she looks at me is tinged with the kind of bad that makes the back of my throat bitter. "I'll get Lee to fix it."

"You will?"

"Promise."

It takes two phone calls, an argument with the head nurse, and a hushed three-way conversation with Iris's doctor and her mother on the phone before they release Iris into Lee's custody. When they finally come in to unhook her and let her get dressed, the smile that blooms over her face is like sunshine across miles of snow.

They put her in a wheelchair, too, but she doesn't protest. "Where's Wes?" she asks. "He was going to come back."

"I saw him downstairs," Lee says.

"We'll get him," I tell Iris, but Lee shoots me a look and shakes her head a little.

"He's with his parents, Nora," she says, like that's going to matter to me.

"We'll get him," I say again, and I shouldn't be mean when my sister looks as wrecked as she does, but I'm not leaving him after this horrible day that was supposed to start with donuts and hurt feelings and end with, I dunno, French fries and forgiveness and our friendship intact.

But here I am again, changing in the span of a few minutes and choices that maybe were bad, maybe were good, and might not be survivable.

He's in the lobby just like Lee said he was. His parents are flanking him, as if he needs protection from the world instead of from his father.

"Steady," Lee says under her breath as we cross out of the elevator bay and head into the lobby.

"Nora." Mrs. Prentiss comes over and hugs me. It's brief and achingly gentle, and it's meant well. She always means well, I remind myself as I grit my teeth and let it happen. "And, Iris, honey, are you two okay?"

"We're good," I say. "We're just going home." I look at Wes over her shoulder.

"I'm coming," he says immediately, and Mrs. Prentiss is right in front of me, inches away; I can see her stiffen.

"Wes." It's the first time he's spoken, but my eyes narrow at the mayor.

"Honey, I really want you home with me," Mrs. Prentiss says, and the pleading in her voice is real, because Wes is just months away from being eighteen and there's not much she can do about the fact that he's spent years dodging time under her roof.

"Lee Ann, please." Mrs. Prentiss lowers her voice, her cheeks tinged with the kind of humiliation a mother doesn't ever want to feel.

Wes bends down and kisses his mom's cheek. "I love you," he says. "I'll be at breakfast tomorrow before we all have to go to the sheriff's station to give my statement."

She strokes his arm, her hand shaky. "Okay," she says, trying to save face but losing the game. Behind her, the mayor is stony silent, the disappointment radiating off him. He probably wishes I had gotten shot or burned up. Things would be a lot easier for him then.

Lee pushes Iris's wheelchair out of the hospital, with Wes and me bringing up the rear like we still need to protect each other.

The sun's shining as we cross the lot and head toward Lee's truck. It seems strange that it's still bright outside, that not even a full day has passed, when everything's changed.

Lee gets us all carefully loaded into the truck's back cab, bruised and raw in more ways than one. It takes a while because the pain pills the doctors gave me are starting to kick in and my seat belt is not working the way it's supposed to.

"Christ," she says, batting my hands away gently and clipping me in. "You're all drugged up. What about you two?"

"They didn't give me anything but oxygen and burn cream," Wes says, and Iris just waves listlessly, which I think Lee takes as a yes.

"You're the designated friend, then," she tells Wes. "Don't let them walk into the pool or anything when we get home."

"I'm fine," I protest.

"I'm not." Iris leans against the window. "I want to lie down."

"Soon," Lee promises, getting into the front seat. Her fingers flex around the steering wheel. "Gotta hand it to you kids," she mutters as she starts the truck. "My life's never boring with you."

"You love us," Wes says easily, like it's easy, even though it's never been, for me or Lee, and maybe that's why the two of us folded him into our family like a missing ingredient.

"Yeah," Lee says. "I really do."

— 64 —

2 safe-deposit keys (stashed in my room)

The sun sets, and we are still alive.

We lie out on the pallet lounge near the pool. It's hot this time of year, dry to the point of danger as we head into the worst of fire season. But tonight it's calm, sky shimmering from the orange heat as the darkness sets in.

Iris is wearing my pajamas, Wes's College of the Siskiyous shirt used to be Lee's even though she never went there, and I wrap up in my robe because the idea of pulling a T-shirt over my raw shoulder sounds like hell. I've got an ice pack against my cheek and two more on the table to break open and use later.

Lee watches us from the house, but she doesn't try to make us go inside to sleep. For a long time, Iris stares out at the reflection of the stars on the pool, and Wes plays a game of solitaire with a pack of cards he brought from his room. He pauses only when she finally speaks.

"I didn't want him to die."

It takes me a second to realize she's talking about Red Cap. I suppose we'll find out his name sometime in the coming days. Does he have people? A family?

"You didn't kill him," Wes says softly. "His partner did."

319

"But if I hadn't made the Drano bomb, maybe . . ."

"Duane was always going to kill him, Iris," I tell her, and it's not gentle, because you can't be gentle with that kind of horrible truth. "He had his escape plan in his pocket the whole time. There was no way he was walking out of there. If you hadn't made the bomb, we wouldn't have either."

She shakes her head like she's trying to shake out the guilt. Lee gave her a hot-water bottle for her stomach, and she curls up around it like one of those roly-poly bugs.

"Don't think about it," I say, because that's my motto. "Lock it away."

"Or talk about it if you want," Wes says, staring hard—admonishingly—at me. It dawns on me that I'm not reacting the right way. *She's not normal.* It echoes in my head. Those words, like Raymond himself, will haunt me forever.

"What are we going to tell the sheriff tomorrow?" Iris asks.

"The truth," I say. "That we stayed quiet until we saw an opportunity to act when they left us alone in the bathroom. We took it, but they got the better of us. Then we got the better of him in the barn."

"So just the highlights. What happens if *he* says something?"

I shake my head. "I don't think he will. He's got a record already, so he knows he's going away for a long time, no matter what information he hands over. Knowing who I am . . . that's much more valuable where he's going."

"Will you run?"

It's not Iris who asks it. It's Wes.

I look across the lounge at him, the depth of all he knows and all we've endured together and separately almost swallowing me.

"No," I say. "But that's why we need to be careful. Because of Lee. No. Don't look over at her," I say as Wes instinctively starts to turn toward the house where she's probably still checking on us.

"Lee can't know," I continue. "She thinks my cover is intact. It needs to stay that way."

"And if it doesn't?" Iris asks.

"She's gone," Wes says, and I shrug helplessly when Iris looks at me like she expects disagreement.

"If she thought Raymond might find out that Ashley Keane became Nora O'Malley, Lee would knock me out and have me on a plane before I came to."

"How long do you think it'll take for him to figure it out?" Wes asks. He's playing it so casual, but there's an undercurrent to his voice, to the shine in his eyes. He's had years of not just being in the know, but living with the results. He's been across the hall, listening to me yell in my sleep, just as much as I've been across that same hall, listening to his pacing and late-night stirring that's part insomnia, part avoiding his own nightmares.

I understand that shine in his eyes. I got to metaphorically throttle the bad man who hurt the only boy I loved in this world. And Wes wants to *actually* throttle the bad man who hurt me. But he'll have to wait in line.

"Yes, how much time is there to prepare?" Iris sits up straighter, like she's going to whip out a notebook from the pocket of her PJs or something.

I shrug again. "Raymond could know already. He could find out in six months. It just depends on who Duane knows and how fast they can get the news to him in prison."

I'll be surprised if it takes more than a month, though. Duane will be determined. Raymond will be eager. They'll probably bond with a big ol' *Ashley Bested Me* party. And then Duane will tell, and Raymond will finally know, and I'll be the thing my sister fears the most: a sitting duck.

"We can talk more about the consequences after we give our statements to the sheriff," I say. "But before we make any plans, let's make sure we get through tomorrow."

We go through our story three times until we have it perfect. Wes walks into the house for a few minutes as Iris stretches out on the lounge, tucking one of the pillows under her head. When he comes back, he has a fresh hot-water bottle for her, blankets for all of us, and Iris is already half asleep. Her lashes touch the dark smudges of purple under her eyes, and I reach out and tuck a lock of hair behind her ear. She twitches under the touch and then settles, dropping off into sleep as Wes and I stretch out on either side of her.

"Sleep?" he asks me.

"No way." The numbness is starting to set in; it'll power me through until tomorrow. I'll crash after I talk with the sheriff.

He hands me a bottle of water. "I told Lee I'd make you drink that."

"Because being hydrated is going to fix things." I take the bottle from him, setting it on my lap.

"It won't hurt." He shrugs.

His phone buzzes. It's been going off every few minutes since he left the hospital with me instead of his parents.

"Him or her?"

"Her," he says, and I feel a twinge of guilt. Mrs. Prentiss is not a bad person. She loves Wes. But she doesn't leave the mayor,

322

and I've tried hard not to resent her for it, and a lot of the time, I fail. I've wondered why, and I've raged against her in my mind shamefully, like this is her fault, when there is only one person to blame.

She's a victim, too. A part of me understands that.

But a bigger part of me will choose her son's well-being over hers, because someone needs to.

"Do you need to go?"

"I'm not going anywhere," he says. He looks down at Iris, his eyes crinkling as he smiles. "I wish I could've seen her throw that flaming petticoat over that asshole's head."

"It was amazing."

"*She's* amazing," he says, and his eyes catch mine, suddenly serious. "You made me feel like a jerk last month when I said I thought she liked you."

"I'm sorry." I am. I could've found a better dodge around it, instead of going for the easy gaslighting.

"You could've told me."

"I didn't want to." It's as blunt as a butter knife, but it's true, and it makes him lean back against a pile of the yellow cushions and laugh softly so he doesn't wake Iris.

"I was avoiding all of it like a coward," I continue. "I thought I could control it this time. How she found out about me. How you found out about us. I thought I could make it neat and new and . . . palatable, I guess." I can't look at him, and I bite the inside of the nonswollen side of my mouth before I continue. "It was childish, thinking I could make my past sound good or somehow okay. It isn't."

"But *you* are," he says, so simply, cutting me down to the bone

323

with three words. They shake my world even more than the three words he said when we were fifteen, when we were all broken and healing and falling at once.

Is it true, though? *Am* I okay? *Am* I good?

"I had the gun on Duane," I say softly. "The sheriff hadn't come yet. I could have—"

"No," he says softly. "You couldn't have."

No.

I couldn't have.

"*She* would have," I say, and I don't have to clarify it's my mother I'm talking about. He can read between my lines in a way no one else can, because he's the only one who knows all the stories of the girls that make me up. "She wouldn't have hesitated. Him or her. It would've been easy."

"You're not her."

"You don't know that. You don't know her."

"I know you."

"Yes, you do," I say, and I can't see it in the dark, his smile, but I can feel it now.

"And you know me," he continues.

"Yes, I do," I say.

"I'd tear the whole world apart for you," he says, and it's not romantic, even though it should be. It's so matter-of-fact, this secret truth now sprouted between us, like my name and my real hair color and the stories behind my scars; also things that only he knows.

"And I'd burn it down for you."

"You almost burned it down around me today," he points out, and when Iris murmurs, "That was me, actually," between us,

324

it startles a painful laugh out of my lungs that sounds strange because it's not hollow.

"I stand corrected," Wes says, trying to suppress a smile.

"I can't let her take credit for my pyrotechnic skills," Iris says, sounding prim even when squished between the pillows and the two of us. "Now both of you need to lie down and try to sleep. You can make vows of loyalty to each other like medieval knights next week. I'll weave some flower crowns and wear a nice dress for the occasion."

"I like poppies," Wes says.

"Noted."

"All your dresses are nice," I add.

"I know. Now, *please*, some of us need sleep. My mom's plane will be landing in a few hours and she's going to be an emotional tornado."

"Lee's getting your mom at the airport. She'll have her calmed down by the time they drive back up," I say gently, but she shakes her head.

"I was a hostage in a bank robbery. Mom will never be calm again. She's going to get one of those toddler backpack leashes in my size and make me wear it."

Wes presses his lips together so tight they disappear trying not to laugh.

"You're okay now, *and* you saved the day," I remind her when I'm sure I won't laugh, because her mom is overprotective . . . and now I have some insight why.

"That last thing is *not* going to help."

"What will?" Wes asks.

"Sleep," she says, her eyelids drooping again. "I just need to

325

sleep a little until the next designated borderline-concussion wake-up call."

So he lies down to her right, and I lie down to her left.

We curve around her like parentheses; Iris is some precious phrase between us that needs the shelter of our crooked knees and tucked hands under chins, breath skating in the space between that makes up all three of us now, along with our secrets, exposed and not.

The world is tilting again. But I have people to hold on to. People to fight for. And that is so different than just fighting for yourself.

I don't sleep. I watch them instead, these people who have become the core of me just as much as the girls who've lived under my skin, and I think about what I have to lose.

It's too much. And I'm not enough.

But somehow, I'll have to be.

— 65 —

2 safe-deposit keys (stashed in my room)

It takes ten days before certain parts of the internet light up with talk about Ashley Keane. There are no specifics—not yet. And it's not enough talk to be totally unusual this time of year. But it's enough to give me the confirmation I need: He knows where I am.

Wes shows up after breakfast the morning my alerts start going wild. His mom's been insisting he stay at home with her, and it's been the kind of tug-of-war we haven't had in a long time. "Have you seen?" he asks.

I nod, but hold a finger to my lips. Lee's still in the kitchen, eating the oatmeal I made. She's actually going to work today.

"Let's go for a drive," I tell him.

He takes us out past the edge of town to one of the lookout points on the winding climb toward the clouds. I get out without asking when he parks, before pulling down the tailgate and clambering into the bed.

He settles on one side and I sit down on the other, my back against the wheel hub.

"They're buzzing about Ashley again," he says. "I'd hoped it would take longer."

"No actual description or location, though. He's keeping the real information close."

"What are we going to do?" he asks me.

The truck bed yawns between us, an ever-widening chasm, and only he has the rope to toss to me. When I told him who I was, I told him everything. Which meant telling him my fail-safe that even Lee doesn't know about.

He tried to talk me out of going down the rabbit hole once, and when he realized he couldn't, he started to help. But I'm worried that this—to fight back in this way—will be too much. This is risking so much more. This is risking him and her and all of us.

Maybe I should go, and when I say it out loud, he does the only thing he can.

"What the fuck, Nora?" he asks, and his incredulity snaps me out of my self-loathing just enough. "Do you really want to spend your life running?"

"Aren't we all running from something?"

"That might sound profound on a mug or a photo of a winding road, but come on."

That's the thing about Wes: He tolerated my bullshit longer than anyone. And now that he can identify said bullshit, he'll never tolerate it again.

"You told me you weren't running," he says quietly. "You told Iris. She won't understand that unless you say *promise*, your truths can get a little shaky."

"Hey," I start to protest, but it dies off my lips, vanishing in the air. He's right that I didn't say *promise*. Just in case. And he caught it. Iris didn't know she had to, yet. Wes would probably fill her in during their next *Nora Lied to Me* club meeting.

"I'm not running," I tell him again. "I *promise*."

There's a warmth in his eyes that he doesn't hide but doesn't want me to see, so I ignore it and continue. "As long as Lee doesn't find out, I have a plan for the fail-safe that is risky and probably doomed to failure, but it's the only one I can think of with a remote chance I don't end up dead."

"Tell me."

I do. I tell him everything I've been thinking, and when I'm done, he's silent. I don't know if it's shock or contemplation.

"We knew this was coming," I say, when the quiet's too much and his face is too much and it's just all *too fucking much*.

"The FBI—" he starts to say, and then stops when I shake my head. He sighs and yanks a hand through his hair, the frustration bleeding off him. It's an old argument.

"I don't know what else to do."

I expect more quiet from him, but instead I get agreement. "Neither do I."

"I don't want to do it." I need him to know that as much as I need to just admit it out loud. I'm not some badass here; I am scared. I'm facing what I've hidden from since I was twelve. The consequences are coming too fast . . . and I see no choice but to charge forward to meet them.

"I know." He tilts his head up to the sky, the sunlight washing him golden. "Are you going to tell Iris?"

"If I don't, you will."

His eyes crinkle. "You girls," he says.

"Bane of your existence?" I suggest, a mix of honey and acid that makes his mouth quirk.

"Family I always wanted," he answers, because there's no acid in him; there's just sweetness and maybe a little sarcasm when the situation calls for it, but it doesn't right now.

I know I'll start doing something like cry if I respond with how I feel, so I kick his foot with my boot and say, "Sap," to give both of us an out, and he takes it gladly, tapping my foot back, because both of us are good at veering around emotional land mines.

"She won't like it. Iris. She'll want to come with you."

For a second all I can do is look at the patch on his jeans that Iris sewed, this little burst of yellow from the fabric she used against the denim. "I have to go alone."

"I know. But she wants to protect you," Wes says. "It'll take her a while to realize that you do the protecting."

"Do you think that's bad?" I can't help but ask.

"No," he says. "I just used to think it was my job. Now I think it's the most honest thing about you."

"I didn't need your protection," I say softly.

"I know."

"No, Wes." I do not reach out. I do not tangle our fingers together. But my voice, the depth of it, it makes him shift in his seat. "I didn't need it. Because you were the first guy I'd ever met who I didn't need any protection *from*."

I guess I've never put it that way before, because his eyes go suspiciously bright, and I love him for it. I have loved him in more ways than anyone else in my life. I loved him gleefully as a friend because it was all discovery, and I fell in love with him before I even knew how, and now we've survived together past that, into Franken-friends. Family.

"When do you want to go?" he asks, and I follow the change of subject, because I'm trying to learn the grace he and Iris have.

"Next time Lee's out of town on a job," I say. "It'll be short notice. I'll need you to cover for me."

"You'll have to be fast so she won't catch you."

"I'll be in and out."

His phone buzzes in his pocket, and he pulls it out.

"Your mom again?" I ask, trying not to feel annoyed.

He shakes his head. "Amanda."

The silly grin on my face is met by a shy one on his.

"She texted me a few days after the bank, when Terry went around blabbing about how we'd survived near-death to everyone we know."

"I'm surprised it took that long. Terry blabbing, not Amanda texting. Have you two been talking? Was she worried about you? What did she say? Can I see?"

He holds his phone to his chest. "No!"

I make a face. "I bet you'll let Iris see," I mutter.

"She gives better dating advice than you."

"*I'm* the one who dated you!"

He laughs, and I barely resist kicking him again.

The sun is high in the sky. We laugh, and I breathe in the moment like it'll be stolen soon, knowing that tomorrow, I'll be doing the stealing.

August 19 (11 days free)

2 safe-deposit keys, 1 fake birth certificate

I've waited until it's not a crime scene anymore and the smoke has cleared and the construction workers have moved in. The bank's still closed, of course, but the two times I drive past it doing recon, Olivia-the-teller's car is parked in the lot. So I make my move.

"Bank's not open," the construction worker up front tells me. But Olivia looks up from the desk where she's sitting and sees me. She's got her arm in a sling; he'd cut her, back in the bank. That's what the screaming across the hall had been. But it looks like she's healing up.

"It's okay," she tells him. "You're Nora, right? That's your name?"

I nod. "I guess we didn't get formally introduced last time. How are you doing? Are you okay?"

"Just a little sore," she says, her eyes tracking over the bruises and swelling that have mostly faded from my face. "What about you?"

It's kind of weird being here with her, because last time, we were both the same amount of scared, but not the same amount of crumbling. And now we're back here, she's the adult again, and

I'm supposed to be the kid. But I'm not really a kid, and she may be an adult, but she's also the mark.

"I'm okay. I'm really sorry to bother you. I know the branch is closed. But my sister keeps the important papers in our safe-deposit box ever since the forest fire a few years back." I pull out the keys. "I have a scholarship deadline in two days, and I need my birth certificate for the application."

"Oh dear." Olivia frowns. "I really am not supposed let anyone down there."

"It's fine," I say. "I totally understand. The scholarship was a long shot, anyway. And there's always student loans."

It's the right knife twist; I know it because I looked into her enough to know she took out a Parent PLUS loan for each of her kids' college.

"As long as you have the keys," she says slowly, "I suppose it can't hurt."

"Really?" I smile in genuine relief. "You'd totally be saving me. My sister will be upset because I kind of put off the application until the last minute. I had three months. I should've gotten my birth certificate earlier."

She smiles indulgently at me, all motherly and fond. "I had to make a spreadsheet for my girls to keep them on track with applications. It's a busy time."

"That's a good idea," I say as she begins to lead me through the back. We're both silent as we pass the carpet that's cut away. I guess they couldn't get the blood out.

"Have you talked to Casey?" I ask.

"I spoke to her mom," Olivia says. "You three looked out for her.

333

I can't tell you . . ." She trails off. "You are very good kids," she finally says, her voice tight with emotion.

I place my hand on her shoulder, and it's not a con when I say, "It's brave of you to stay here."

She lets out a shaky laugh. "Oh, honey, I don't have a choice. I've got mouths to feed and a mortgage to pay." She clears her throat as she unlocks the steel-barred door that leads into the safe-deposit box vault. "Just call for me when you're done, okay?"

"Will do."

I step inside and head farther into the vault, waiting for her footsteps to fade. And then I move: not toward the box where Lee keeps Bailout Plan 3 (of 12). No, I go to box 49 and insert the key I found in Frayn's office. The flap opens, exposing the box, and I try to slide it out.

I don't know what I expected, but when I can't even pull it out because it's so heavy, the weight tells me what it has to be. I knew it was going to be valuable; I thought maybe cash. Some old coins. Stock options or art. A bunch of jewelry you could yank diamonds out of. Something like that.

I did not expect, once I got the box inched out of its slot enough to unlock it, to find gold tucked beneath an old copy of *The Wind in the Willows*. And not a bottle of tiny nuggets—we're talking six 400-ounce bars of gold bullion.

Definitely enough reason to rob a bank. Over three million reasons, because that's about how much this is worth, if the quick search on my phone is right.

Well, shit. I look over my shoulder, knowing that I'm on borrowed time. If I take too long to "get my birth certificate," Olivia will come looking for me.

I've done the research: Howard Miles, the owner of the box, was a widower with no family and no heirs. So there was no one to give this to, no one who knew about it. Did Mr. Frayn steal the keys off the old man? Were they entrusted to him? I'm not about to ask, and I know Casey's dad isn't going to be talking anytime soon, if he has even remotely decent lawyers. It doesn't matter, in the long run. I have the keys now.

A prickle runs down my spine, and the temptation; oh, the temptation . . .

Money enables you to run, if you have to. And it gives you a chance to fight back, if you choose to.

My fingers curl around the box. Who am I kidding? Isn't this why I brought my messenger bag? Isn't this the reason I didn't tell anyone I had the keys? Wes wouldn't like it. Iris . . . well, I'm not sure where she'd fall. *We're more alike than you know.* Would she understand?

This isn't about satisfying my curiosity. This is about being who I truly am: a girl who finds a way through everything thrown at her.

So I take two of the bars. I don't take all of them, only because it'd be too heavy, not because I'm struck with some sort of moral fortitude. I slip the gold and the book right into my bag, and shove the box back into its slot in the wall, locking it shut. Safe and away, no one knowing any better, and only me with the key. By the time Olivia's footsteps come clicking down the stairs again, I'm already on the other side of the steel bars with the birth certificate I brought from home clutched to my chest.

"You're the best," I tell her gratefully, and she smiles again. "If I somehow get this scholarship, I owe you dinner."

"I'm glad I could help. After the last week and a half, I think we could all use a little break from the universe."

"I'll say." And I just got one.

I follow her up the stairs, keeping my shoulders straight beneath the added weight in my bag.

"Thanks again," I tell her, and she waves at me as she walks back to sit behind her desk . . . and I stroll right out of the bank with the biggest score of my life, just like that.

My hands don't start shaking until I'm driving out of the parking lot, but I press harder on the gas, speeding down the long, straight stretch of ranchland highway, moving forward.

Already, the plan is solidifying in my mind.

Step one: Book a flight.

Step two: Throw down the gauntlet.

Step three: Survive, somehow.

— 67 —

1 long blond wig with bangs, 1 vintage plaid skirt,
1 black cashmere cardigan, a truly impressive
array of makeup

Iris's fingers card through hair that isn't mine. I can feel the pressure through the wig cap. She bends down so she's at eye level with me, pursing her lips as she tugs at the back of it, straightening it just a little.

Then she steps back. Comb tapping against her arm, she examines her handiwork.

We've waited for my face to heal up, and now my stomach is spiky with nerves, like when I asked her to help me with this. Now I don't want to turn around and see my reflection in the mirror. I haven't looked like this since I was twelve. No—I haven't looked like this *ever*. The almost-grown-up version of the girls never walked the world, and now I'm looking at Iris, expectant, instead of in the mirror.

"Well?"

"Truth?"

I lick my lips and then make a face, because lip gloss is sticky, and I don't like it when it's on my lips and not just rubbed off from hers. "Yeah."

"I like your short hair. And your T-shirts and boots. You look really weird right now. Well, no, not *weird*. Just . . . not like you. At all. Actually, you look a lot like Brigitte Bardot."

I would narrow my eyes at her, but I think the mascara might smear. "Who?"

She points to my right, at her collage of various classic film actresses and vintage fashion ads. Her mom could easily clue in on the whole *Iris likes girls* thing just by looking at her room, but straight people do really love to gal-pal us up rather than face the truth—even when it's hung on the walls.

I look at the actress she's pointing to, and then I turn, staring at myself in her vanity mirror.

All I see is my mother and memories. But before I can lose myself in the thorns that come with all that, Iris's door jerks open.

"Iris, do you and Nora want—" Ms. Moulton comes into Iris's room without knocking and comes to a dead stop when she sees us. "Oh." She frowns at the sight of me. "Nora! You look . . ." She stops, completely thrown by the change. That's good. I do not want to look like Nora when I go.

"I'm thinking of doing makeup and hair for the senior musical," Iris says. "Nora said she'd be my guinea pig. Her sister has some wigs because of the PI thing. What do you think?"

"It's very Brigitte Bardot," Ms. Moulton says.

"That's what I said!"

The two of them share a smile, all conspiratorial and warm.

"You always look great." Ms. Moulton smiles at me. "But this is cute, too. You did a good job, Iris. The theater department would be lucky to have you."

"Thanks," Iris says, like she didn't just come up with that lie on the spot.

"Did you two want something to eat? I was going to order pizza. Half vegetarian, half pepperoni?"

"Sounds good," Iris says. "Nora?"

"That'd be great. Thanks."

"I'll holler when it's here," she says, closing the door behind her.

We're quiet for a moment, Iris fussing with the collar of the black cashmere cardigan she put me in. Finally, she lifts her gaze to meet mine in the mirror.

"You're good at coming up with stuff on the spot," I say, careful not to call it *good at lying*, even though that's what it is.

She shrugs. "I spent a lot of time finding ways around my dad's rules." Her hands are suddenly still, like she's as surprised as I am that she's brought him up.

We haven't talked about what she told me in the bank bathroom. I don't want to push her, but I worry if we don't talk about it sometime when there isn't a bomb she built between us, she'll think that what she told me is another kind of bomb, one that's ticking down. And it's not. She was strong, then and now. It's one of the reasons I love her.

I'd like to punch that asshole ex-boyfriend who didn't like wearing condoms, *and* I'd love to destroy her father . . . but that's another matter.

"I had a lot of rules to follow, too." I hate how tentative it comes out, but that's how I feel. With Wes, everything came out in a horrible flood of stories that never seemed to end until suddenly, there weren't any more to tell, and then we just had to endure in the space between them.

This is different. This is giving pieces up and getting some in return. The ground was tilted toward me when I was with Wes because I had the truth and he didn't. But with Iris, she and I can be on even footing. We can know each other, piece by piece. We can build something with that knowledge.

"I bet," she says. "Are you scared?" She fiddles with my collar again, and then her hand settles on my good shoulder. There's a little catch to her breath when my shoulders relax under her touch, and I lean back into her, trusting her to hold my weight. Her fingers stroke my shoulder as the back of my head presses into the soft heat of her stomach.

"I can't be scared," I tell her.

She bends, a lock of pin-curled hair swinging over her shoulder. She presses a kiss to my forehead, then the tip of my nose, then an upside-down kiss on my sticky lip-glossed lips.

When she pulls back, she says the thing that burns the doubt and worry away and replaces it with something more. Something stronger.

You can be scared with me.

— 68 —

the truth

Lowell Correctional Institution, Florida

I'm not surprised when they take me to a private visitation room. She'll have made friends in here, dazzled a guard or two, maybe even a whole handful. If there's one thing my mother knows, it's how to work a person and a system. It's why I've never worried too much about her in here.

I'm alone for a minute or two, and the nerves flutter. Lee never talks about her visits here, and the nights after she comes back are the only times all year she drinks. Glass after glass of wine until she's stumbling and I have to help her to bed. One time, as I covered her up with a blanket, I heard her whisper, *I don't want to, Mommy,* as she curled into it, and my heart burned in my throat for days after, because I knew.

I knew.

The time alone gives me a chance to assess the room: the table and two chairs bolted to the floor, the metal loops on the table and floor for the chains.

Do they shackle her in here? Of course they do. What a naive thing to even wonder. I can't think like that. I know better.

The back of my neck tickles from the wig, the weight of hair on my shoulders unfamiliar after all these years. I take deep breaths and keep my back to the door I know she'll be coming in from, even as I hear the footsteps and the scrape of the lock, the clank of what I know are her chains, because I am not naive. I'm *not*.

I can hear her settle in the chair, the murmur of the guard's voice, and then his footsteps, leaving us alone. Definitely against regulation. Absolutely not a surprise.

But I still don't turn. I show her my back and the spill of long hair that looks real, and I wait.

"Natalie."

It's strange, to hear it. My name. But it isn't. Not anymore. Natalie was the touchstone. She was supposed to be my secret forever. The name I kept for myself. For my family and no one else.

I had been Natalie longer than any of the other girls. I'd been Natalie much longer than I've been Nora, but someday, that won't be true anymore.

And that is my new forever secret. Just like all the girls and names I carry.

The girl my mother loves, the girl she thinks I am? She's no one's touchstone. I let her go. She became something that needed to be killed so Nora could flourish.

I left some of her behind in the bloody sand, banished pieces of her with a bottle of hair dye in a dingy motel, and he doesn't know it and I won't ever tell him, but Wes's love helped me destroy whatever was left of her, because my mother's daughter can't be loved or known by anyone.

Natalie's gone. Nora's become real. Stranger, more secret things have happened, I guess. But it's knowledge that is mine and mine alone, and I know the value of things that belong only to me.

I finally turn. Her breath catches, and I know why. I look so much like her, like this. Looking at me must be like staring at a photo of herself at seventeen, and looking at her is like I'm seeing the path I would've ended up on if I hadn't fought my way out.

"You're so grown up."

Walking forward, I slide into the chair across from her. I can see the guard in the hall through the tiny window on the door. I wonder how long we have. I fold my hands in front of me, placing them on the table. I meet her gaze head-on, but I stay silent.

Her eyes track all over my face, and anyone else would think of it as a mother drinking their kid in after so long apart, but I know better. She's searching for clues. For tells. For anything she can glean and use.

"I've been so worried. I thought maybe . . ."

"I was dead?"

"On the bad days," she says, and oh, it sounds so sincere. Her fingers knit together, but I won't let it affect me. I'm glass. A reflection. Everything bounces off me instead of getting inside. "I searched for you. The best I could, in here."

"I'm sure you did."

The little twitch of an eyebrow—they're not as elegantly shaped in here, a little wilder, just like mine—lets me know I'm getting to her.

"I wondered if they put you in witness protection. Your sister's been trying to find you, too. Is that where you've been? With the marshals? Did you finally get away?"

Relief bursts in my chest. The trap I laid with Duane worked. Lee's cover is still safe for now. My mother doesn't know how I got out. She still thinks it was the FBI and the marshals.

"I could've slipped my handlers from day one," I say. "I didn't bother until now."

"What are you doing here, baby? Do you need help? Are you okay?"

Her eyes swim with tears that'll never be shed, because the only motivation behind them is information, not emotion.

"You know why I'm here."

I take my hands off the table and lean back in the chair, unblinking, staring her down. She breathes, in and out, so damn steady, but her eyes are roving my face again.

And then she leans back, too, the best she can, chained to the table. Those tears are gone in a blink, and the smile that curves around her lips?

That's my mother.

"The wig's good," she tells me as her smirk deepens. "You cut your hair, I hear."

She's trying to unsettle me, so I let the silence drag. It's the simplest trick in the book: Make the mark fill the silence. But it's also the easiest when it comes to her, after this long. I know she has questions.

But I'm not willing to provide answers. They'll just become weapons in her hands. Everything always does.

"You never divorced him." It's a statement. No, it's not. I want it to be; I want to be that strong. But it comes out like the accusation it is.

"I love him," she says, and truer words, I don't think they've ever been spoken. Because goddamn, she really does, doesn't she? It's twisted and it's broken—a fun-house mirror reflection of what I know love is. But what she feels, it's real. It's *so* real, she barreled forward into the gator's mouth, knowing he might bite down. And when he did, she dragged me into the water with them. Chum for the taking.

"He was going to kill you."

"But he didn't," she says, her voice softening. "It was a misunderstanding. Then you had to go and put yourself in the middle . . ."

"I put myself in front of the *gun*."

Her lips press together, the lines around her mouth deepening. There's no filler in here.

"You're alive because of me," I tell her. I want to say it one time. Have it acknowledged.

"I'm in here because of you," she says, flipping it, making it cut, because it's just as true.

I shrug, determined to be equally cruel. "I did what you told me to do, Abby. I was a viper."

"You bit the wrong man, baby."

"Because he's your man?"

"Because you're being foolish. You came here knowing full well that as soon as you walk out of this room, I'll be letting him know you paid me a visit. I'll give you a head start, baby, because I love you. But I have to tell him."

I hang my head, staring at my feet. The feeling inside me isn't resignation or hurt. It's a kind of click that locks away any hope forever.

She doesn't want her husband to kill me. But she also doesn't want to be on his bad side.

Can't have both, Abby.

"What are you doing here?" she asks again, and this time, the question is real, there's true confusion behind it.

I lean forward, and my eyes are wet and my mouth is vulnerable when I finally look up again. Her eyebrows scrunch, that flash of anger gone, replaced by the concern that I know is almost real.

"Do me a favor." And I wait a beat, so she can hover on hope just a little longer. So it hurts when I deliver the words to crush her. "And actually think for once. You taught me everything you knew. *Everything*."

I want to lick my lips. They're dry, but it's a sign of nerves. "You've been trying to piece together what happened that night and right after. And this whole time you've been asking yourself: *What would Natalie do?* But that's not the right question."

She swallows. Her throat bobs a little—weakness. My eyes flick, and she knows I've seen. Her mouth flattens. Mommy's angry.

So I go in for the kill.

"What would *you* have done?" I ask her. "If he'd been a mark, and not the love of your life? What would you have done, with all your tricks and sparkle, if *your* mother let a man put his hands on you? Not in the name of the con. Not for money. Not for any of the things that you taught me were important. No. You did it for the love of an abusive man who tried to kill you and wants to kill me. So don't ask yourself what Natalie would've done. Ask what *Abby* would have done. What would the woman who raised me to bite back do?"

She shudders, and God, I want to be the kind of person who smiles. I want to be that hard. I want to feel triumphant.

But I'm just sad.

I'm just trying to survive. Her. Him. Myself, whoever that is.

"What would you have done?" I ask her again.

And this time, she finally gives me the answer.

"I would have made a plan and allies. And I would have found my way out of it."

I can see it clicking together in her head; dominoes falling down, leading her farther into the tunnel I dug with bare hands.

"Keep going."

"I would have gotten a weapon . . . made my move whenever the opening presented itself. I would have run and never looked back. I would have done whatever it took."

"And that's just what I did," I say. "*Whatever* it took."

It's there, the hint at more, and then the goose bumps prickle across her skin, telling me I'm digging in exactly where I need to.

I've played this out in my head a hundred times on the plane ride over, in the hotel room bathroom, on the drive to the prison. I had a script of how it'd go, and she's playing her part. Now we're at the moment.

Don't falter now, Nora. Home stretch, then home. Back to them. *Please let me get back to them.*

"What's the most important thing, Abby?" I let my voice go high. I ask the question whose answer she drilled into me with each different name and hairstyle and personality. I mimic her right to her face, wearing her damn face, and those goose bumps across her skin spread down to her neck.

"*Always have leverage,*" she whispers.

I smile. It is cruel this time, because I have reached the moment when I have to be.

"What did you do?" she asks, and I am finally ready to tell. The secret I've kept so close, for so long.

"Alongside the hard drives in his safe, there was a thumb drive.

It was encrypted differently than the others. I handed the big stuff over to the FBI so they could put him away and I'd get the protection I needed. They didn't need to know about the thumb drive."

"You kept it."

I push forward. "It took me years to learn enough to break through the encryption. But I did. And what I found . . ." I just smile then. What I found is nothing to smile about—it's fucking wretched, a sick treasure trove of sordid secrets and dirty deeds—but it's also the reason I'm going to win.

How I'm going to protect everyone.

"He really did deal in the dirtiest kind of information, didn't he? Kindred spirits, the two of you." I stare her down and I resist throwing in a hair twirl, because I'm afraid she'll lunge at me.

She's never put her hands on me—never needed to. There was always a bigger threat to sacrifice some part of me—my self, my body, my innocence, my safety—to them . . . her marks and the love of her life who turned her into one instead.

But it's just us now. No marks. No Raymond.

There's nothing but the truth between us, and it's never been this way before. It's always been lies and slippery dodges. But she can't hide anymore.

And I've chosen not to.

"You have his blackmail file?"

"It was a mess when I got it open. Barely organized. But I took care of that. Color-coded it. You know, red for politicians, blue for dirty cops, green for drug dealers, et cetera."

"Natalie . . ." she says, and there is warning in her voice. There is a shred of motherly concern that I can't be sure is fact or fiction, because at this point, what of her is fact and what is fiction? "You need to run. Far and fast."

"No."

"Baby, he is up for an appeal next year. It's an uphill battle, but he's got the best lawyers."

"And you're cheering him on," I say, and she can't look at me. She's got six years left on her sentence, and if he's free by the time she's out, that'll make things even sweeter for her. They'll fight and they'll fuck and scream and throw things and make up, all in the span of twenty-four hours, and the cycle will turn and turn until one day, something breaks it and I won't be there to tilt the ground to save her anymore. He'll kill her. That's the only way it ends. She knows it. I know it. But she can't stop. And I had to let go.

I've known about the appeal since the start of the summer. Lee and I had a fight about it. She'd wanted to run then and there. I wanted to wait and see. No. That's not exactly true. I want to wait and fight. That's who I've become.

That's who loving and losing and then making Wes family has made me. That's who loving and keeping Iris has made me. Maybe not hopeful, but determined.

"Natalie, he will kill you."

"And you'll help him, won't you?" I ask, looking at her dead-on, wishing it was different. "When it comes down to it, you'll do whatever he asks."

She looks away. Her shrunken chest rises and falls in deep breaths. I can see her collarbone jutting out from under the khaki scrubs. She's thinner in here. And not in the cultivated gym-rat way she'd been when I was a kid. In a *the food's shit, sleep's shit, everything's shit* kind of way.

"Baby," she says, her voice breaking, and it's the answer, even if she doesn't want it to be. A woman torn, that's my mother's constant state. Teetering between her daughters and her man, between good and bad, true and fake, love and hurt. She is all blurry lines and bad ideas, and too drawn to danger. I hate how much I see myself in her, even now.

But her loyalties are not with me, no matter how much I wish they were. And my loyalties are not with her, no matter how much she wishes I'd fall back into her hold.

"I have to survive. I'm in here a long time because of what you did."

I let out a laugh. "You're in here because of what *you* did. You let him put shell companies in your name and laundered money through them. And you refused to turn on him even after he pointed a gun at you."

"You always antagonized him—"

"Bullshit." I bark it, and I sound so much like Lee, I think it startles her. She flinches in her seat. "You can't con me anymore," I tell her. "You have nothing left to teach me. How does it feel to realize that I didn't only outsmart you, but I outgrew you . . . at *twelve*?"

"I'm so damn proud I can hardly stand it," she snaps, and it's this bolt of truth between us, shearing our anger in half. "You are everything I wanted you to be. Everything I raised you to be, and everything you have to be. But you won't be *anything* if you don't run. You'll just be dead."

"Fuck you." And I want to snarl it, but it comes out in a sob. She's just said everything I've ever wanted to hear from her, but it doesn't mean shit anymore, because she's going to go to him. She's going to tell him *everything* I said, and if he gets out . . .

That's it. That's *it*.

"You and I are the same," she says. "You should be able to understand why I do what I do. You and I, we survive. No matter what life throws at us. We find a way. I know you'll find a way. Just like I did."

"Life didn't throw this shit at me, *you* did. You made me like this. You brought him into our life. You brought *all* of them into our life. We aren't the same. I would never do what you did."

"But you did," she says. "You chose yourself, baby. You left me behind, with the Feds coming in. I would never have done that to you."

"Yeah, you just let me get beaten in the name of love and molested in the name of the con."

Her chains scrape against the ring on the table. I've never said those words out loud. Not to her, at least. I've said them to my therapist and . . . well, that's it. Just Margaret. Lee knows because it happened to her, too, Wes read between the lines of all the stories, and Iris I told in the way girls sometimes tell each other. But those words, that bare truth, they are hard to say just like that . . . out loud, and I was taught to be quiet. It's harsh, and I was taught to soften my words. It hurts. Me and her.

"As soon as I realized—" Her recovery is so damn swift, like she's had it ready this entire time.

"Stop," I say. I order it, because I'm afraid if she continues, it'll spill out of me: the stories Lee told me, about the con that came before the sweetheart con. I can't. They're not my stories. And I think I might kill her if the words exist in this room between us, and I can't, I can't. (Some of me wants to, for Lee, for myself.)

"You know what I did to get us out of Washington," she hisses.

"Too little, too late."

"That's—" Her mouth flattens, her lips nearly disappear. My skin crawls, terrible little shivers up my spine. She's angry. Not remorseful. Not guilty. No, just pissed that I even brought it up.

I want Iris's hand in mine, squeezing tight. I can almost feel it, I want it so bad. I nearly close my eyes, imagining it. But I steel myself instead.

"I came here to deliver a message," I say. "I want you to tell Raymond something for me."

She raises an eyebrow, expectant.

"If anything happens to me, there aren't just people who will make sure certain items on the thumb drive go to the FBI. I wrote an entire program that'll trigger if I die. All that blackmail material he spent so much time gathering and dealing in will flood the market, and it'll look like he's the one selling it. Do you think he'll survive long in or outside of prison then? Do you think *you* will?"

Her lips pinch at the question. She may be proud of me for outsmarting them, but she hates me for it, too. It's why she's in here: She did too good a job raising her baby girls into vipers. She didn't think we'd turn around and bite her, even though she gave us no choice.

But Abby doesn't know how to be when she isn't the center of my universe. She doesn't know how to exist when the axis of my world—and of everyone else in her net—isn't tilted in her favor. I've yanked the ground back toward me, and now she's the one who's off balance.

"Mutually assured destruction, Abby. If he sends someone to kill me, worst-case scenario, he dies via toothbrush shank before the appeal even happens. Best-case scenario, he gets out on appeal and all the people whose secrets leaked will come for him. Because I've had years of freedom going through all the files on that drive, tracking down every twisted thread and person involved in every dirty secret. There's a lot of powerful people doing a lot of bad things on that thumb drive. I know about Dallas. And I know about Yreka."

"What happened in Yreka?" she asks, which is so damn sloppy of her, because it tells me she knows about Dallas. About fucking *Dallas*, and what he set up there. My stomach flips. I have got to get out of here before I lose all composure. I've done what I've come for.

"You'll have to ask him. He has a choice to make. It's very simple: I die, he dies. I live, he gets to."

"He won't let you keep all that dirt," she says. "The FBI having it is one thing—they can't use it the way you . . ." She fades off. Shakes her head. "He'll come for you, no matter what. You need to *go*. Far away. You need to change. Become another girl. I know you can do it, baby. You were always a natural at slipping into someone else. You can hide from him." Her voice, it's like it was that night, when she begged him. She's begging me now. It seems like it's for me, but I know; it's for him.

I've scared her, shaken her with how I've grown and sharpened into something she can't quite grip.

"I don't *want* to hide."

"This isn't about what you want!"

"But it is," I say, and there's the truth, the one I've created for myself. "This is absolutely about what I want. Because I have the

353

leverage. I was smarter than you then. I'm the better con artist now. I'll be out there, armed with everything you've taught me and everything I taught myself on top of it. And if he ever gets free and is stupid enough to come for me himself? The pieces I cut off him, I won't give back this time." She sucks in a breath, but I stay still and strong. *She's not normal.* I can hear North's voice in my head. I can see that realization on my mother's face.

And maybe I'm not. But maybe I don't want to be.

"This isn't a game you should play." She shakes her head. "You're good at hiding, baby. But you're no good at fighting."

"You have no idea what I'm good at." I get up, and just like the last time I left her, it is easy.

It is necessary.

I'm at the door, and the guard steps forward to open it for me, when it bursts out of her: "Natalie!"

I look back. One last look. One last time. Because either way, if I win or if he does, I don't come back. This is it. I need her to know.

"That's not my name anymore," I tell her.

And then I'm gone.

— 69 —

Nora: Sister, Survivor, ?

I'm strong until I get through the metal detectors and out into the lobby with the rickety chairs. I sink into one, and my face is wet, but the guard up front doesn't pay me any mind. She's used to it.

I cry. I let myself flat-out ugly-sob in the prison visitor lobby like I'm in a bad movie about teens overcoming adversity. But I'm not overcoming anything; I'm just plain overcome.

Finally, I pull it together. Kind of. And I look toward the doors and the parking lot. I have to get to the airport and be home before Lee gets back.

The thought fills me. Home. I scrub at my cheeks and take a deep breath, but it's a shudder and shake in my lungs.

Girls like me, we prepare for the storm.

When I was twelve, I made a choice. Her or me. Him or me. Survive or slaughter.

Abby might be right; he might still come for me, even if it signs his death warrant along with mine. But I am done running and hiding.

I'll fight if I have to.

He ever comes for me, he won't just find scared, panicky Ashley who thought fast but couldn't shoot straight. He'll find all the girls I've been. Rebecca taught me how to lie. Samantha taught me how to hide. Haley taught me how to fight. Katie taught me fear. Ashley taught me survival.

Nora put all their lessons into practice.

Deep breath.

Rebecca. My name is Rebecca.

Get up.

Samantha. My name is Samantha.

Wipe away the tears.

Haley. My name is Haley.

Shoulders back.

Katie. My name is Katie.

One foot in front of the other.

Ashley. My name is Ashley.

Push the doors open.

Nora.

I walk into the light.

My name is Nora.

Resources

_____

Much of *The Girls I've Been* is centered on the journey through surviving abuse. If you're struggling, know that you're not alone, and if you're in an abusive situation, know that it's not your fault, no matter what anyone tells you. The hotlines below can help.

Hot Peach Pages
An international directory of sexual and domestic violence agencies, giving information and support for every woman and girl on Earth
hotpeachpages.net/index.html

Women Against Violence Europe (WAVE)
A network of women's organisations combating violence against women and children in Europe
0 1 548 272 027 wave-network.org

Men's Advice Line
A helpline for male victims of domestic abuse
0808 8010327 mensadviceline.org.uk

Southall Black Sisters

Help for Black (Asian and African-Caribbean) and minority ethnic women and children who have been victims of violence and abuse
0208 571 9595 southallblacksisters.org.uk

Galop

Emotional and practical support for LGBT+ people experiencing hate crimes, domestic abuse or sexual violence
0800 999 5428 galop.org.uk

The Survivors Trust

The largest umbrella agency for specialist rape, sexual violence and childhood sexual abuse services in the UK and Ireland
0808 801 0818 thesurvivorstrust.org

SurvivorsUK

An inclusive service for male sexual abuse survivors, supporting anyone who identifies as male, trans, non-binary or has identified as male in the past
0203 598 3898 survivorsuk.org

Love Respect

Aimed at 16-25-year-olds, exploring what is and isn't a healthy relationship – from physical violence to coercive control
loverespect.co.uk

A note from Tess

———

In chapter 43, Iris refers to her endometriosis as a "heavy bleeding condition" as a way to get Red Cap to leave her and Nora alone in the bathroom.

While heavy menstrual bleeding is one of the many serious symptoms of endometriosis, I would be remiss if I didn't clarify that endometriosis is not a condition but a disease that often causes debilitating chronic pain, and Iris is simplifying for effect.

An estimated one in ten cis women have endometriosis—and this statistic does not begin to include *all* the people who have endometriosis, since it's not just cis women who have uteruses or who menstruate—and it takes an average of ten years to get a diagnosis because period pain and problems are often not taken seriously or are dismissed as "normal."

If you would like to know more about endometriosis and how to advocate for yourself medically if you do deal with menstrual pain, please visit endowhat.org.

If you are living with endometriosis like myself, I send you love and strength and all the spoons.

—TS